THE NEARLY DEPARTED

The Eldritch Twins | Book Two

NICK VOSSEN

ISBN: 978-17357-7-7696

Published by The Parliament House

Cover design by Shayne Leighton

TRANSMISSION

SEAN WATCHED the small bulb of red light blink in and out of existence. The sun had set on the Chihuahuan, and the hyacinth sky was fading off into the dark blue hue of twilight. Several streaks of cloud vapor, left by whatever sort of experimental shadow government or black ops flying vehicle that had just flown by, were slowly dissolving overhead.

He flicked the extinguished butt of the cigarette out into the desert night and headed back inside. There, he performed the elaborate scheme of tilting antennas, hitting switches, and tuning dials to get his ancient radio equipment functioning.

"Hmm, this oughta do it."

Following his words, the speakers cracked and came alive. Sean looked up as the distinct voice of his good friend—and radio host for the freethinking people—Harold Summer drifted into the small confinements of his motorhome.

"*…absolute mayhem. Oh, how I wish there was something the* GDF *could've done for those poor people.*

"*In other news, I have gathered trustworthy intelligence that* Haven *might in fact have planted spy equipment into all of our homes. It apparently involves a pocket-dimension created by a* Tuba, *which is a small, lesser daemon that many of us have had the displeasure of encountering. Usually, they like to hole up in our attics for the winter; nevertheless…*"

Static burst forth from the big speakers and Sean, used to faulty equipment, cursed under his breath before he slammed a hand down, hard, on the top.

The voice that returned on the radio wasn't Harold's.

Sean held his hand aloft and listened closely.

"*Stop what you are doing.*" The voice was deep and full of authority. "*Everything you know is wrong. There are no monsters. There have never been any monsters.*"

Sean slid his chair toward the desk and sat down, eyebrows raised. "What the hell?"

"*Supernatural and paranormal phenomena do not exist. Everything is an illusion. We expect better of you.*

"*You believe in lies.*

"*You have seen no truth.*

"*We expect better—*Haven *expects better.*"

Forcing himself away from the speakers, Sean played with a couple of dials on the tuners. The voice shifted in pitch slightly, and a faint rumble could be heard over the strange broadcast.

"Let's see," he murmured and turned another dial, flicking some more switches. "Aha! I knew it." Sean laughed and pulled a switch slightly to the right of the mess of cables running from the elaborate setup to the speakers and the wall. One of the sound channels fell away from the broadcast, and the voice returned, sounding more hollow and sinister than before.

"*There are no monsters. You have been told lies.*"

"Subliminal hypnosis," Sean groaned. "They're actually doing it. They're covering up."

He ignored the light rumble beneath his feet, turned the dial off, and started pacing around the room. After a minute, he grabbed his smartphone and sifted through his usual channels of communication to check if he had any new messages.

Annoyed then at the empty inboxes and lack of notifications, he spent a good ten minutes trying to put into words whatever it was he was trying to relay to whomever he wanted to contact when a text message from Harold Summer sent shivers up his spine:

Got pulled off the air. They're f#^@$(g onto me, man. Pulling the rug underneath all of us. Popped the Swansong twins a while back too, I heard. That right? You gotta help me out here man. H.*

A wave of panic washed over Sean. He tried hard to keep a steady hand while he nervously typed out a reply to Harold, asking him what the hell he was talking about.

Did Harold just casually mention that the twins got killed by Haven? He couldn't believe that. He knew the twins long enough now to know that they were about as hard to kill as a rock is to shave. Haven couldn't possibly have gotten them—*especially* not them. They'd talked on the phone just a few days prior, or was it a week? He was sure it couldn't have been more than a week.

Sean was running all kinds of disastrous scenarios through his head when the radio suddenly burst alive with static again.

"H-he-hello?" called the voice of a young woman. There was a distinct distance and echo—a delay like when someone calls you from the other side of the world. "A-anybody t-th-there?"

Sean dropped his phone onto the floor in awe and relief, then snatched the microphone up and checked to make sure it was plugged in. He couldn't help but smile as he answered,

"Hey! Lilly! Can you hear me?"

"Sssssean, g-ggood to hear y-your…you-your voice, b-buddy!" a male voice rang out from the void between the desert and wherever the place was from which the transmission originated.

"Quince!" Sean fist-pumped the air awkwardly. "Wait one second while I fix this." He pulled at some wires, turned a dial all the way off, and then gave the setup a good kick. "How's the connection now?" He didn't wait for them to respond and continued talking. "Glad to hear you guys are okay! There were rumors going around you guys died. Gave me quite a scare."

"Yeah, it seems a lot better." Quincy still sounded robotic and hollow, but less far-off, at least.

"Funny you'd mention that last tidbit, Sean," Lilly interjected with her trademark sarcasm. "You still believe in an afterlife?"

Sean's smile dropped. "What? Whatcha mean?"

"We don't know where you get your info from, exactly, but you're going to want to sit down." Radio waves made Quincy's voice sound very analytical and droning, like a high school math teacher Sean had years ago. "You see, we are temporarily indisposed of…"

"We're dead, Sean." Lilly ripped the proverbial band

aid off as best as she could; which meant with no subtlety whatsoever.

"Well, okay… Just tell him directly, then," Quincy complained, his voice drifting further away in the background.

"He's seen and heard worse!" The radio static cracked and buzzed as Lilly hissed vaguely at her brother.

"Doesn't mean you can just drop this bomb on him without giving him proper warning."

"What else was I supposed to do, then?"

"Guys," Sean interjected. He held the microphone tight and tried his best to keep his hands from shaking. "Please tell me what the hell is going on. You tell me you're dead, but I'm talking to you right now. That doesn't seem right, does it?"

Lilly started laughing. "Have you been living under a rock? Is this the same guy that got his brains almost turned to soup by a Mindflayer? This is perfectly normal stuff."

Sean felt a wave of embarrassment cascade over him. He knew she was right, but as far as dying goes, he thought that was at least something that'd stick. "So…how?"

"We're not quite sure…" Quincy was interrupted by a barking off in the distance.

Sean scratched his head "Wait, is that a dog?" He heard Lilly softly murmuring sweet nothings toward something too distorted to make out now.

"We'll get to that," Quincy replied. "Point is we're… half-dead? Is that what you could call it?"

"Sounds about right," Lilly added.

"Half-dead," Quincy repeated. "We're stuck in this

void, this limbo that's apparently a plane between life and the afterlife. It's a shadow-riddled place of emptiness and depression… Anyway, we're not sure how we got here, but we've got it on good authority that we can get back."

Sean couldn't believe his ears. Lilly and Quincy were the strongest people he knew. He'd never thought in a million years they would end up in a situation as sticky as this one. "So… How *are* you going to get back?"

"It's a long story, and we're kind of going off on a hunch," Lilly answered.

"Kind of figuring that out right now," Quincy added.

"WOOF!" the unseen dog piped in.

The glass of scotch nearby was empty; Sean was sure the half-filled bottle beside it wouldn't make another sunrise. "Okay… So, how are we talking right now?"

There was some shuffling heard on the other side before Quincy answered, his voice trailing with a bit of embarrassment. "Y'know, we're not really sure. Nothing quite makes sense here."

"We found this old radio setup and kinda tuned into…whatever we tuned into. I don't know what to tell you, Sean." Lilly sighed. "But we ended up right where we had to be, apparently!"

The floor beneath the motorhome rumbled again. Sean made a mental note that he really needed to get moving before the quakes turned out to be something worse—Primordial Wurms.

He sighed. "Okay, then. What's it like there?"

"The near-afterlife?"

"Yeah."

"Well, it's like…" Lilly fell silent for a moment and mumbled something which sounded too distorted to hear, then the barking started again. "Hewie, sit down!" She cleared her throat and restarted. "Uh, have you ever been inside a mall after all of the shops closed down for the day? Or a public bathroom when the cleaner's been by and all the lights are turned off, and you're unsure whether or not you're supposed to be there?"

"Actually, yeah, I can quite vividly imagine that."

"That's how it is all the time here. Only with deeper and longer shadows; vague, yet menacing figures always staring just off in the distance and random screams during the night, which is all the time. It's always night here," Quincy supplied coolly.

"That's terrifying." Sean gulped and reached for the bottle of scotch, pouring some in the glass, downing it before sloppily replacing the cap. "Anything else noteworthy?"

"Neon streaks that light up the sky, cloaked hermits knowing everything about our past and possible futures— an afterlife, or near-afterlife mafia?" Lilly said. "Perhaps it's best to just start at the beginning?"

Sean lit up a cigarette and popped the cap back off the bottle of scotch before taking a big swig. "All right. Have at it."

Lilly's sigh reverberated through the little cabin. "So it all kinda started when we were down in Georgia, right before we met someone you oughta know…"

PART I

Demons of the Fall

Chapter 1

WE LEFT *New York in the spring. It wasn't long after that the Daemonic Depths swallowed this huge part of the Eastern coast from Portland all the way up to Nova Scotia. You must've heard about it. In the tragedy's wake, enormous tidal waves crashed down onto the broken, debris-littered coast every single day. Floods went rampant. The survivors didn't even have time to mourn.*

So, me and Quincy…we ran—

fled south.

Somehow it was all too much to bear in that moment. The feeling that nothing we'd accomplished really mattered in the grand scheme of things. It was as if we'd wandered in some kind of dreamscape, desperately clinging to some hopeless ideal that one day things would get better.

But we knew they never would.

So, we retreated even more.

Hiding in abandoned and forlorn places away from the prying eyes of the world, listening to the warm nostalgic tunes of piano music straight from the vinyl on some wonky old stereo system. It took us back, you know? Back to the days as they were before. Just for a little bit.

Something had changed, however. As much as we would like to forget the horrifying things we'd experienced and seen, the things that were still very much there, all around us; it seemed as if the common folk already kind of did.

Listen, I know it sounds crazy, but do you think it's possible that people's minds, on a global conscience level, can be altered to not see the monstrosities all around them? Like, out of mind, but still very much in sight, but with people being oblivious.

Every day we saw more disappearances, more murder, carnage…but folks seemed to blame everything but the monsters, demons, and other horrors they had come to live with on a daily basis over the last couple of years.

The streets emptied after sundown. People started hiding in their fortified homes, peering out of the windows in search of dangers they had all but forgotten existed.

Our Global Defense Army remained absent wherever we went, but in contrast, the looming shadow of Haven appeared everywhere. There were rumors of strange and thin, slightly inhuman-looking men in black lurking around abandoned train yards or staring off in the distance somewhere just out of plain sight.

Always staring.

Always just out of reach.

We learned all of this from those few people we talked to that still believed in and saw the rotten reality in front of them.

So, we listened. We listened well, and we knew we could not keep hiding away and turning a blind eye toward these horrible happenings.

We ended up back where we started, back where we belong, and doing what we do best. We were helping people. Helping them, even though they themselves did not realize they needed it…

. . .

Lilly and Quincy both shuffled uncomfortably in their pew as they watched the silent, see-through specter glide across the upper balcony of the church. The rest of the congregation, whether they were too engrossed in their spirituality or dazed from a trance caused by the loud droning of the organ, did not notice.

"Look at her, walking, hovering, whatever you wanna call it. So slow, so graceful." Lilly pointed as the female ghost peered over the railing. "Why do ghosts always walk that slow?"

"What do you mean?" Quincy yawned and folded his arms in disinterest. His gaze landed on the left-most parishioner sitting two benches in front of them next to the aisle. Their target was still keeping quiet—for now.

"I mean… When in your entire life have you ever had the luxury to wander off *that* slow, ever? It just doesn't make sense. Why don't we ever encounter spirits that run around or walk up the stairs like normal people do?"

"Not everyone jumps up the stairs with the ferocity of an excited mountain goat while simultaneously almost breaking their kneecaps in the process," Quincy muttered, smiling then when he saw Lilly's cheeks flush.

The ghost, in the meantime, had floated off. It was probably pretty bored of humans coming and going in the church. So, it went back to doing its ghostly things like moaning, whispering from dark corners, and stomping on stairwells. The usual, really—nothing special.

"Are you sure this is our guy?" Changing the subject, Lilly nodded toward the nervous-looking man now fidgeting in his seat. "It's kind of hard to distinguish the afflicted from the rest of these kooks sometimes." She turned a quarter on the pew and faced Quincy.

"Lemme tell you, I'm getting pretty sick of these hidden little towns out in the sticks. We need to figure this stuff out soon." She groaned. "I'm like the number one main course meal for these mosquitoes, and I don't know how but I *swear* they've become like the size of rats, at least." She shook her head and swatted her hand around her ears. Her messy curls fell across her face. "*Abnormally large rats*, Quince."

There was a faint buzzing sound and Quincy chuckled. "I'm sure we'll have our big breakthrough soon." He gently grabbed his sister's swatting hand and smiled. "It's gone, Lil'. You're *safe*."

"Easy for you to say." She glared at him playfully. "They seem to leave you well enough alone." She sighed. "I want to go home."

"*Ssssst!*" One of the parishioners in the pew in front of them turned around in annoyance and glared.

"I know," Quincy whispered, ignoring the parishioner and the pastor's call for silence and prayer as the service officially began. "But you and I both know that this thing looks like it could be pretty damn big. I'm not ready to just pack up and leave, at least not until more Haven agents show up than we can handle. I don't think we could do anything about that except run."

At her huff, Quincy awkwardly scratched his nose and tried to not look his sister in the eyes. "I know that we're like…very close to Louisiana, Lilly. I cannot put into words how much I want to go straight there. I feel the pull too. But it's too dangerous for us to return yet; Sean said it was teeming with Haven agents. New Orleans is—"

"*SSSST!*" A couple in front of them had murder in their eyes when they turned to stare at them.

"Alright, already! *Sssst* yourself!" Lilly looked ready to go on a tangent, so Quincy placed a hand on her wrist.

"Hey! Eyes on the prize, sunshine," he whispered. "And to answer your earlier question, I'm about ninety-five percent sure it's the guy my contact told me about. Same symptoms and all. First the drooling, the twitching, the"—he cleared his throat—"shedding of the skin."

The pastor droned on in the background, unaware of any commotion. Two benches ahead, however, the twitching man the twins were shadowing started to convulse heavily with each passing lapse of a verse. His mouth released strange, garbled noises and his head started to lop toward the side of the middle walkway. The parishioners around him were murmuring and whispering in disgust—perhaps even fright.

"Here we go." Quincy nodded. He got ready to move.

"Please don't do it here. Please don't do it here. Please don't, not yet. Not yet. *Not yet,*" Lilly whispered frantically as she and her brother watched the gross figure of the shuffling farmer try and make his way out of the church.

As soon as the door slammed behind him, the congregation seemed to let out a sigh of relief. Quincy had read that it was believed to be an ill omen if a man or woman got sick and stayed within the confounds of a holy place.

After a brief pause, the pastor, seemingly satisfied now that the commotion had died down, went on rambling.

The twins slipped out of their pew and headed for the door.

"Stop convulsing like that, you're seriously making me sick!" Lilly snapped as soon as they found the man lying in the alley beside the church. She immediately cocked the hammer of her revolver back and aimed at him as he twitched on the ground. "I said stop it!"

Dusk had cast the entirety of the small town in a strange muted orange light. The bare branches of the churchyard trees in the distance creaked in the wind. Dark clouds were gathering from the east.

No one was around and although both of them were technically in disguise, Lilly and Quincy had the distinct look of outsiders emanating from them—the gun didn't help either.

"Where's the rest of you lot hiding?" Quincy pressed his foot against the man's stomach. The man cried out and his moans echoed through the cramped alleyway behind the church. "No one's going to hear you, buddy. The Faith's still strong in the south; everyone's in church."

"Raaarggh, you sacks of meat and marrow, you will pay for this. Release me at once. I shall say nothing." The man's face was swelling up and pus started running out from every orifice. His voice cracked and twisted, sounding less like a man's and more like that of a demonic entity with each uttered syllable.

"Please." Lilly shivered, but kept the gun firmly pointed at the man. "Sir, if the *real you* is still in there, we need your help. You've got to tell us where the affliction is coming from. We're trying to save—"

"Come…closer," the man interrupted in a whisper, his voice turning somewhat back to normal voice.

Lilly leaned in. "Please, you can tell me. Help us."

"Lilly, watch it," Quincy warned.

There was a roar of thunder in the distance as the man stretched his neck to get his mouth close to Lilly's ear. "Why don't you burn in the deepest heart of a dark star, *whore*."

Then…

The man then exploded in a shower of blood, viscera, and a mysterious green substance. Big chunks of flesh and bone splattered against the church wall; Lilly got utterly soaked.

Emerging from the gore was a pair of alien-like worm creatures that were trying to make a quick retreat from the twins. However, Quincy had anticipated their appearance and made quick work of one of them with the switchblade pocketknife he concealed. He crushed the other under his shoes.

"Ah… Aaaah. No… Not *agaaaaain!*" Lilly ran her fingers through her slime and blood-coated hair. Face twisting in a grimace, she leaned away and heaved.

As if completing some twisted tableaux, rain began pouring down, accompanied by crashing thunder. Mysterious velvet pink lightning and the ominous tolling of the church bell soon followed.

"Well, at least most of this will wash away, I guess." Quincy stuck his hands in his pockets as he watched a furious Lilly stomping toward their car.

His eyes fell on the gory mess and he swallowed, having trouble keeping his lunch down. Then his gaze fell on a piece of paper sticking to the protruding bloody ribcage and he reached out to grab it.

The heavy rain clattered against the windshield. Their grey Ford Fiesta sped into the night away from the doomed little township and the gruesome scene they'd left behind.

Quincy clicked the rearview mirror up and kept his eyes concentrated on the dimly lit and badly paved roads ahead while Lilly rolled around in the back, trying her best to change into clothes that didn't reek, weren't sticky, and didn't have blood all over them. With her head out of the window, she'd then tried to rinse some of the visceral splatter out of her hair and achieved moderate success.

"Next time, *you're* going to be the one holding the gun and *I'll* be standing seven feet away being the 'good but intimidating cop' for a change, okay?" Lilly yelled as she dragged her wet mop of hair back inside and wrapped a complimentary motel towel around it.

"Jeeeeez, you don't have to yell."

"Oh, I'm sorry, *there's* alien *mucus in my* ears!" Lilly threw the towel down. "Seriously though," she whined. "I don't know when you acquired this tenacity for justice and, believe me, I *agree* with you, but…"

"But what?"

"Five towns, five guys afflicted with the green glowing stuff running out of *all* their orifices, good *lord*. Four of them were talking about some kind of entity called '*Mother.*' Three of them exploded upon questioning… Am I forgetting something?"

"Two of them were spotted in contact with Haven agents."

"*Right.* Are you familiar with the game called '*In Over Our Heads?*' Because we really seem to be having some kind of winning streak over here. We don't even have a new lead."

Quincy threw a brown and green stained wad of

paper toward the backseat. "*Au contraire,* my dear sister. I found this flyer on the...*body* of the deceased. Check it out."

"I'm so tired," Lilly whispered under her breath. But she unfolded the sticky paper, trying not to touch any unsightly stains or breathe in too much. "Huh, the Wyrewood county annual Harvest Festival." She continued to skim the words. "Okay, pumpkin contest? Uh-uh. Food, drinks, and games? Yum. Corn maze? Yes, okay, terrifying. That's it?"

"That's it," Quincy repeated. "Wait, what's terrifying?"

"Don't you remember? I used to have these nightmares all the time when we were little. You know, the ones where I was lost in a cornfield?"

"The one with the shadow man in the straw hat coming to get you?" Quincy's eyes narrowed a little. "Yeah, I remember. You weren't just having bad dreams and afraid to go back to sleep. You were genuinely terrified, waking up as if you were in real mortal peril."

"Don't remind me." Lilly squeezed her eyes. "Just thinking about it is giving me a hell of a headache."

Quincy stared at the white road marker lines flashing by, then checked his phone. "There should be a diner just a few miles up ahead. Let's get our bearings straight, okay?"

"Okay, I—Quincy, *watch out!*" Lilly yelped and pointed toward the windshield.

Quincy managed to swerve the car to the right just in time to avoid hitting the creature that was perched in the middle of the road. His hands trembled as they gripped the steering wheel tight.

Lilly stared through the rear window at the dark-winged beast sporting goat horns and the face of a horse. It flashed its red eyes eerily toward the car before it took off.

"Are you okay?" Quincy asked, sighing in relief. He slowed the car down considerably once they could no longer hear the beating of wings.

"Think so." Lilly eased in the seat and tried to let her heartbeat slow back to normal. She nervously tied her hear back in a messy, curly knot and started turning the cap off her plastic water bottle. "Interesting day," she said, glaring out the window.

"What is a Jersey Devil doing all the way out here?" Quincy wondered aloud. But when no response came from Lilly, he figured it was perhaps better to forget about it. They both needed something to eat and were likewise *desperate* for sleep.

"Bacon and eggs, extra bacon, extra eggs, and a barrel of coffee, please!" Lilly strode in the diner like she owned the place, calling out her order before they were even seated. The prospect of a well-lit building with food inside always seemed to lift her spirits.

The diner, a typical one as far as Southern U.S. roadside dining experiences go, was almost empty. There was a rough looking trucker sitting in the front at the bar, an elderly couple taking the 'Unlimited Pancakes' challenge, and a blonde new-age-y type of girl sitting in the far-right corner. She appeared to be of similar age as the twins as far as they could see, considering she appeared to be engrossed in the book she was reading.

"Go ahead and take a seat, darlings. I'll be right out for your orders, hmm?" the little woman behind the bar called out, giving them a sweet smile that pulled up her impressive black unibrow.

Quincy and Lilly gave a polite nod and headed over to the far-left corner booth. From here, they could easily keep track of who entered the diner and have enough time for a sneaky getaway if the wrong people came knocking. It was only a precautionary method, but it was one the twins had discussed often. They were still very much fugitives and wanted by Haven personnel all across the States—it was of grave importance for them to be vigilant all of the time.

And today, it appeared their careful precautions had proven to be right. After the food had come and gone and the twins had some time to settle in, the jingle of the bell just above the diner door and the onset of footsteps in heavy boots announced their fears to be coming true.

"Shit!" Lilly exclaimed. She dove down, her head soon only slightly peering out from above the greasy table.

"What?" Quincy replied. "What's going on?" He lowered the coffee cup back to the table.

"Hush!" Lilly whispered. She stared intently toward the door, where only mere moments earlier, a man dressed entirely in black and wearing odd black sunglasses entered. He was standing at the front bar counter speaking to the unibrow lady. Lilly spotted a handgun tucked away in a holster on his belt.

Quincy made a quick 180-degree turn, took a hasty look, and spun back around. "Shit," he said, repeating his sister's earlier statement. "Okay, we've gone over this situation a thousand times already, right? Where are our nearest exit points?"

Lilly scanned the room and saw the lady nod toward their booth. She flinched and dove back down.

"Lilly?" Quincy whispered.

"Yeah?"

"The exits." Sweat was dripping from Quincy's forehead. "Exits, a bathroom, anything?"

"Allontheothersideoftheroom," she peeped.

The sound of the heavy boots was fast approaching.

"No… You can't be serious. Did we…"

A long shadow stretched out over the table. The sinister looking agent blocked out most of the fluorescent lights hanging on the shabby diner's ceiling. "Excuse me." His voice was strained and gravelly. "I'm going to need to see some identification."

"Identification," Lilly said and faked a smile. "Hah, yes, of course. One moment, I…"

"I think what my…*girlfriend* is trying to say is that we kind of left the identification in…"

"The car!" they said in unison.

"Yeah so," Lilly continued, "if you'll excuse us for a moment."

As Lilly was about to get up, the strong and broad arm of the agent pressed her back into the booth. "I don't think so," he grunted and peered over his sunglasses.

"Hey! Silly me, I think our IDs are actually in my handbag. It's under the table. Let me have a quick look-see." She glanced at Quincy, clearing her throat. "Come and help me look…*honey.*" Lilly's face contorted into mild disgust for a brief moment.

The pair dove underneath the table and proceeded to have the fastest and strangest non-phonetic conversation they had ever had. The summation of the ten second wordless exchange was approximately the following:

What do we do?

I don't know.

Think of something!

Why should *I* be the one that has to think of something?

You're the smart one!

I can't think under this stress!

We can't just kill him, can we?

No!

"Hey!" a female voice called, approaching the booth.

From beneath the table, the twins saw a pair of dark green Doc Martens skip over toward them. Quincy noted her shoes weren't unlike the one's Lilly used to wear.

"Sir, you don't need to see their IDs. They're just my cousin and her boyfriend coming to visit me all the way from Atlanta."

From under the table, Quincy could see the girl's hands making strange gestures. He nodded at his sister, who nodded back, confirming she saw it too.

"I don't need to see their identification?" The agent's voice creaked in confusion.

"Shit, man, no. Them's just Cassandra and Pete from Georgia. You know them, don'tcha? You used work with Pete's dad over at the newsstand in Macon," the girl continued.

Her arms crossed; her left hand made a wave.

"The news…stand?" the agent mumbled.

"Better go and check out if it's still there. I bet the

boss will be very angry if someone made away with the entire stack of the Times, huh?"

"Oh, dear no!" the agent exclaimed. The floor shook a little as he ran back toward the exit.

Quincy and Lilly finally crawled out from underneath the table, sitting together on one side of the booth, and came face to face with their apparent savior. The blonde new-age girl they had seen earlier was awkwardly staring at them. She didn't say a word; instead, her hands were making a gesture like she was tying a knot when at the exact same moment, the loud bangs of trashcans falling over could be heard from outside.

"Shoelaces," the girl said with a laugh. "I couldn't resist." She stared them down for a bit more before continuing, "Uhm, mind if I sit with you? I have a feeling we have a lot to talk about."

"Ah, sure." Quincy peered at his Lilly, who shrugged. "Go right ahead." Quincy gestured toward the other side of the booth.

He couldn't help but stare then a little at the peculiar woman as she slid into the booth across from them. She had a very distinct look. Her hair was wild, with strands of dreadlocks near the front adorned with silver and bronze jewelry. She had a septum ring and was wearing dark lipstick. Her clothes were loose, colored in royal purple and black. And she was wearing a beautiful aged-copper pentagram necklace.

Quincy was quite spellbound by her appearance. Lilly noticed—she was staring too. "

You…You just *jedi-mind-tricked* that guy into leaving us alone," she blurted out in fascination.

"Well…Not quite. But eh, I guess it works the same

way. I usually stick to harmless fun, but I could make him walk off a cliff if I needed to." She shrugged. "With these Haven assholes you never know, huh? I know they can't be trusted, so when I saw you two in a pickle, I knew I had to step up."

"How'd you do it?" Lilly asked while eying the girl from head to toe.

"It's a kind of magic." The girl winked but pulled away her gaze, seemingly a bit embarrassed.

"Seriously, though," Lilly pressed. "Oh, and I like your boots, by the way."

"Yes, I'm dead serious. I'll explain later. And, *by the way*, thanks." She laughed out loud and Lilly smiled, cheeks reddening.

"So, uh." Quincy finally cleared his head a bit. "Whatever you did, thanks. You really did get us out of a potentially nasty situation."

"Lizbeth," the blonde said, introducing herself. Her rose-colored cheeks negated some of her pale overall complexion. She held out her hand, her fingers covered in marvelous rings of all sizes "Lizbeth Borden. But please, call me Liz."

"Lizbeth Borden?" Lilly shook her hand but raised an eyebrow nonetheless. "As in… Lizzie Borden? Are you related to…?"

"Nah," Liz countered. "I get that a lot. But no. My parents just kind of had a dark sense of humor."

Lilly lit up. "Ha! That's pretty funny!" She looked over to Quincy and saw him smiling as well.

"I know!" Liz grinned.

Quincy had a strange feeling, as if he had known Lizbeth for a very long time already. It was only there for a moment, but he instantly knew where it had come from. Her demeanor was exactly like his sister's, which was probably why they seemed to get along immediately. *Good lord, there's two of them now,* he thought and cleared his throat.

"Ahem. Anyway, nice to meet you, Liz. Again, we're very grateful for the help. You have no idea." He paused. "By the way, this is so rude we haven't introduced ourselves yet. I am…" Quincy stopped, eyes widening, and looked toward his sister.

"You see we're…" Lilly started, but a pang of doubt started gnawing at her conscience; she knew they couldn't leave a trail. Like always, they had to lie in order to stay safe. She shuffled in discomfort.

"You two are the Swansong twins," Liz said, smiling in satisfaction when both of their mouths fell open.

Chapter 2

LIZ WAITED for the initial shock to clear, then held her hand up. "Please, by all means, don't start to panic." She smirked. "You two are kind of infamous…if you weren't already aware of that."

By this time, the diner had emptied out completely, save for the counter lady, who was now cleaning the kitchen in the back.

Quincy, however, still glanced around, keeping himself on his toes at all times. "Yes, we're *very* aware of that, which is exactly *why* we're trying to keep this super low profile." He stood up and started to hover near Liz. "How'd you know? *Who* sent you and *how* did you bewitch that agent? Tell us—"

"Hey!" Lilly jabbed Quincy in the shoulder, and he stopped, flinching back into his seat. "Would you sit the hell down and act like a human being, please? She helped us!"

Liz laughed. "Jeez, talk about the size of the stick in

your…" But despite the huge grin appearing on Lilly's face, Liz refrained from finishing the sentence. Her tone became a bit more serious. "Okay, okay. I understand the caution; I just thought me getting rid of that agent for you would net me at least a *few* cool points with you both." At Quincy's silence, she huffed. "No? So, let's put the cards on the table. I'm kind of a *friend* of Sean Cooper. I believe that name will ring some bells, yeah?"

Quincy sighed while Lilly peeped as soon as she heard the name escape Liz's mouth. "You know Sean?"

"Yeah. We're not like the greatest pals in the world or anything, but he trusts me, and I trust him. Call him if you think it'll help sort this situation out." She put her mobile phone on the table and shoved it toward Quincy.

He shoved it back toward her. "We have our own ways of contacting him," he muttered, narrowing his eyes. "Besides, if we're to trust you, I'd rather have it be based on our instincts." Soon though the stern look flushed from his face and for the first time in a while, Quincy actually looked relieved.

Lilly scooted over toward him and gave her brother a soft pat on the back. "So, to make it official: I'm Lilly. And this is my stupidly skeptic but lovable twin brother Quincy—who I wouldn't trade for the world. We're kind of inseparable. And we bear the burden of being a Swansong… It seems like our reputation is preceding us," Lilly stopped and waved. "Again, and properly this time, nice to meet you, Liz."

Quincy smiled at his sister's words.

Liz chuckled. "Hi." She sat up straighter then. "Well, no use putting it off. I *was* really using magic back there, but not the bad kind, if you can believe that. I'm a witch, actually. A white witch.

"A white witch?" Quincy whispered, looking a little confused. "How does that work?"

"It's simple, really." Liz's eyes trailed along with the waitress as she came by with the mop. Once she was out of earshot, she continued. "My coven and I practice Good magic. I know you two have seen your fair share of destruction, but I promise we use our powers only to help and heal those in need. We thrive on growth and rebirth, not chaos and death."

"I like the sound of that." Lilly's eyes grew big and wide. "Tell us more."

"Have you ever heard of the Night Lights?"

Lilly and her brother exchanged glances before she joked, "Well, of course we know about the little sleep lights, but somehow I doubt that's what you mean." Lilly took a sip of coffee and drifted off toward heaven as she felt it warm her soul.

"The Night Lights. It's the name of my Coven," Liz explained. "There's a myriad of stories to tell but I'm not quite sure we have the time. I'm currently out on my own."

"Oh, you can at least share one interesting tidbit, right?" Quincy laughed. "Do it for Lilly. She used to want to be a sorceress when she grew up."

Lilly smiled and went red; Liz mirrored the warm gesture.

"Okay, one interesting little fact—you'll never guess who our High Priestess, eh say head-witch, is."

"We probably won't," Quincy said. "So, go ahead."

Liz leaned in toward Lilly and whispered something in her ear. Quincy couldn't quite hear what she said.

"Get out!" Lilly exclaimed, her eyes wide. "I love her!"

"For real!" Liz shouted back. "She's amazing, you've got to meet her!"

"I really have to!"

Quincy watched the exchange and rolled his eyes. "Fine, keep your secrets," he remarked to deaf ears, wondering if he could ever get back into the conversation again.

"Makes a lot of sense," Lilly added with a nod.

Quincy shrugged, only half-paying attention. "It *totally* does." He smirked sarcastically, but the two women only shot daggers at him. "Anyway, back on topic, for I'm very curious about this, as is Lilly, I'm sure. What brings you to this neck of the woods?"

Liz tapped the plastic rim of the table. "You know, it's complicated. I've been tracking a series of peculiar deaths related to some kind of Outer-World illness that's been afflicted certain individuals as well as corrupting a lot of wildlife around the state."

"Well, I'll be damned," Lilly bellowed. "I think we're investigating the same thing." She looked over at Quincy, who nodded. "I guess we'll be sticking around each other for a while," she happily stated.

Quincy threw the still-sticky Harvest Festival flyer on the table in front of Liz. "This is the one thing we've got going for us now." He turned to his sister and grinned before turning back to Liz, who was trying her best to dissect the information in the flyer without touching it. "So, what's *your* take on corn mazes?"

A huge racket from the front of the diner threw the trio off, and one by one they peeked over the back of the bench toward the entrance. With a lot of noise, four men came in hollering and laughing. They were dragging something behind them in a net. Liz and the twins heard the lady at the counter yell out in fright, which caused the men to laugh even louder. Above the ruckus, the soft cries of what sounded like a wounded animal arose, which made Liz look on-edge in an instant.

"Look at it jammerin' and squealing, har, har!" one of the men bellowed.

Without a word Liz, stood up and stampeded across the diner toward the group.

"This'll make a mighty fine stew for ya to sell all throughout the winter, Misty. I tells ya there's a lot of meat on these things, even the smaller ones ya see right there. Yeh, do ya?"

The twins hurried after Liz, who now stood in the middle of the diner, arms crossed and furious. "What the hell is this?" she demanded.

On the floor entangled in the net was a small Jersey Devil crying out in fear and pain. Its wings had been ran through with buckshot and clipped. It also sustained multiple hits from a baseball bat to its mouth.

"What the *hell* have you done?"

The Jersey Devil's eyes darted around the room as it let out a big yelp, a pool of blood starting to form underneath it. Lilly turned around and buried her head in Quincy's neck, who stood equally speechless.

A bucktoothed, not-too-bright-looking fellow tipped his Bud Light hat and dared to step up to Liz. "We here caught ourselves a Horse Monster, and it's a big-un! Isn't it, boys?"

The rest of the men cheered and hollered.

"This isn't a big one, it's a *baby*!" Liz turned to the twins with pleading eyes. "It's must've gotten lost. Jersey Devils aren't usually seen around here." She turned back to face the men. "They're harmless to us! They just want to be left alone!"

"This-un tried to bite me! How's that for harmless, huh, girl?" a broader looking man with a filthy and stained shirt meandered up to the bleating beast and kicked it in the ribs.

It cried out and strained against the net. Its hoofs were beating against the side of a table, its poor, useless wings flapping inches from each other having no effect.

Liz stepped up to the man with the gross shirt and screamed in anger, "You mother*fucker*! You'd rather subject yourself to kicking a baby animal when it's down than look me straight in the eye?"

When he winced and stayed silent, she snapped, "I said look me in the eyes! *Look*!"

Quincy saw that Liz's hands starting to glow with streaks of white and green pulsating light. She made her hands into fists and pointed them down toward the ground. Pieces of old bark suddenly sprouted from beneath the diner tiles and shot up the man's legs. Slowly, both of his legs below the knees had turned to wood and fastened themselves to the floor of the diner.

The other men tried to overpower Liz, but some kind of pulse wave sent them flying into the chairs and booths surrounding them. The lady behind the diner counter screamed and ran off into the kitchen.

Liz lashed out toward the captured man. Her flat hand hovered just inches in front of his cheek, which started to redden and sizzle. Soon enough, big, bulbous blisters started to appear.

"Let me tell you something about harmless," Liz continued. She looked around the room at the myriad of terrified individuals. Lilly, and especially Quincy, included. "Harmless are ninety-nine percent of the beasts in the world around you. You want to know who's not harmless? Those that protect all matter of life from *shit stains* of society like you." Liz kicked the filthy man's right wooden tree-trunk leg. It snapped in two immediately, and the man howled.

"Look at you all," Liz hissed and started gesturing again, more branches, roots, and trunks coming up to ensnare the other men, who started pleading in fear. "In times like these, mankind is supposed to come together and look after each other to save each other from the *real* threat." She scoffed. "Instead, you go and torture a harmless creature and call yourself men? You call yourself human?"

The filthy man's blood was spurting everywhere around him; Liz was coated in it, yet she didn't flinch. She bowed down toward the trapped Jersey Devil and with gentle care and precision, placed her hands against its wounds. The creature's wails became softer, its breathing less laborious and more regulated.

"Liz, I think that's enough, okay?" Quincy stammered. "You've made your point, okay?" He struggled at finding the right words to speak. "Let them go and we'll release the Jersey Devil together."

"Let them *go?*" Liz responded, outraged. "No, my

dear, I will *not*. In fact, my Coven believes in a thing called karmic justice, and whenever such an opportunity allows, who are we to get in its way?" Tears welled up in the corners of her eyes. She was shaking. "I told you I could make men walk off cliffs, and I told you that's not what we're usually about. But this is different. I *can't* let this go."

In the distance, perhaps a few miles away from the diner and further up in the air, harrowing howls and cries could be heard. Shrieks of confusion, fear, and anger.

Liz walked up to the bucktoothed man, who was now fused by his waist with the roots sticking out of the floor. "You hear that? You see, the *big-un,* as you like to call it, is circling around above looking for its young right now. Jersey Devils are harmless, yes, but oh so protective of their young."

"Liz, come on!" Quincy shook his head. "It'll rip them to pieces!"

But Liz was already half-way through the front door. "I know."

Lilly, who still hadn't said a word ever since the men walked in, stepped away from Quincy and grabbed her coat; she started trailing after Liz.

Quincy couldn't believe his eyes. "Lilly, are you serious? This isn't what we do. This isn't us! C'mon, we've got to let them go!" He couldn't believe what was happening. This was not like his sister at all.

Lilly turned around and gave Quincy a deadly stare. "Let 'em..." She looked at the creature caught in the net. Its eyes brimmed with tears, but Liz had done *something* to at least give it a fighting chance. It would pull through, but those pleading eyes would go on to haunt Lilly forever. "Let 'em rot," she told Quincy and disappeared after Liz.

Quincy's gaze met the group of crying and pleading men, but all he could do was look away as a thump of something huge shook the diner's roof. "I'm—I'm sorry!" he told them and quickly headed toward the door.

Chapter 3

IN THE CAR and back on the road, with an extra companion to boot, nobody said anything for a good couple of hours. Eventually the rain subsided, and a thick fog crept up through the entire woodlands of Georgia. Further up in the treetops an eerie wind started howling during the latest hours of the night.

It was as if an evil omen followed the Swansong twins wherever they went.

And it wasn't much of a stretch to think that way, especially for what the twins had gone through ever since having to leave their secretive shelter in New York. During the course of just over a year, they'd had a fair number of encounters with harrowing paranormal events. Some had proven to be more innocent than others, but with each Nightstalker preying on little children, each ancient curse, each stretch of lost highway fissured away from current time and space, the twins got that gut feeling a little bit more. That voice inside their heads complaining and asking them, *Why us?*

Eventually, it was like a revelation when they realized it was, in all probability, impossible to avoid the burden that came with bearing the Swansong name. From that moment on, it was as if being a Swansong was a genuine curse—their first curse, and the one curse they could never fully lift or escape from.

The realization seemed to bring a sort of peace of mind to Quincy, but not to Lilly. Even though she was loyal to her brother and to keeping him safe, perhaps now more than ever, she struggled with her fate and her place in the universe. Thus, every day her mind and sense of self crumbled away just a little bit more, and there was absolutely nothing she or Quincy could do about it. Neither Quincy's kind, soothing words of encouragement nor her own fantasies about a life with more purpose than to solve everyone else's problems could dig her out of the hole she'd found herself in.

Hours later, the car was still as quiet. Quincy saw the first streaks of morning sunlight reach out from behind the dark rain clouds that now served as a mere distant memory of a gloomy and terrifying night. He looked over to his left as an exhausted Lilly pulled into the parking lot of some shady motel on the edge of whatever part of deep forested United States territory they were in now.

In the backseat, Liz was quietly murmuring in her sleep.

As Lilly was getting ready to get out, Quincy finally broke the silence. "Don't get up, sis. I'll handle it."

It was well past noon when the dusty, but to be fair otherwise remarkably clean, three-bedded motel room stirred back to life. Having slept the most before getting to the motel, Quincy was the first to wake up, but Lilly and Liz followed soon after. Only a few words were spoken during this time, and when (late) breakfast and simultaneous lunch had come and gone from the nearby mom-and-pop market, Liz couldn't help but finally address the huge elephant in the room.

"So," she began, "I'm really sorry for the way I acted back in the diner. Man, you two hardly know me and I hardly know you, and I snapped at you as if—"

"You know what, just leave it," Quincy interrupted. "That was some really messed up stuff, but a few hours before, *we* literally watched an innocent man exploded into bits so…"

"A man that was carrying the disease and the parasites with him," Liz filled in. "Lilly told me when you were asleep. You had no other choice. Me, on the other hand? I'm just seriously surprised to even be here with you. I'd have left my ass there in that diner."

Lilly, who was sitting upright on the bed and finger combing her messy hair and cursing at all the knots and tangles, interjected, "We don't leave the good ones behind. Quincy knows this, and just the fact that he ultimately walked out with us means he felt the same way about those…monsters. He just doesn't want to admit it."

Quincy said nothing.

Liz grabbed her smartphone and hopped up on Lilly's bed next to her. "Okay, you want to know why I felt so strongly about what happened?" She fiddled with the phone for a bit before looking over at Quincy. She patted the blankets next to her. "Come and see."

As Quincy sat down, Liz navigated a video app to a strange video. In it, they saw a life-size mannequin doll which appeared to be moving on its own while being accompanied by unsettling, noisy synthesizer music.

In the video, the doll spoke in a very chilling robotic singing voice, spouting phrases such as, "I feel fantastic," but eventually turning toward the ominous, "Run, run, run, run!"

A few shots of a forest were spliced in the video near the end, before ending back on the doll now in full view standing up.

"Yikes… For real. Why are you showing us this?" Lilly complained. "I hate mannequins, truly hate them—this is going to give me nightmares!"

"After everything we've seen, *this* is going to give you nightmares, Lil?" Quincy laughed. "Come on!"

"I'm telling you, there's something wrong with this video." Lilly nervously rubbed her elbows. "Something is *off*."

Liz stood up and started pacing the room. It was pretty obvious from the way she was shaking and rubbing her arms that she was very nervous about something.

"You're absolutely right about that." She sighed deeply, then continued. "What you're looking at is the only known recording of a serial killer from Lookout Mountain, Tennessee. The doll in the video supposedly represents his last victim and the sounds you're hearing her make are the actually vocalized recordings of her being forced to read made-up gibberish and pleas." Liz fiddled with her phone some more. "The actual recordings were found at his dilapidated shack a couple of years later and sound like this…"

Lilly and Quincy listened in shock to the horrific recording of a woman pleading for her life, being told to say that she felt fantastic while she wept uncontrollably. When the hoarse male voice on the recording asked her what she wanted more than anything, she said she wanted to run.

"As far as anyone knows, these are the last known words my mom said before she was murdered," Liz revealed, her lip quivering.

Lilly sucked in her breath and felt tears burning at the corner of her eyes. Quincy simply looked down to the floor in shock.

"You see the stretch of woodland in the video?" Liz continued. "That's where they found her body. It's not too far from the place he held her, or so they claim. When the police were doing their rounds, it was our shepherd, Sammy, that eventually started digging up the place where that maniac had buried her remains." Liz got back on the bed and buried her head in the palms of her hands. "Sammy was put down for *destroying* vital evidence."

"No," Lilly murmured, heartbroken.

"Yup. And they stopped looking for the guy a few years afterwards, since the murders stopped… They *killed* my dog, but the guy that *murdered* my mom got away with it! The only thing left is this sick video, shared all across the internet, and this recording, which I can hardly bear to listen to but can't get bring myself to get rid of."

"I'm so sorry about all of this," Quincy spoke softly. "I had no idea—"

"Of course, you didn't. Don't be sorry, 'cause none of it is your fault. But now you know why I acted the way I did." Liz rubbed away her tears. "Two innocent souls close to me lost their lives, let alone all of the other victims, while the killer roams free. And keep in mind that this was *nine* years before the obelisk in Egypt. This wasn't any demonic possession, paranormal phenomenon, and/or supernatural type of deal. This was one hundred percent human malevolence. Pure *evil* distilled in the twisted mind of a single rotten individual."

Lilly scooted over and wiped away her own tears, then grabbed one of Quincy's and Liz's hands and squeezed. "We have to stay strong. It's like you said, Quincy—people *need* our help and if we *can* help, who are we to deny them? But we have to stay vigilant and we have to realize we can't save everyone, even if it's by their own wicked faults."

She turned toward Liz. "Humans can be awful, *awful* people. We've seen it, just like yesterday, and just like the story you just shared." Lilly sighed. "But we've also seen the good in people. People who did everything in their power, who risked their lives to help us fight an ancient Sumerian demon that was ripping apart their loved ones. We've also met those who were afraid of a so-called monster at first, until we uncovered its true nature—how all it wanted was to make toys for their children. You know what the people did? They celebrated the little nature spirit; they got over their fears of the unknown and everyone and everything triumphed in the end."

Liz nodded. "I kind of lost my purpose after all that

stuff with my mom happened. I wandered around aimlessly until the Night Lights found me and took me in. They taught me a lot, about everything, and I learned so much from them. They're like family to me, you know?" She smiled. "Still, I went on this quest to find out about this affliction all on my own. I felt as if something was still missing in my life and I couldn't put my finger on what it was. However, I do think there is no such thing as a coincidence, so us meeting must've been fate in some way or another."

"I think my sister would wholeheartedly agree on that," Quincy said with a laugh. "We're very glad to have you around, Liz. And whatever happened back there, you seem like our kind of person."

"What kind of person is that?"

"A good person."

Liz let out a very long, drawn out sigh of relief, giving Lilly's hand a squeeze. "I guess we're going to be preparing our best harvest festival get-up, then?" she asked, smiling.

It was a warm smile that made Lilly and Quincy feel like things were looking up again. With a whole new member to the team of misfits, they'd definitely stand a chance to solve the case of the mystery affliction now.

Moira lit the black wax candle and threw the still-burning match into the darkness behind her. The walls of the little room were filled with racks on which rested all manner of reagents, ingredients, and other peculiar knickknacks. In the middle of the room a white circle, adorned with occult symbols of unknown origin, was drawn on the floor. Black candles dotted the inside, and surrounding the circle stood a host of jarring and genuinely off-putting curios. There was also a glass of strong unknown liquor, a box of cigars and, surprisingly, a chicken clucking around near the edge.

The drab black curtains that hung over the single window were shut tight. Still a slight humid breeze, unusual for the time of year, circulated the room: Its presence confirmed what could be described as aura of weird hanging slightly off-balance in the air.

Moira slid the candle she'd just lit in with the others and sat down in the ritual circle. She tucked in the frizzy lock of black hair in her velvet turban and let the light of the candle flames wash over her dark, exposed skin. She moved to sit cross-legged and began murmuring unintelligible gibberish.

Very softly, whispers started to surround her. Moira couldn't quite make out what they were saying, but she knew well the consequences of opening her eyes at the wrong time. She listened close for a single voice, that single silent whisper that she was looking for. And when she heard it she reacted—with her mind's eye she grabbed it from the fissures between worlds.

When she opened her eyes, she noticed the light in the room was dimmer. The flames, though still burning at their full intensity, had their light now absorbed by a void that appeared to be a living presence, awake and aware in the room. Moira looked to her left to see the wooden walls of the house looking as if they were bending off toward the outside—it was as if the ceiling was steadily dropping down closer and closer above her head.

"Do you enjoy distorting aspects of the natural world? To me, you aren't as unnerving as you might think you are, Master Loa."

The candlelight suddenly intensified tenfold.

A pitch-black silhouette of a tall, crooked old man wearing a top hat appeared on the illuminated, impossibly angled wall. The shadow picked something up from the floor—a cigar—and lit it. Moira recognized the familiar smell immediately, but the box of cigars in the circle remained untouched.

"What you ask is a lot, you know, Mambo. Hm?" It was a voice like an old grandpa's, but turned slightly off-pitch and just a tad more Caribbean. "Do you truly know what forces you deal with?"

"You haven't heard my plea yet," Moira hissed in anger. "Do not treat me like a child!"

"I know everything already."

The silhouette loomed over the reflected shadow of the chicken clucking around in front of the flames. A little tuft of smoke escaped from the old man's mouth, and the shadow of the chicken dropped dead: The actual chicken meandered around clueless until some fifteen seconds later, it collapsed on its feet—dead.

"What you ask," the silhouette of the old man continued, "is not simply an exchange of goods; you ask a service, ongoing, until certain conditions are met. Whenever and wherever."

"That's right."

"You are aware of the price you must pay?"

"Yes." Moira was shaking. These deals weren't to be taken lightly. She knew, and she was terrified.

A gust of hot wind blew through the room. The wall

straightened back out as if nothing happened. The candles blew out for a few seconds before coming back to life and radiating their normal amount of light. The liquor, the cigars, and a handful of the curiosities were gone, swept away into whatever realm the strange shadow returned to.

At the tail end of the unnatural wind, one last sentence carried to Moira on the flow of the air: "Let it be done."

For a few moments, Moira sat there perplexed, not quite knowing what to do, when a knock came from the door. The noise made her jump a little, and she knocked over one of the candles, which spilled wax all over the wooden floor. She blew it out as the door opened.

A white man of average height with fancy hair and a very expensive suit stood in the doorway. He was wearing sunglasses and constantly looked to be listening for orders to come in through his visible earpiece. "Miss LaGrande," he said to her, "boss wants to know if you're ready to head out to Wyrewood County. We've got every-thing set up." His eyebrows went up as he shifted to eye the room.

"Thanks. Tell him I'll be with him shortly," she snapped with a wave of her hand. She pushed past him and disappeared into the adjacent bathroom.

The Haven agent looked around the room a final time before turning heel and meandering back outside. "Creepy voodoo *shit*," he muttered under his breath.

Chapter 4

MAKE NO MISTAKE: The world is still a very scary place, my friends.

It took the twins and Liz about a day and a half of travel, with enough breaks for food and rest in-between to reach the aptly named town of Darkness Falls in Wyrewood County. Wyrewood was a hidden slab of swamp and woodland on the very edge of Georgia, just a stone's throw away from the Alabama border.

Quincy remained skeptical about traveling the main roads and highways with so many of Haven's obscure black cars driving around while their sinister black helicopters hovered around above the well-traveled routes.

And so, they once more traveled as incognito as possible, which meant taking the most backwater roads possible, often not more than a muddy streak in-between a sea of trees closing in around them. It finally gave the trio enough time to get to know each other on a level that was a little bit more basic and fun and had less soul-crushingly awful events or horrifying tales scattered throughout.

They had encountered a few peculiar events along the way that some would've once called *supernatural* phenomena a long time ago.

First, they had stopped to pay toll to a goat-man for crossing his bridge over a small but distinct enough little river that couldn't be traversed otherwise. As a small thank you for paying the goat-man's toll (a meager three fresh salmon) the benevolent creature shared a little tidbit about the ghost children of a railway crossing about sixteen miles ahead.

And sure enough, after leaving a shiny silver coin on the road near the railroad, a bundle of about five phantom kids manifested behind the car. They not only pushed the car across the railway with ease, but apparently were so impressed with the offering that they had pushed the car on for a fair number of extra miles afterwards—Quincy was certain they had saved a lot of gas this way.

The twins were surprised and glad none of the encounters had been malignant in any way, and even claimed to enjoy the experiences. Oh, how times have changed. Liz had explained to them the essence of universal harmony and balance. After the twins had jolted the protection of the God-machine back to life in Antarctica nearly two years ago, the balance of light and dark had all but shifted back to a more neutral space.

Malevolent, *evil* forces would eventually disappear on their own (hopefully), but with them, so would the global conscience, the awareness of what was happening… At least that was the going theory. The twins had seen this conscience fading before, but they had also seen their fair share of abysmal things still happening all around.

The worst part was that just about all of these wicked events the twins had encountered or heard about could be traced back to the intervention of Haven, who now had freer roam than ever since it appeared that the world governments had abolished the Global Defense Force program. Not even the rising of the Daemonic Depths had brought them back, the old GDF leaders claiming that while the events were tragic, if there weren't any creepy nautical crawlies coming out of the trenches and onto the broken shores, they couldn't do anything about it.

All was not lost, however. For from the ashes of a lot of GDF chapters rose small groups of resistance against Haven and their nefarious doings. The twins knew of their existence but never dared to reach out for help. They were famous amongst those few people that still remembered what the events in Egypt did to the natural world around them, so any interaction would plant a huge target on their backs.

Sean had often tried to convince them that the scattered resistance groups could rise up against Haven and would need the twins' help. But they would always refuse. Lilly and Quincy believed that being wanted dead or alive by Haven meant putting everyone they loved in danger at all times. So, they never stayed anywhere for long, and they never made lasting friends: Sean, and perhaps now Lizbeth, being the exception to the rule.

The Ford Fiesta rolled into a parking spot underneath a weeping willow tree on the edge of town. Darkness Falls looked exactly like whatever kind of stereotypical back-woods little town someone would imagine if they were to be told, '*Hey, imagine a stupid little hick town near the woods in Georgia.*'

It had one main street filled with red-brick houses sporting such locations as a bar, a bed & breakfast, a mom-and-pop grocery, and an antique store. The short little street ended in a square bordered by the local church and town hall with an impressive clock tower. Lively oaks and willows brandishing lovely yellow and orange-colored leaves were scattered throughout the small side streets, which eventually ended up as little cobbled roads leading up to some of the many farmhouses scattered around the town. Grey overcast clouds floated high up in the air and masked the town in somewhat of a constant shadow. Quincy parked the car on an empty lot opposite an unremarkable brick building.

Liz slammed the car door closed. "Well, welcome to *Hill Valley*, population *zilch* and"—she cupped her hand into the air and managed to catch a few raindrops—"yes! Permanent *shitty* weather!"

Quincy rummaged through the trunk of the car and presented a couple of umbrellas. He threw one to Liz, gave one to Lilly, then opened the last one for his own. "Oh, hush!" he chided, smiling weakly. "I'm sure a bit of rain will not dampen the festivities, eh, Lil?"

"I cannot tell if you're being sarcastic right now or not," Lilly replied and ran her finger through her curls. "Look what it's doing to my hair!"

"From what you've told me about having only treated it with the complimentary motel shampoo packets for about half a year, I'm surprised it hasn't all fallen out yet!" Liz snorted.

"Please don't scare me like that," Lilly mumbled. Her eyes drifted off toward Quincy, who had already wandered a ways a head. "Hey, wait up!"

A small pathway led out of town and into the fields beyond a line of trees. A tiny pumpkin sat at the junction where a big sign indicated the direction of the Wyrewood County fair. With the rain now steadily coming down, a bank of fog rose through the tree line, but the sound of music clearly signaled the festivities were still taking place.

"Huh, that's actually closer than I initially thought," Quincy remarked. He halted when he saw Lilly shifting uneasily beneath the umbrella she held. He could nearly feel the pang of doubt coursing through her mind as she stared at a construction of hay bales stacked near the edge of the trees. An ominous-looking black scarecrow wearing a straw hat stuck in the ground next to it.

"Reminds you of the shadow man, doesn't it?" Quincy carefully asked.

Lilly just nodded.

"Yeah, I never really liked all these fall festivities myself. I guess many stem from ancient harvest rituals and stuff like that. There's something *just not right* about them." He stepped toward Lilly. "But we need you now, Lil. You know that."

"In the fall, when the shadows grow longer and deeper and the sunlight is chased away, our own demons will try to rear their ugly heads. And if we don't fight them, they will take over, and we will be driven mad by our own worst nightmares." Liz turned to Lilly and grabbed her hand.

"Whatever is troubling you right now, Lilly, know that it is the season of doom and gloom out there, and your mind can be your worst enemy. Do not let your demons win."

Lilly straightened her back and nodded again. "Right. Thanks." She made a single step on the path that went in-between the trees toward the festival. "Good talk," she added nervously.

Liz held Quincy back for a bit. "What about you? What strikes fear into your mortal heart, hmm?" She saw him eying Lilly in concern. Lilly was staring off in the distance, lost in thought. "Hey, she'll be alright, I promise. So, c'mon, tell me. What's your fear poison? Is it spiders? I bet it's spiders."

Quincy scratched his neck and looked away for a spell. "Well...I...uh, you know, I used to be really scared of Gregorian chanting. When I was little, it reminded me of darkness, spirits, and evil things."

"You mean it put the fear of God into ya?" Liz grinned. "But c'mon, seriously, something must terrify you now, right?"

Quincy closely watched his sister meander up ahead of them. "I don't kn—uhm—let's talk about this later, okay? Let's go."

Liz shrugged and followed him; both quickly joining up with Lilly.

Just around the bend of the muddy road, past the dense line of oak trees, a wide rolling plain stretched out ahead. Luscious green grass and farmland formed the border of the woods. On the other side of a big red farmhouse, a field of corn sprawled out across the horizon as far as the eye could see. Children were playing on and around a dilapidated tractor that sat nearby—it seemed to have been stuck in the mud for years.

People all around seemed happy, dancing and singing to the country band performing up on stage. Rows of colored tents lined the dirt paths leading around the site and featured all kinds of tasty snacks or fun games. The dreary weather appeared to have no influence over the day's festivities at all. The crowded field of people was a stark contrast to the empty town they had stumbled upon just a little bit earlier. It appeared that the people of Wyrewood County held on to their tradition steadfast.

But for all the fun and happiness that the Harvest festival seemed to portray, Liz and the twins could not shake the feeling that something was devilishly wrong with the entire affair.

Quincy noticed it first and was convinced he'd have felt it whether or not he had grabbed the event's flyer off an exploded corpse infected by a parasite of unknown origins.

"Do you two feel that?"

Liz stopped walking, clasped her hands together, and breathed out slowly. She closed her eyes for a split second —they darted around fiercely when they opened again. "It's like the ground is buzzing. It's almost unnoticeable." She knelt down and plucked a little bit of dirt from the ground and rubbed it between her fingers. "The land is upset…"

"I—" Lilly laid her eyes on a cart of produce, but a shiver ran down her spine as she watched the freshly picked eggplants pulsate every few seconds. It was as if something was living just beneath the vegetable's skin. She pried her eyes away, and they landed on a farmer who had just started pushing the little cart that the greens were nestled in by them. The man's hollow expression made her nervous, but it was the tiny flash of green in his eyes, visible only for a second, that really set her on-edge.

"These people are afflicted," Lilly said through gritted teeth. "All of them!"

Quincy watched a group of children play near the tractor. They were running and cavorting around like children at their age should be doing, but there was something very unsettling about the whole display. The children weren't smiling; they weren't laughing. It was like they were brainless automatons, programmed to act one certain way.

Quincy's hands tightened around the umbrella handle. The rain was unrelenting. "Let's get away from the crowd for a bit, okay?"

They gathered a little bit further into the field, near the edge of the fog and about fifty yards from the back of the country band's stage. It was relatively quiet here, but they stood out like a sore thumb. They were the outsiders snooping around with big black *here we are, come get us* umbrellas. Luckily, the harvest festivities seemed to distract any curious onlookers enough so Liz could try her hand on a guidance spell.

The twins followed Liz as she slowly paced around the field. She seemed to murmur an occasional unintelligible word or two, but for the most part, she made gestures with her hands or traced arcane symbols onto the ground with salt and oil from her pouch.

"How does it work?" Quincy knelt down beside Liz after she'd fallen quiet.

"Wha—" It was like she had snapped out of a dream. "You mean magic? Witchcraft?"

"Ehm... Yeah? Whichever of those you prefer, I guess?" Quincy fumbled with the words.

Lilly was eying the carefully drawn pentagram and the wavy symbols next to it.

"I'm trying to commune with land and its spirits, to seek guidance on where we should concentrate our actions."

"That's sounds complicated." Quincy raised an eyebrow. "I'd love to know more about the exact process of it all."

Liz laughed. "Well, it's not like it's an *exact* science, if that what you think." She opened her little hip pouch and the twins could see various bottles, cloth bags, and things tied to hemp rope within. "It's all about being in tune with the world around you. Having feelings and empathy are the important, not a list of ingredients and a recipe. It's give and take. It's about respecting the Earth and the resources it provides." Liz pulled a little bottle of pink Himalayan salt out of her pouch and poured a bit of it over the symbols she'd drawn, which now started glowing. "And using them wisely."

"Why does it feel like I learned something, but I still don't get it?" Lilly sighed.

Liz's big blue eyes met Lilly's. "It's—it's also willpower."

Lilly flushed. "Oh."

"Lil', Liz..." Quincy muttered.

"Ingredients are important; otherwise, the arcane

forces can wear your body down. Also, you'll need to know some Latin for most spells, but for the most part…" Liz traced her finger over the heart-lines on the inside of Lilly's hand, which she was unaware that she grabbed. "You'll need that special spark." She winked.

"L-ladies," Quincy stammered.

Lilly's cheeks turned a deeper pink as she let Liz's hand go and looked away. "I'd love to try magic one day, when times are better."

"*Hey, seriously now!*" Quincy yelped.

"What?" Lilly turned to him in anger. "What is it now?"

Liz sucked in her breath. "Lilly, I think what Quincy was—is trying to convey is that we appear to have company."

The trio had unknowingly wandered back toward the fair grounds and did not initially notice the group of townsfolk gathering around them. The group of people stared wide-eyed at them.

Quincy saw the same emotionless void in their eyes, while Lilly noticed things burrowing just beneath their grey skin in their cheeks, below their eyes and in their throat. Liz could feel the earth beneath her tremble and weep.

As the country band got back onstage and a musician struck the first few chords on his banjo, a bolt of lightning came crashing down and hit a lone tree across the field that wasn't that far from the fairgrounds. The noise exploded, accompanied by the roar of thunder and terrible music.

One of the men in front of the group surrounding them let out an inhuman shriek and lunged forward. Lilly yelled and pulled her umbrella closer in response, keeping the pointy end held forward like a weapon—the man screamed as he ran his mouth right onto the end of the umbrella. The disgusting choking and retching sounds of the poor impaled individual drowned out with the screaming noise of the worm-like parasite that tried to crawl its way out.

Lilly's hand shook as she released the umbrella handle and felt for the gun hidden underneath her jacket. "Trouble!" she yelled back, knowing it was quite the redundant statement.

The group of infected individuals crept forward, pushing the twins and Liz closer together. Flakes of dry skin and entire slabs of wet meat plopped off the poor people's faces, arms, and hands as they moved. There was not a single shred of humanity left in them.

Liz's hands clumped together and, as she muttered something unintelligible beneath her breath, they waved outwards, forming a spell that pushed the townsfolk back somewhat. "What now?" she yelled frantically toward the twins, who were standing with their backs together.

"Wooheeey! Are ya'll ready for some great country line dancing out there in the field or what?" the burly man on stage called out. He adjusted the reed hat he wore, scratching behind his ear until it fell off with a wet *plop*. "I'd tell you what, rain or shine, ain't nothing gonna stop us from having some good ol' fashioned country dancing, cow-poking, heathen-burning time, are ya'll with me?"

"Heathen-burning time?" Lilly whispered to Quincy.

The crowd of sickly-looking people yammered together in monotone moans and encroached closer.

"Alright, here we go now," the singer belched, and the band started to play—

I'm going down the river,
let the fresh spray hit my face.

One of the infected closest to Quincy shrieked as it ran up to him and threw up a hissing, green mucus-like foam from its mouth. At the last second, Quincy opened the umbrella, and the gross gurgling stuff spattered against it. It wouldn't hold for long. The umbrella started smoking, and patches of green started leaking through.

Quincy swallowed hard and followed in his sister's footsteps by jamming the end of the umbrella right in the retching man's eye socket.

Mississippi dreams of mine,
like stars up in the sky.

With pinpoint accuracy, Lilly jerked her brother back and shot a bullet point-blank into the parasite worm emerging.

Hold me clooooooose…

Three infected exploded in an instant. Acting quick, Liz cast a quick spell that formed a protective barrier around them. The green and grey viscera splattered against its invisible border.

Lilly slipped under the outreaching arm of another infected and shot the once-human woman's jaw off.

"Hey," she called to Liz and waved at the protective bubble. "We once had a Fire Vampire that could do that!"

Drink me innnnn…

Two heads caught aflame.

"Cool beans!" Liz yelled back. "I'll wanna hear all about that one soon!"

Quincy threw his jacket toward another spitting infected. When it wrapped around the man's head, a bright green glow shone through the fabric—it reached a sparkling, crackling climax, the crackling mostly being the partially dissolved head falling off the man's shoulders and tangling with what remained of his jacket.

Mississippi dreams of mine,
stay with me for all time.

The trio was pushed back by the encroaching mob; their backs now turned toward the entrance of the huge corn field. Liz fired off bolts of magic but started missing more than she hit.

"I don't know how long I can keep this up," Liz yelled in exhaustion.

"We got this!" Lilly held her hand on the trigger and swayed the barrel of the gun from left to right, keeping a close eye on any infected individual that dared come closer.

"We can lose them in the corn maze," Quincy panted, convinced.

"Hell no!" Lilly protested. "That's a freaking trap and

you know it! They're pushing us *in* this direction for that very reason."

"I agree with Lilly," Liz sighed. "It's too obvious."

Lilly fired the gun again; Quincy and Liz shielded their faces from the slimy brain splatter that resulted from the shot. "I'm out of ammo," Lilly called out dully. The situation was so frantically dire, so unimaginably stupid, Lilly thought it was almost boring. This could not be the way they'd go…

Quincy squashed one of the parasite things under his foot. "Of course, it's a trap! I just don't see any other way to go."

"Ssssttooop! Just give uuuuaaapp!" a half-melted woman hissed.

"I'm not going in there," Lilly snapped, standing her ground.

The flesh-dripping woman came closer and reached out for Lilly. "Run away, little girl! Run away!" she garbled.

Lilly pushed the woman on the ground and let her Doc Martens and gravity do the rest. "I'm gonna need a sign or something."

Liz bobbed her head to the band's still-playing song absentmindedly while she expended the last of her powers pushing the infected back. *Huh,* she thought. *I swear this isn't how the lyrics go.*

Meanwhile, Lilly was still ranting: "Seriously, I'd like to hear *one* good reason why we can't stomp our way through the fail-squad here and make it back to the car in one piece."

…and if I can't go home instead.

Then may the true dark ruler of the cosmos strike me...

As if it were divine intervention (of which they all knew that was *evidently* impossible), a bolt of lightning struck the stage. The explosion was massive and extremely loud. A brilliant flash of white-hot heat seared through the fields and the collective screaming, screeching, and moaning came to its zenith exactly 0.1428 seconds after impact. The result was what could only be described as a lake of blood, mucus, and gore pooling around the entire field. Some arms and legs stuck out from the body of acid-like, hissing fluid.

And yet, they *still* moved toward them.

Very meticulously, very slowly. Very all-encompassing.

One of the *Cajun Fried Delights* stands sunk into the blubbering pool and dissolved.

"Sweet Celestian Sun!" Quincy cried over the deafening ring in his ear.

"Lil—" Liz began.

"Yeah, okay, I'll take it," Lilly yelped. She took her brother and Liz by the hand and together they sped off into the corn maze.

Chapter 5

WE HADN'T ALWAYS LIVED in New Orleans. In fact, we grew up in the depressing downpour of a permanently shadow-cast mansion on a little island just off the Massachusetts coast.

You'd think growing up with the sharp, icy winds of the Atlantic would teach us a certain sense of danger, or instill a certain fear in our young hearts. For sure, the waves crashing down hard on jagged shores of our little island and the constant, temperamental storms always brewing in the silty air certainly acted as a well enough warning not to take the wild, primordial sea for granted.

That old crooked and creaking mansion by the sea was our home, and we were children of the waves. Children of that old Swansong family up in New England, those of the old blood from the old world—an island race.

Yet, Quincy and I, we were outsiders—we knew we were and always had been and always would be. We had surely learned to recognize the many dangers of our nautical surroundings and thrived among them, but it was everything beyond our little island world that was alien and strange to us.

Once, we visited some of Mom's relatives in rural Nebraska, in a small town in the middle of nowhere surrounded by cornfields, deep, dark woods, and a whole lot of nothing. We were both out of our element, but I felt it the worst. The ancient forests chilled me to the very core. I couldn't explain it.

Every night while looking out of the guest room window of that farmhouse, I shivered at the thought of ancient things, things that were here before the human race, things from a time beyond that had existed. In my head, it would spread out and into the corn fields that stretched out just a few feet below the window I was looking out of.

From that fear, something manifested deep within me, something that would haunt me for years to come. A demon born not from ash, brimstone, and occult ritual, but from the delicate psyche of a poor outsider girl with an uncertain future.

Lilly put the journal she was clutching back in her pocket and opened her eyes. She was alone in the middle of a small open space in the corn maze. Above her, a gigantic tree creaked in the wind. From one of the highest branches, a rope dangled down and from it hung the limp body of a young man. Ice-cold jabs of pain ran up and down Lilly's spine—the man looked like Quincy for a split-second. It was only very brief, and she wondered if she had imagined it. She was sure she did.

Then, the man's head fell off and splattered on the ground: It was a pumpkin. Lilly sighed with relief…until the clown appeared in the corner and began laughing menacingly. Lilly managed a small peep before running off in the first available direction. *You've got to be kidding me,* she thought, biting her lip as the sharp leaves of the cornstalks hit her in the face.

"Lilly? Quincy?" Liz took a good look around the narrow, fog-filled lanes of the corn maze. She couldn't hear anything except for the distant sounds of rain and thunder emanating from a very strange pink and turquoise-colored sky above the field.

"Oh, shitballs," she whispered.

Before opening his eyes, Quincy could not help but shiver at the baritone voices booming around him. He was lying on something cold and hard. Was it a slab of thick concrete, or an enormous stone won in some forgotten quarry ages ago, now serving as the sacrificial altar for whatever entities skulked near him?

Either way, Quincy still wouldn't open his eyes. The melodious chanting was distinct in its style and language. Quincy knew what it was, and he hated it.

Something rustled past his left ear. Was it a bit of fraying rope? Was it a human finger teasing his unfortunate predicament? Was it some blood hungry companion animal quietly sneering as it watched a lamb go down for the slaughter?

Quincy still did not want to open his eyes—yet he did.

The thing that tickled him was a leaf. The voices had gone. He was alone, and there was a lot of corn. Like, seriously, a lot.

Liz stripped a third cob of corn of its leaves and finished the star pattern on the dirt. The leaves weren't perfect, but they'd have to do for now.

In the middle of the pentagram, she had dug a small hole in the earth in which she had carefully placed the following ingredients: a half-melted tic-tac (as a replacement for a leaf of mint); a shiny quarter from The Netherlands with their queen's facial profile stylized on it (it would hopefully replace the drop of royal and/or blue blood); and lastly a rubber chicken with a pulley in the middle (no doubt a more than adequate for the two-to-three wishbones required).

As her hands waved around, Liz tried her best to remember every vivid line of the incantation. Her fingers weaved complex patterns in the air and she suddenly felt the spark—something was going right. Liz smiled when she felt the currents of arcane energy zip from the core of her being, through her fingertips and out into the open air right before the energy shot out in front of her. It made a hard left after about two seconds and proceeded to dissipate a handful of feet into the cornfield.

It also lit quite a large amount of corn on fire.

"Ya—ouch! Wow, okay!" a voice came from the same direction. Liz could hear someone rustling just a stone's throw away.

"Quincy?" she called with relief. "Quincy, is that you?"

A sweating, mud-stricken figure emerged from the blackened corn. There was a disheartened look in his eyes and smoke rising from his pants. "Yeah. Yeah, it's me." His expression lightened somewhat when he saw her.

"All right!" Liz bellowed. "My interdimensional-translocation-beacon-incantation worked!"

Quincy squatted and coughed up a patch of black soot. "Your what?"

"My interdimensional-transloc—"

"Yeah, yeah, okay," he interrupted, "and that does *what*, exactly?"

Liz perked up. "Well, what it *does* is locate you through the ether with lightning speed and accuracy and then conjures an arcane thread for me to follow. And I've found you! It worked so quick!"

"That's probably because I was about ten feet away from you to begin with," Quincy groused, rubbing his temples.

Liz blushed.

A crack of orange lighting flashed through the cloudless pink sky as the wind picked up and blew a haunting flute-like tune softly over the cornfield rows. What little of the strange white sun that had hung in the air was now being completely covered by the ominous purple clouds up in the sky—it was getting darker.

"Where's Lilly?" Quincy asked. "I'd figured you'd been searching for her first, seeing as you two are having that kind of *BFF* thing going on."

"I don't know," Liz answered. "Sorry to burst your bubble, but I actually *did* look for you first. We're going to need each other when finding her; she's troubled."

"Troubled?" Quincy raised an eyebrow "What do you mean, *troubled?*"

"Tell me," Liz started, "did you see anything that particularly scared you when you first regained consciousness in the field?"

Quincy swallowed. "Uh, yeah, I—"

"Spare me the details for now, a *yes* will suffice," Liz shushed, pointing a finger up toward the sky and then gesturing all around her. "This place, it's not real. What little horrors we both may have experienced waking up do simply not compare to this. This is Lilly's nightmare. All of it."

"Her nightmare?" Quincy had a dire look in his eyes. "This place…"

"It's a conjuration of some sort. Someone or something reached out into her mind and pulled these fears to the front. Whatever it is that's doing this, it has the power to manifest her demons and weave it through our real-world. The cornfield was the perfect transitory gateway."

Liz looked grave. She cracked her knuckles as she looked up at the peculiar violet and purple clouds drifting above their heads. "These harvest fields are rows and rows of the same thing. It's a perfect diversion to make the transition nearly unnoticeable."

"And so, when it's not clear whether someone transitions into a nightmare, the fear is much stronger after the first bad thing happens." Quincy rubbed the black soot he wiped from his shoes between his fingers. "Am I getting close? How do you know all this?"

"Quite right," Liz confirmed. "Oh, and I know because I've seen it before. But not like this, not by a long shot. It was a Spore Crone back then—she used hallucinogenic mushrooms. But this, this is way bigger. Have you ever heard of anything, any type of creature, monster, or being that is able to do this on this kind of scale?"

Quincy gritted his teeth. He wanted to find Lilly as

soon as possible, not sit around and discuss whatever grave dangers could be threatening her right now. "There are some tales in folklore," he relented. "They mostly talk about beings that feed on fear or can smell it out of a person," he gulped. "Things like Mindflayers can influence an individual's mind, but we're not dealing with the likes of them. They're rare—they don't distort the world around them as far as I know, and lastly…" Quincy fell quiet.

"Yeah?" Liz tried carefully.

"We'd already be either dead or gone insane if it were one of them," Quincy continued. "A handful of things can also create tiny otherworlds, or pocket dimensions as we like to call them, but again, I don't recall reading or hearing about anything that can conjure up such a thing from a person's mind."

"I don't like the sound of not knowing what we're up against. What else can y—"

"Okay, that's enough!" he interrupted her. "I don't like this either, but what I really don't like is hanging around speculating what kind of harm can befall my sister. I'd really appreciate if you could help me find her first, and then…"

Quincy fell silent as piercing howl echoed over the rows of corn.

Whatever or whoever it was, it sounded terrified. It rose even above the rumbling of the thunderstorm and the drizzle of rain that had gradually turned from a drizzle to downpour.

A murder of crows that had hidden themselves between the corn rows, pecking at imaginary worms and small seeds in the soil, shot up into the air immediately with one fell swoop. Their cries mimicked the horrified shriek heard just moments before. One by one the birds took on a look of bloodthirst in their eyes, or so it seemed. And as if moving as a single hive mind, the collected omens of misfortune and death shot off toward the direction of the outcry.

There wasn't much to add to the scene.

"Let's go," Liz said as she hastily gathered some still usable spell ingredients back into her pouch.

Quincy simply nodded.

Moira shivered when some of the drops of wet, green goo dripping from the ceiling hit her in the neck and earlobe. The mucus was strangely hot, tingling against her warm skin and...

Is this stuff buzzing? she thought, closing her eyes and taking a few deep breaths to get herself through the horrible sensation. When she opened them back up, the walls of the old farm shed were pulsating ever so slightly as a sort of membrane, barely visible to the naked eye, and glowing in a chromatic hue now and again.

Shit. You're in way over your head and way above your paygrade, LaGrande.

A broad-shouldered tank of a soldier appeared in front of her and Moira bounced back from the unexpected sight. The soldier wore a hazard mask which looked like a modern-day military plague doctor mask. He also carried one heck of an assault rifle.

The few bits of skin visible through the edges of the uniform showed him to be tattooed, presumably all over his body. Moira was almost sure it was part of a warding spell. It was a brilliant move actually, to protect oneself from the supernatural by ways of ink pierced into the skin. A lot of malevolent things can take away your crucifixes, talismans, or bijous in a flash, but removing one's entire top skin layer was a lot less viable an option. Which didn't mean it wasn't at all possible, of course.

"Didn't you hear what I said?" The soldier groaned, apparently tired of repeating himself.

"I'm sorry, what?" Moira felt as if she had just woken up from a dreamlike daze. "Again, I'm sorry," she repeated. "This just happens, kind of comes with the job you know, ha."

The soldier shook his head and gave a complaining snarl. "Central command would like to know if everything is in order on your side of the plan."

"Yeah, yeah," she said, then yawned unintentionally. Behind her back, under the robes she wore, she was gripping the stone jars as tight as she could. "The ritual ingredients are all in place, so once the trap is set and sprung, it's a quick one-way trip into the absolute Nothing for both Swansongs, courtesy of the LaGrande family recipes in superior necromantic Hoodoo." Moira gave a weak smile.

"A simple 'yes' would've sufficed," the soldier snapped before he spun around and walked off. "Fucking witches!" Moira could hear him say before his ramblings died off further into the twisting wooden hallways.

Such a cursed place. Moira eyes darted around for any other nosy Haven personnel. When she didn't find any, she took both jars from behind her back and placed them in the spots she had previously chosen for them. For the casual shadow government employee onlooker, they wouldn't stick out that much, but they were essential for her plan.

"*WHY DOES THE CHILD BRING FORTH THESE NON-ESSENTIAL OFFERINGS?*" the alien-thing whispered to her.

She could again feel the erratic buzzing on her neck and ears, an afterglow effect of the otherworldly organic matter that had once been present there. Moira ignored the thing. She had tried her best to do so ever since she came here and first laid eyes on whatever the hell it was. Now it even plagued her mind and dreams when she wasn't even close.

"*ANSWER ME. SUCH INSOLENCE. NO WAY TO TALK TO MOTHER,*" the thing cried before it wracked her head with sharp pains.

I'm not part of your flock! Moira wanted to scream out, but didn't. She knew that to acknowledge the thing was detrimental to the truly secret corners of the psyche.

For now, she simply walked away from the scene entirely, having done everything she needed to do for now.

In the hallway, it did not take long for her to bump into another one of the Haven enforcers. This one seemed a bit friendlier though, as far as she could tell with the masks on and all. "Miss LaGrande," he beckoned. "ETA is about ten minutes, you good, yeah?"

She nodded absentminded.

Here we go, let's hope this works… Man, I'm overthinking a lot these days.

～

Lilly was fleeing for her life. Or so she thought.

Tears welled up in the corners of her eyes as she stumbled through the patches of mud and loose soil in the small pathways between the corn. She hadn't looked back yet, but somehow she knew exactly what horrific thing was pursuing her.

With a big *splash* and a dull *thud*, Lilly slammed hard into the mud. She bit the inside of her cheek as the surge of pain flowed through her ankle and side. She desperately tried to be as quiet as she could—any type of sound would betray her presence. Once again, she did not know why, but somehow, she knew this for a fact.

Her breathing consisted of short bursts, and every gasp stung her insides with sharp pains. She wondered if she would ever be able to distinguish reality from hallucination again. Even now as she let her eyes wander across the top of the corn rows, she swore she saw streaks of flames rise up through pillars of black smoke a little way away. At least she had ditched the clown, which was a small comfort.

She lay there silently for a while, just by herself in the mud. She was contemplating every sinister and mocking move the universe could've thrown at her and her brother. She knew she didn't want any of this anymore, but how could she possibly leave her old life behind? Especially with every bad and horrid thing ever dreamed up by mankind and beyond following her now, just two steps behind.

Lilly rose from her muddy half-grave and gazed in the direction from which she was running. There, on the edge of the cornfield, was a man cloaked in everlasting shadow with a perpetual darkness covering his face and features.

And he was wearing a raggedy straw hat. Hot streaks of terror shot through Lilly's spine—she screamed.

She screamed like she had never screamed before. It was a primordial shriek, a tidal force of pure terror and anguish.

Around her, flocks of birds rose up from the fields and joined her in her harrowed cry. They would fly up toward where the shadow-man was and circle around above him. Then the birds would peck each other menacingly, and more than one would eventually lose the infighting and slam into the earth below. A black-feathered carrion cannibalized through some ancient evil force beyond their control.

She started to shake.

The shadow-man was lumbering toward her, and Lilly started her desperate flight all over again.

The lone figure had very little discerning traits to speak of. He was not overly broad nor was he super thin. His black clothes were not distinguishable from a distance, yet it did not appear to be any style or brand or sort of clothing at all. The shadowy figure was like many a nightmare manifestation, an embodiment of fear and inner turmoil and struggle. He had no face, for he needed none, just like he needed no discernable clothes or traits. He only needed to convey one simple message: *If I catch you, you will die.*

Lilly tried emptying her mind. She tried to think of pleasant things like a box of kittens or a bunch of puppies or cherry pie from a diner near a small town in Washington state they had once passed through. She tried thinking of more pleasant memories together with Quincy and her parents, but each of the memories eventually ended up in the same place—with her going to sleep fulfilled and happy and then ending up trapped in the corn maze with the shadow-man.

Lilly barely managed to avoid slamming face-first into the red farm shed that seemed to have popped up from nowhere right in front of her. She turned around with her back toward the shed and immediately went into a hyperventilating panic when she saw the shadow-man creeping ever closer. She could not actually *see* him move or walk at all—it was as if the thought of him coming close made him inch forward with every blink of the eyes or every flash of lightning.

It was now fully dark with only the thunderstorm lighting a path or, on rare occasions, the moonlight peeked through the exaggeratedly fast-moving rainclouds to light up small patches of earth and corn. The rain slammed hard against Lilly's cheeks. She let herself slide down the back of the shed.

She started to sob in defeat, only startling for a bit when she thought she heard her name being called in the distance.

"Lilly! *Lil!*"

Was it another dream or figment of her imagination?

"Lilly, *please!*" A familiar voice rang through the air like a fresh meadow breeze on the first day of spring.

"Quin-Quince?" Lilly whispered.

"Lilly! Are you okay?" Another voice, slightly less familiar, but warm and welcoming nonetheless joined the first.

"Liz?" Lilly mumbled. She opened her eyes, and through mystical light of an unknown origin, she saw her brother and newfound friend Lizbeth standing on the edge of the corn, just a few feet behind the shadow-man.

"Do-Don't come closer!" Lilly managed to yell out. She grasped her sides in pain and looked down at her hands. They were bloody. She must've cut herself on a jagged rock when she fell down. She ignored it for now. "He will kill you!" she yelled again. "Don't do it!"

"Lilly, he's not *real*! None of this is, except for all of this damn corn! Well, and the rain, possibly. That feels real," Quincey mumbled.

Lilly made herself as small as she could as she inched against the wall of the shed entirely. She pulled up her knees toward her face and squinted. "He's right there! You can see him, can't you?"

"He's only there because you made him appear your-self!" Quincy called back. "We're in your nightmare. You always gloat about how you can control your dreams, right? You can control this as well."

Liz cleared her throat. "Lilly, do you remember what I said when we first arrived in this hellhole town? When the days shorten and the air gets colder, the demons of the fall will rear their ugly faces and try to get those negative thoughts in our heads. Do you remember? This is your demon, Lilly, but he can't be beat with a fistful of blessed buckshot and a whole bunch of attitude. Are you getting the gist of what I'm saying here?" Liz was shouting, her voice going hoarse near the end.

"I-I don't know," Lilly exclaimed, feeling defeated. "It's too hard."

"No, it's not, sis." Quincy called out. He started to walk toward Lilly, just behind the encroaching shadow-man.

From the corner of his eyes, he could see several figures dressed in stylish black appear on the edges of the field and corners of the barn. Besides their suits, they also had the sunglasses in common. "Lilly…" Quincy shivered. He was more wary of the agents surrounding them than Lilly's nightmare manifestation. "Stay still. It's going to be okay, I'm coming, yeah?"

"Quincy, don't!" Lilly called out. "He'll get you; you're right behind him."

"No, he won't," Liz said calmly, her eyes tracking the Haven agents as they crept forward.

"He cannot hurt me, just like he cannot hurt you." Quincy stood right behind the shadow-man now. "I know this is hard, Lil, but trust me."

Lilly gasped in relief and wonder as Quincy stepped right through the shadow-man, which evaporated on the spot as soon as he did, like a bad dream vanquished by the merciful morning light.

Quincy ran up to his sister and embraced her. "You're alright, sis. Yeah?" He tried to get her to stand up, but quickly noticed the bloodstains seeping through her shirt.

"I don't *think* I'm alright." Her eye lids fluttered. She threw him a weak smile.

Quincy returned the nervous gesture. "You'll be okay; we'll figure it out. Most important thing is that this nightmare of yours is over, okay?" He grabbed his sister's shoulders and looked her in the eyes. "I'm really proud of you, Lil."

Lilly was nodding when the two of them fell through the side of the shed.

It was a very peculiar turn of events: For a moment, there was no shed but rather a kind of starry doorway into another place, and that other place also turned out to be a doorway toward the other side of the shed. The whole ordeal lasted maybe half a second. Its harrowing effect, however, could be felt like a deep nauseating seed in the stomach of those who underwent it for anywhere between two and forty-eight hours.

From the outside, the aftermath was nothing more than what looked like a slight ripple in the air around the side of the shed, like heat off the asphalt in the heat of the summer. One moment, the twins were there—the other, they weren't.

Liz saw the wobbling shed very clearly. She had ducked down in between the cornrows and laid flat on the ground. There was no time for anti-detection spells or any sort of magical intervention. Haven agents were already circling the field. She had to move as quickly as possible while staying out of sight.

"There was a third one, I am sure of it," a smooth and very articulate voice said just inches from her hiding spot.

"Orders, sir?" a rougher, hollow voice asked.

"Kill on sight."

"Affirmative."

Drip… Drip… Drip…

The walls were oozing. The ceiling was oozing. There was a smell nearly indescribable—incomprehensible, unconceivable, unfathomable. It was humid, thick, and impossible not to inhale with huge gulps at a time. It was acidic, and it hurt a lot. It was something the human body naturally rejected, leading to a very unfortunate conundrum for anyone who found themselves trapped in this lair of foulness without some kind of breathing apparatus or protective suit.

Then there was the other thing… Namely, all the eyes jittering everywhere. They were flashing about in perfect unison and sought out any sudden or unexpected movement.

The eyes were everywhere. Literally.

The entire inside of the shed consisted of some sort of pulsating blanket of filth and rot with those upsetting bulbous lookers hanging out all over. Every once in a while, a glowing aura ran across the entire mass. From top to bottom, an indiscernible light lit up beneath the thing, making it shine in an array of colors all at once.

From the corners of their eyes, the twins could also make out the now familiar parasite-critters that had been infecting the brains of the poor people they'd encountered. Luckily for them, the things appeared to have no interest in them—for now.

Then there were the teeth. Needless to say, the orifices were aplenty, and they had the yellow and brown rows of razor sharp chompers and fangs (and tusks?) to go with them. But a mouth wasn't a requirement, apparently. Many who would lay their sights on this tableau would definitely never have seen a jagged tooth grow out of a seeping eye socket before.

Once the initial shock of the temporal displacement had dissipated and they had gotten their first whiff of the toxic fumes drifting in the dilapidated barn, nearly choking in the process, it was Quincy that managed to form the first sentence between them.

"Is your foot…" he wheezed. "Hey, it's both. Are your feet stuck in these alien pods as well?" His last few syllables ended with a very nasty coughing fit. Quincy struggled for breath, but most of the air entering his lungs was immediately expelled by his body's tendency to preserve the functionality of his vital organs.

For a little while, Lilly said nothing at all. She simply stared around in horror at the gruesome scene. Her breaths were very small, slow and laborious, but after a bit she noticed that this method would allow just enough oxygen to reach her lungs in order to stay conscious, at least. "Slow down your breathing," she sputtered. "Short little pockets of air. That's right…" She smiled weakly. "All right."

No talking before mass, little lambs, a voice shrieked inside their heads. It was shrill and very loud, and it hurt as if small razorblades were cutting across their scalps. It was also instantly recognizable as being one of those specific *not of this Earth* kind of voices.

Lilly groaned. "Oh, not some extraterrestrial crap *again.* We don't do that kind of stuff anymore, man."

Silence.

"Have you seen that alien-owl movie with Mila Jovovich in Alaska? That's us right now. It's above our paygrade. Way up there," Lilly joked, her voice weak.

"Are you telling me we're getting paid?" Quincy joined in on the banter and coughed. Then he laughed until one of the teeth-hole things started to slither toward his feet.

A nearby bulbous mass exploded outward in the

twins' direction, and both were covered in an outburst of toxic fumes seeping from the dripping extremity.

Suddenly, the twins couldn't speak anymore; all they could do was cough—then they realized that breathing was one hundred percent impossible. Panic grew.

Their surroundings became vague, their tunnel vision growing until the inevitable point came when they'd pass out and presumably never wake up again.

When a fuzzy outline of a man appeared in front of them, the twins thought they were hallucinating. He was clothed in a full-fledged hazard suit, which strangely also came with a tie. Furthermore, he seemed to be wearing sunglasses behind his protective mask.

The figure leaned over and pulled oxygen masks over their mouths. He then waited until a faint spark of life returned to their eyes. Soon, both Lilly and Quincy gasped for air. The green, grey, and brown blubber surrounding them sounded as if it was bawling with disappointment.

"I wouldn't *anger* anything before knowing what I'd exactly be dealing with," the man chided and shook his head. "Then again, you are *not* highly trained spec ops personnel, but rather two increasingly annoying pests needing to be dealt with ASAP." The man chuckled and raised his hand.

Several beams of light came down from the ceiling and lit the twins up in a harsh brightness that felt as if it burned the skin; it definitely hurt the eyes. There was a second story balcony on which several more men in black with special operative soldiers nearby stood at attention. The alien growth that covered the inside of the farmhouse building was likewise splashed all over the balcony, but it did not seem to affect the people standing there.

"So supernatural farm buildings are a thing now as well, huh?" Quincy panted, and the mask fogged up a bit.

"Now," the man in the suit continued, ignoring Quincy's comment, "let's get the formalities out of the way. My name is Special Agent Dutch. You two are the meddlesome Swansong twins, no introduction needed. Are you ready to comply?"

"We don't work with Haven scum," Lilly hissed through the mask over her mouth. "You're the people to blame; you caused all of this. And this…" She waved around at the gory spectacle around them. "What the *fuck* even *is* this? What in the Ancient's name are you doing here?"

SUCH DISRESPECT, the voice in their mind came again. It gnawed at the twins' heads like a cheese rasp.

"That *thing* is a formidable outer-worldly being Haven was absolutely fortunate enough to find out here before the GDF dogs would get at it." Agent Dutch seemed to quiver from delight when speaking about the being. "Oh, if only you know the things it can do! Fully cooperating as well, especially in tracking you to down and getting you here."

"Why is that?" Quincy asked.

Agent Dutch caressed a slimy tendril lovingly. It slid across his arm before crawling back to wherever it came. "Well, you kind of threw things in its favor when you…" He shrugged. "You know, I rather don't see the point of explaining things you don't need to worry about."

"Oh, right." Quincy laughed. "We'll *surely* talk now that you won't give us *any* explanation at all."

Several of the teeth rows started gnashing again and moving toward him. It would have made Quincy break out in a profuse sweat if he wasn't already doing exactly that. All he could do was chuckle nervously, considering he had no clue how they'd possibly walk away from any of this. He was thinking about it, though—a solution, that is—when he saw Liz lurking in a corner on the balcony, ready to help when the chips came down.

A young woman of African-American descent, dressed in turquoise, deep blue, and gold appeared behind Agent Dutch. Her half-long, straight hair was dark, but the tips were shades of light blue, purple, and pink.

"You're early, Miss LaGrande," Agent Dutch chided. "But okay, might as well make this quick." He scoffed. "Miss Swansong, Mister Swansong. Let me assure you that what you've witnessed up until now in Darkness Falls and the surrounding counties—the infestation, the amnesia, the nightmare-hallucinations, the total compliance and subjugation of will—it's only a *fraction* of what *Mother* can do."

"Mother?" Lilly spat. "What a perversion. You're all sick."

The terrifying voice of 'Mother' let out a shrill cry. It was a sound encompassing absolute terror. A wail of malevolent laughter and maleficent moaning. It was unearthly.

Although they did not say, both twins were mortified. There was something itching in the back of their heads. It was as if something wanted to get in, to claim them as its own, as its property forever. Quincy could swear he heard furtive whispers just on the inside of his temples. He swallowed hard.

"So that's all this was? A ruse? An elaborate trap to get us where you want us? What the hell do you want?" Quincy pleaded. He was stalling, having figured out that Haven likely wanted something from them, and the longer as he could bide their time, the longer Liz had to prepare a spell, incantation…anything to help.

"A trap? Perhaps yes, but Mother was going to work her magic one way or another, with or without you two sticking your noses where they don't belong. As for what I want; just one thing, really…" Agent Dutch grinned.

"Cut the Bond villain act and tell us." Lilly rolled her eyes.

"You *know* about the forgotten Celestian tomb, the *last* one in North America. And no, I'm not talking about Three Rivers in New Mexico. Where is the last tomb?"

"Tomb? I have no freaking clue what you're on about!" Lilly yelled. "But know you're gonna pay for all of this, you *fucker*! Just you wait!"

"We—" Quincy began, but he was interrupted by an insufferable noise of retching and high-pitched cries.

Agent Dutch held his ears to one of the mucus-spewing orifices. "Yes, uh-huh. I understand, thank you." He stood up and pulled out a standard caliber 9mm handgun. "Mother tells me you're telling the truth. So, I guess you two are indeed, as suspected, absolutely useless. Now, let's see…shall we do the infection or…" He stopped and shooed away one of the clacking parasite-beasts that had come and taken an interest. "No, that'll take too long. Oh well, boring route it is."

Agent Dutch shot both Quincy and Lilly point blank

in the head. He did not even so much as flinch when their limp, lifeless bodies sagged to the floor.

"*NO!*" Liz bellowed in shock and horror as the unreal scene unfolded in front of her eyes. She felt rooted to the floor. Her body wanted to collapse, but her mind told her to run—*Run like hell*. Around her, the shuffling of feet and the drawing of weapons was another indication that it was time to flee.

"Moira, you know what to do with these," Agent Dutch said, sighing. "Agent Pickman, Agent Gibbous, make sure that witch is terminated." He pointed to Liz before he took a handkerchief to his gun and wiped the blood off with zero emotion. "Oh, and you, Agent Adams…"

"Sir?" a raven-haired woman with a grotesque scar above her left eyebrow answered.

"Call you-know-who. I'm sure he'll be very pleased to hear that the Swansong twins are dead."

____

Chapter 6
THE TWINS

____

IT FELT LIKE A SWIRLING VORTEX. There were fleeting moments of extreme triggers in sounds, sight, color…and everything between. It all happened in a split second. One snap of the fingers and it was all gone.

"NO!"

The twins could just make out Liz's terrified scream from the balcony right before the world turned to black and white. Helpless, they could only stand (or float) there and watch as their bodies hit the ground, blood and mucus gushing from the holes in their heads.

Special Agent Dutch said something to the fading voodoo girl that accompanied him, but it was already too vague to make out.

The twins could only stare in disbelief.

They wanted to say something. They wanted to reach out and do something, anything. But before they could react, they realized that the monochrome façade before them was a simple reflection of the last few seconds of their lives. It was a fractured mirror held before their eyes, and from in between the cracks of shattered glass, it was as if their subconscious selves spoke to them and told them that they had failed. That this was all for nothing.

The twins closed their eyes.

The scene, together with the entire waking world, faded from existence.

There was a crossroads now when they opened their eyes again: Everything was still colorless and there was nothing that resembled life anywhere as far as could be observed. The sky was pitch black and void of stars. Trees, grey and forlorn, surrounded the twins on all sides, except for the dark expanses toward which the various pathways seemed to lead. There were symbols carved into the dirt in the middle of the road. It was as if a distant humming could be heard from them. The twins took a step closer toward the pattern of symbols, and it felt as if the earth beneath their feet buzzed with anticipation.

Lilly looked at her brother. He looked sad and lifeless; she felt the same way. It was as if they had been robbed of not only their lives, but their souls, their humanity. Everything felt bleak and hollow.

For the first time in a while, Lilly felt compelled and able to speak her mind. However, the most difficult thing for her—and Quincy as well—was to acknowledge that which they both already knew had happened. She said nothing at all, for there was nothing to say that would make it better.

Crossroads were a well-known concept in mythology. They symbolized the pathways between worlds and dimensions. Those wandering them would more often than not have to come to terms with the transition from life to death. This was, after all, as far the twins both knew, their death.

Lilly wanted to discuss all of this and more, for she saw the same observations burning on Quincy's lips. She was just about to open her mouth when her head shot to the side where she noticed something moving. Her eyes grew large and welled with tears. Perhaps a part of their soul was still intact. A soft whining came from just beyond the underbrush in front of them.

"Hewie?" she called toward the little grey shape that darted in and out of the tree line. It was the only thing she could muster. She had forgotten about everything else.

Quincy followed with some hesitation. "Lilly? Woah, is… Hey, be careful."

"What for?" she called back. "You know what's happening here, right? Look, it's Hewie. It really is—he waited for us all this time."

The bushes in front of them rattled, and from them emerged the spectral image of a corgi. It was entirely transparent, and every bone in its body could be seen. Yet, for those with a keen eye, looking very closely would reveal the intricate fur pattern the little critter used to wear in its living days. Sure enough, Lilly was one hundred percent convinced it was the old Swansong family pet, Hewie. She threw herself on the ground and wrapped her arms around the dog. To her surprise and relief, her arms did not phase right through.

Quincy knelt next to his sister and patted the little dog on the head. "It really *is* him. Wow, how are you, little buddy?"

Hewie barked enthusiastically and with anticipation.

"He's dead, just like us," Lilly responded distantly. All of a sudden, she felt struck down again, unclear of what to do or say. "What the hell are we going to do, Quince? I mean, shit. There's no coming back from this. We failed."

Hewie barked happily at the sound of Lilly's voice. It was a strange contrast to their direness of the situation.

"I don't know what to say," Quincy said, having to raise his voice over the increasing echoes of Hewie's barking. "There's no real denying the facts here!" he yelled. "LET'S HOPE THAT PERHAPS LIZ GOT AWAY AND CAN RALLY SOME PEOPLE TO STOP THIS MOTHER THING!"

"Hewie!" Lilly huffed. "People are talking! What's the matter with you?"

The corgi barked and wagged his tail fiercely before he sped off down one of the crossroad lanes. Lilly quickly jolted up and ran after him. "Hey! Wait up, buddy!"

Quincy followed. "Lilly, wait, can we stop and think about this? This is a crossroads, right? Won't this determine our ultimate fate or whatever in the afterlife? Feels like kind of a big deal? Right? Wait up! Dammit!" He stopped to catch his breath. Then, after realizing there was no such thing as breathing when you're dead, he sped off after them again.

The path ended at the edge of a lake. The water's surface was silky smooth, and it shone like silver. At first glance, it looked thick, like mercury.

Hewie ran three laps around Lilly's legs first before diving in the lake with a happy yelp. The ripples from the ghostly corgi's splash were mesmerizing, each tiny wave reaching the reed-filled water's edge seemed as if it cascaded right back toward the center of the lake. And with every ripple, a soft neon glow could be seen deep beneath the water. It was the first bit of color the twins had seen since, well, their death. They were both utterly engrossed by it.

The only real downside to it all appeared to be the fact that Hewie was not coming back up. Soon enough, the lake was still again, and there was no sign of him at all.

"I'm going after him," Lilly said after a couple of minutes.

"Uh, I'm not sure that's such a great idea. We don't know what's in there," Quincy countered.

"Uh, yeah we do. Our dog is." Lilly rolled her eyes. "Besides, we're dead. There's nothing to hurt us. Here, look." Lilly grabbed her right pinky finger and snapped it into a less than subtle off-angle. "Oh, holy *shit*, I was just trying stuff out, that really works!" She laughed.

"Gross!" Quincy squinted at the oddly angled appendage, then turned away to look around. "Okay, point made, I guess." He shrugged. "What's the worst that could happen anyway, right? Right, Lilly?" At her silence, he turned around to see his sister diving into the silver lake.

Groaning with annoyance, Quincy followed.

The twins did not expect the lake to be a one-way type of deal.

As soon as Quincy had dipped his head underwater, his whole body felt as if it fell through the inside of a tornado. Yet in mere moments, he had emerged on the other side and fell hard on his butt. He looked around bewildered and saw his sister had already wandered off a hundred feet or so with Hewie. He caught up with her quickly, and only after being reunited did they get a good look around and let the world around them sink in.

Around them were buildings, trees, lamp posts, and even cars, but not a single living being could be seen. They figured out soon enough that it was actually the town of Darkness Falls, near which they had lost their lives. But it wasn't *their* version of the town—it wasn't the *living* version. Everything was, for lack of a better term, distorted somewhat. Buildings and houses had weird angles or features that perhaps did not belong or weren't logical at all. Everything was cast in permanent shadow. The same monochrome tone of grey that permeated the crossroads was also the norm in whatever this place was.

But not everything appeared dark and lifeless, however. In the sky above them were great streaks of ghostly neon lights dancing and twirling across the vast blackness of the ether. Now, there *were* stars, but Quincy (having dabbled in astronomy for a semester) could not recognize or place any of the constellations. The bright pink, blue, and purple neon lines pulsated now and again. For the twins, it was impossible to determine where it came from, how high or low the lights hung or what their purpose was. They could only discern that, like its closest living world counterpart—the Aurora Borealis—it was majestic in every way.

For the accomplished *listener,* there was another thing that set this plane apart. Coinciding with the pulsating lights was a slight breeze flowing through the dreary abandoned city every once in a while. When listening very carefully, tonal sounds could be heard carried by this wind. It was very soft and almost unrecognizable, but those with keen ears could hear the whispers of a flute or the slight humming of synthesizers droning alongside the flashing of the lights high up in the sky.

Pretty as they were, the few 'pulses' of light and perhaps *life* did little to dissuade from the darkness-clad ghost town and its less than picturesque environs.

The twins slowly wandered along the main street with an anxious feeling that something could be, and was, lurking around every possible corner. Hewie strolled only a few feet ahead and looked back at every few minutes, keeping a close eye on them. Lilly was convinced the little dog felt that dreaded feeling of impending doom as well, but she was slightly relieved at the confidence with which the little corgi traipsed over the abandoned streets. *Shouldn't be afraid of anything* she reminded herself. *You're already dead, kiddo. Tough shit!*

"What the hell is this place?" Quincy asked eventually with bated breath.

"Well, it has once been described as '*the living world as seen through a fractured mirror in a dusty old forgotten room.*' It certainly has a nice ring to it if you're into the whole poetic thing," an unfamiliar voice answered. It was close too.

From behind one of the cars across the street emerged a crooked old man with a long grey beard and a bald head. More peculiar was that he didn't seem to have any eyes, just empty dark sockets. He clenched a rickety walking stick and was dressed in black tatters. Despite the somewhat unsettling first impressions he did not come across as having any kind of malevolent intent.

"Woah! Okay. Wh-who are you?" Lilly was taken aback by the man's appearance.

"Eh, it's not important right now." The man treaded slowly toward them, Hewie sniffing his feet. The little corgi sneezed and quickly back off. "This old hermit has got a few wisdoms to share yet, but they are probably better left until a later time."

"Okay, then let's share some straightforward ones, please. Where are we?" Quincy asked.

"Yes, good, very good question indeed," the hermit praised, then took a big breath. But his chest did not expand, nor was there any need for any air to be breathed here, the twins had noticed. "You two are currently residing in what is commonly known as the Inbetween."

"Ooo-kaaay?" Lilly raised an eyebrow. "Elaborate? Please?"

"Other such names given are: The Hinterland, The Shadow, *Purgatory* if you're into the whole biblical thing or, lastly, the Realm of the Nearly Departed." The hermit coughed. "So, you're in luck there, Swansong twins."

"What do you mean, we're in luck?" Lilly asked.

"Wait, how does he know who we are?" Quincy chimed in.

"And how do you know who we are?" Lilly repeated. "Is this some kind of ruse? Another hallucinatory spell? Is there a way out?"

The old hermit shook his head. "Too many questions at once: Your past and possible futures we will perhaps discuss these another time. For now, you only need to know one thing."

"And that is?" Quincy was growing impatient.

"Your mortal bodies have died, but your souls...have

been preserved. You have been tethered to the Inbetween, but the other side is still back in the living world. Check your pockets."

Lilly and Quincy both ransacked through their clothes and conjured up a small piece of glowing string.

"Do not lose that," the hermit instructed. "That could be your ticket back to life."

"Really?" Lilly gasped. "So, what are we supposed to do now?"

The hermit shrugged. "I could tell you the entire ordeal and how to fix it, but where is the fun in that?" He laughed. "You need two things: to contact the entity that holds your tether here in the Nearly Departed Realm—his name is Samuel Hain."

"Samuel Hain. Sam Hain? You're kidding, right? That's the name we're going with here?" Lilly groaned.

"Two," the old hermit continued, ignoring her remarks, "you will need a guide through the realm to ensure you don't stray from the path and encounter a more *permanent* state of being deceased. But it seems you already got that covered."

"Oh yeah?" Quincy raised an eyebrow. "Who's that going to be, then?"

There was no response—the old man had disappeared.

Hewie began barking with fervor, hobbling up and down as he chased his tail for a couple of laps.

"Hewie?" Quincy asked aloud and the see-through corgi yelped in acknowledgement.

Lilly smiled wide. "Hewie! Yes!" Something resembling happiness crept up from the gaping maw that felt was left of her soul. "Well, this will be one for the books, right? *Swansong twins find world threatening alien, get killed, come back, and proceed to kick alien ass.* It has a nice ring to it." She then grew more serious, twirling some of her curls between her fingers. "Then again, I don't know what *Mother* exactly is, but that nightmare—for me it was very real. Are we in over our heads?"

Quincy shrugged. "We've lost our heads. There's nothing we can do about it right *now.*" The situation had gotten so absurd, he almost felt immune to it. "We should concentrate on getting out of here. Maybe we can contact this Hain fellow through that broadcast tower on the hill over there."

"Woooah, that's strange. There wasn't any broadcast tower in Darkness Falls back in real life, was there? Come to think of it, there weren't any hills either."

"Well, we're not in *real life* anymore. We're half-dead, hanging-in-the-balance, *nearly departed.*"

Chapter 7

LIZBETH

THE LIFELESS BODIES of Quincy and Lilly sagged to the ground, blood and mucus spilling out of the fresh holes that had opened up through their skulls just seconds before.

"NO!" she screamed. She couldn't hold it in even if she wanted to. The pain was too strong; her body quaked with anger and hate. There were a thousand things left to do, and a million things left to say. But Liz realized that for now, to save herself and to make sure someone would make it back to see this abomination destroyed, all she could do was run.

Immediately after the outburst, the soldier perched on the balcony to Liz's left spun around and flashed his headlight—he saw the heels of her boots disappear from view. A hail of automatic machine gun fire blasted through the wooden planks of the farm shed moments later.

Liz ran as if the Devil had given chase, which in some way or another, could be considered fairly accurate considering the circumstances. She followed the same way down that she'd taken up to the second floor with gunfire and yelling and a host of angry men and women in hot pursuit.

At the bottom of the stairs, just shy of the backdoor leading outside to the fields, a huge burly-looking soldier caught Liz off-guard, and she ran right into the elbow he'd flung toward her in anticipation. It hit her straight in the gut and she moaned before gasping desperately for the air that was knocked out of her. The soldier, ugly with a patchy beard and yellow, crooked teeth, grinned widely as he grappled Liz up and into his bulky arms.

"This'll surely be a promotion for old Bobby," he laughed. "Stop kicking. You'll only make it worse, pretty one."

"Since when did you fuckers become so militarily organized?" Liz struggled as the big arms clasped around her torso, squeezing tight. With her left hand, she tried to reach into her back pocket. Her other hand reached for something in her front right pocket.

"Since when? Ever since we became the only ones left between *you* and the things that go bump in the night, sweetheart."

"*I* am the thing that goes bump in the night, asshole," Liz responded. She flicked the lighter she'd grabbed from one pocket and burned the sunflower seeds she'd grabbed with her other hand for just this occasion.

"*Luminosus!*"

The entire room lit up in a blinding flash of pure white-hot solar energy. The soldier released her in surprise, and Liz took advantage by skittering out of the shed and back into the fields as fast as she could.

Back outside, the world seemed to have been returned

to its fairly normal self. The sky was now a burning orange indicating that darkness was, well, falling, on Darkness Falls. With Lilly dead, the nightmarish drape that had befallen the fields had dissipated. The feeling of oppression was mostly gone, and so was that nagging feeling of constantly being watched.

In the split-second Liz got to think about everything, she was relieved. It meant that whatever *Mother* was, it could only partially conjure up the demons of the psyche and place them in the waking world. It could only do so when the mental state was weakened enough. There was no doubt, however, that breaking the sane mind was definitely another one of *Mother's* specialties.

Liz sped off through the cornfields. She kept a close eye on the sun and whispered a small prayer under her breath in the hopes that she had still remembered the right direction from which they had come into town.

The butt of an assault rifle to the temple got Liz heading face-first for the mud. The dull *thud* came from her left, and for a moment, Liz's world was spinning out of control. It wasn't so much the pain as it was the bile forming in her throat—her luck was waning. Her powers were all-but drained. She hadn't the energy nor the willpower to fight any longer.

She could not get up; her head felt like it was bursting at the seams. Liz cursed her misfortune as the barrel of the gun pricked her neck.

"End of the road," a woman with a raspy voice said. Agent Pickman was standing over Liz with her boot planted in Liz's lower back and the gun keeping her head down.

Liz could see the woman's hair tucked in a neat bun,

complementing the simplicity but also elegance of the flawless black suit she was wearing.

"Shades out at night, huh?" Liz huffed at the woman's sunglasses. "Are you an actual idiot?"

A man, in the same attire, walked up next to the woman in black. "Always the feisty ones, right, Agent Pickman?" he spoke mockingly.

"I like the feisty ones, Agent Gibbous. Reminds me of the days when I was *undisciplined*," she replied.

"Then perhaps it's time for a lesson." Agent Gibbous laughed.

Liz braced for impact, letting go of any and all bits of energy she had left. She felt herself slowly slipping to sleep when she heard a third voice join in.

"Leave her to me." A young woman approached them; it was the dark-skinned voodoo girl Liz had seen earlier accompanying Agent Dutch in the shed with whatever the hell they'd end up calling that horror show.

"LaGrande? What are you doing so far away from Dutch's heels? Orders were to kill on sight—we're following orders," Agent Pickman said.

"She asked you a question earlier," the girl said. "Are you actual idiots?"

"I swear…" Agent Gibbous groaned.

"She's a *witch* and she can end both of you in seconds. Let *me* deal with her."

Liz felt the butt of the gun leaving the back of her neck. She also felt the weight of Agent Pickman's boot lessen. It seemed absolutely crazy, but her first instinct at that very moment was to get up and start running again. Liz sighed laboriously as she tried getting up, fighting the pain and vertigo.

"Shit," Agent Pickman exclaimed and cocked the gun.

Moria LeGrande rolled her eyes. "Really?" she asked. "Fine, you asked for it." She

snapped her fingers, and the ground around Agents Pickman and Gibbous stirred wildly. They both started taking several steps back but were caught completely unaware by the myriad of snakes that started flying up from the ground.

The earth itself cracked open and spat serpents of all colors and sizes, which soon attached themselves quite vigorously to the pair of Haven agents. Needless to say, their horrified death screams could be heard far and wide. It was unclear whether the agents' skin started to color purple due to a particular kind of poison, or if it was to be attributed by 'merely' suffocation. Nevertheless, both agents had put up a *very decent* dance-off before plopping to the ground unceremoniously.

"Damn, that was way louder than I thought." Moira gritted her teeth. "Get ready to run," she ordered, turning to Liz.

Liz was back on the ground, lying with her face sideways in the mud and her bum sticking up in the air—she was snoring.

When Liz opened her eyes, two things immediately became clear: She was somewhere inside, and all of the corn was finally gone.

There was also the voice, slightly familiar, that was saying, "Hey, do you have *The Cajun How-to-Voodoo Cooking*

Guide and You by Francois von Salad? Yeah? Nice, that's definitely going in the check-out pile."

Liz looked around. She was lying on a bunch of pillows in a cozy but dusty corner of an old library. A few oil lamps hung to the sides of the walls, lighting up a little bit of the room, which was mostly filled to the brim with stacks of books, papers, and floor-to-ceiling bookcases.

"*Eldritch Cathuria and Trips Around the Great Basalt Pillars of the West—A Travel Guide* by U. Kadath? Closer, but not quite. Need more on dimensional tampering."

Liz spotted the sign saying *Darkness Falls Public Library* and the feeling of defeat from earlier came back, rising within her. She was still in town, which meant she was still far away from safety.

She started to wonder now how she even got to the library in the first place. She spotted another sign: *Restricted Section—Occult and Magic*.

"*A History of Time-Space Anomalies on Edwards Island* by Maggie Adler. Closer still…" The voice kept on mumbling. "Very interesting, but not local."

Liz stood up and followed the sound of the voice around the corner of one of the bookcases. Her head spun around like she was on a merry-go-round going seventy miles-per-hour. She grasped the bookcase tight. She felt the bile rising in her throat as she looked around for an exit, but couldn't immediately find one.

"Oh, shit, I think this is it! *Sticky Things on Infinite Planes* by Wyoming MacLeods!" The voice belonged to the dark-skinned girl that was also present in the barn. Liz remembered her name—Moira. Moira was partially to blame for getting the twins killed…

Moira needed to die.

Moira looked up from the table she stood at and smiled at her. It wasn't an evil, mischievous, or even a crooked smile. It was actually kind of sweet. "Oh, hey, you're up. Good, now listen real close for a moment—"

"What the flying fuck?" Liz burst out. "Give me *one* reason why I shouldn't *evaporate* you right fucking now?" Her face was dark red with anger and sadness.

Moira threw her hands up in the air. She was taken aback by the outburst, but couldn't say she was completely surprised. "Hold up, hold up!" She took a step back. "Let me say my piece and I'll give you, I dunno, at least three or four reasons not to kill me."

The pain on Liz's face was almost tangible, but she said nothing. She simply stared.

"Okay," Moira continued, "reason one: Me working with Haven, that wasn't my idea… It's my family, and they have a lot of influence. It's complicated."

"You're a LaGrande, right?"

Moira nodded.

"Not helping your case at all," Liz hissed.

The LaGrande family was a notorious clan of voodoo practitioners that had a reputation of having members sticking their hands in evil and otherwise unsavory businesses on more than one occasion. The LaGrandes and their few allied cults and organizations were rivals of pretty much every other witch coven, druid circle, or warlock sect in the continental United States—even at 'war' with some of them.

Liz stared at the ghostly apparition of an old lady librarian listening eagerly onto the conversation from one of the empty chairs. She growled, and the spirit faded away with a grimace.

"I'm not like the rest of my family," Moira said, ignoring the preceding scene. "I'm against all of this crap. And there's your second reason right there: I want to join the rebels, the people going against all of Haven's doings."

The fists Liz had been clenching loosened somewhat. Still, she was very skeptical and most of all, still very angry. "I'm not with any rebels, so frankly, I don't give a shit. You killed my friends!" The tears started to well up again.

Moira took a deep breath and sighed.

She had a pleading look in her eyes that Liz tried to ignore at first, but there was something genuine about the girl.

"Look, I know this'll sound crazy, but I actually made sure your friends have a chance of making it back."

"Wait, what?"

"There's your third reason." Moira gently lifted two stone jars engraved with voodoo symbols up onto the table. "I made a deal with a spirit of the crossroads. The souls of the Swansong twins have been preserved right here in these jars. They are tethered to the afterlife, and we can help them get back if we work together."

"I can't believe…" Liz's head swirled. "But what about that monster in the barn?" she asked. "It has powers we've all never seen before. Haven can ruin everything if it isn't stopped."

Moira smirked. "Reason four"—she tapped the last book she'd taken off the shelf—"I may have found the book from which we can at least figure out what that amalgamation of everything unholy that is back there, and hopefully learn how to stop it as well."

For a little while, the two women sat in silence: Moira knew she had to give Liz some space to let everything sink in.

Eventually, Liz spoke.

"Alright, let's go. I want to hear everything."

Chapter 8
INTERMISSION

"HOLD ON, hold on! You're telling me that, right now, you're talking to me from a broadcasting tower that somehow managed to materialize in the *Inbetween* spirit realm in a town in which there is no such thing in real life?" Sean started to wander around the little room again.

"Wrong," Lilly muttered before sighing. "Sean, have you been paying any attention at all to what we've been telling you? I mean, yes, the broadcasting tower really *is* a very cool detail about what this strange place can do and manifest and all that, but I'm very sorry to say that contacting you was not the very first thing that sprang to mind."

Sean could hear Quincy in the background clearing his throat.

"What Lilly means, Sean, is that contacting the *living* after shedding part of our *mortal coil*, so to speak, did not seem to be the logical first step to undertake."

"Or even steps two through seven," Lilly added.

"Back at it with the fancy words again, Quincy." Sean chuckled. "I thought we agreed you'd speak plainly as to only having then to explain things just the one time…" He scratched his beard. He had shaven just a couple of nights earlier, but the thick stubble had already returned with a vengeance—it was itchy, distracting.

"Well, you see, Sean—" Quincy started.

"I know what a mortal coil is!" Sean interrupted, sounding a bit insulted. "Now, go on. You were heading up to the broadcasting tower, and…"

A loud knocking coming from the door of the trailer interrupted the conversation.

Sean groaned. "Ah, now what?" He took out the 9mm handgun tucked away in the back of his pants and slowly inched toward the door. He held the gun up at shoulder height. "Who is it?"

No answer.

"I said, who is it?" Sean yelled. "C'mon! Identify yourself, or you have ten seconds to get the hell away from the door before I start shooting. Do you think I mind a couple of holes in my door? I live in a trailer, man."

It was silent for a few seconds more before the muffled voice of a young woman, perhaps a tiny bit confused sounding, came from the other side: "Huh, what? Oh, darn it all!"

Confused, Sean opened the door.

Staring vaguely toward the first rays of morning sunshine coming up over the vast emptiness of the desert was Liz. At the sound of the door opening, she spun around quickly and smiled wide as she saw him. "HEY!"

"Jeez!" Sean covered his ears. "What's wrong with you?" he yelled back.

"WHAT?" Liz's head bobbed. "Oh yeah, SORRY!" She pulled out her headphones, and Sean could still hear the music screeching through them at top volume. "Great value, these things. Topnotch sound. I mean Fleetwood Mac sounds *phenomenal,* but don't expect to hear a *thing* that's going on around you anymore." Liz let herself in and looked around the trailer. "So, how's…life?" she asked cautiously.

"Is that Liz?" Lilly echoed from the speaker. "Hey!"

"Hi, Liz," Quincy joined in, "have you been making progress?"

Liz rolled up her headphone wire. "Yeah! That's why I'm here picking up this big old log before he throws himself into the chipper." She slapped Sean's back, who was unprepared for the sudden movement and lost his balance.

Sean scampered back up. "Wait. Liz, you know about all this already?" He turned toward the radio and slapped the top of the installation. "You contacted *her* before *me?* C'mon, Lil…" He sighed. "And Quincy? That's harsh, bro."

Liz rolled her eyes. "Really? Out of all the things you can be worked up about, this is the thing you pick?" She grunted. "You are unbelievable. And for the record, it was *me* who contacted *them* first."

Sean poured another drink—Liz snatched the glass of scotch from under his nose and downed it in one go. Disgruntled but understanding, he pulled out another glass and filled both of them up to the rim.

"Excuse my harshness," he said then, only half sincere. "This is all still kind of a big shock to me. Here I've been sitting for just about the entire night listening to what you three have been up to and so far, the only things I've learned have all been terrible. And this only adds to the confusion." He scratched at his beard. "What are you doing here, Liz? What's happening? I want to help, and I know you all need it, but I'm freaking *clueless* here."

"WOOF!" Hewie chimed in through the radio speakers.

"Oh, and seriously, what the hell is up with that dog? I mean you told me just now, but I don't—"

Liz held up her hands. "Sean? Hey, Sean..." Her voice was now slow, steady, and soothing. "I know, man. Shit is all kinds of messed up. I promise you, you'll be up to speed in no time, okay? For now, I'm going to need you to try and relax for a bit. We're working on a lot of stuff at the moment and yeah, we really need your help. So, stick your head in a bucket of ice or something and clear your mind a bit, okay?" She stood up and started to snoop around again.

"Yeah, okay." Sean nodded.

The speaker crackled to life again: "Don't forget we're all in this together, Sean," Quincy said. "This isn't about saving me or Lilly per se, but Haven is cooking up something huge, and we have no idea how to stop it as of yet. It's just that..."

"It's just that we'd really like to get back to breathing humid swamp gas and smog on Earth-proper. I mean, we'd *really* appreciate it!" Lilly finished in a manner only she could.

"You know we're working on that, Lil." Liz threw a dingy old gym bag she'd found under the bed into Sean's arms. "Pack some light stuff; I think it's better if we get out of here as soon as possible."

"Why?"

The ground rumbled again. It was closer than before.

"Yeah, okay," Sean conceded. "I was planning on moving anyway. The desert belongs to whatever those things are now."

"Primordial Wurms are our *least* concern, believe it or not," Liz sighed out; she looked exhausted.

"You do *not* want to mess with those either way," Lilly peeped up. "I swear, the only thing they *don't* like to eat are feet."

Sean threw some loose clothes in together with an assortment of electronics and conservable food and zipped the bag up. His heart was pounding. "Okay, ready."

Liz was already halfway across the threshold of the door. "Great, we can fill you in on the rest along the way."

Static blew from the speakers as if to protest, and Sean raised an eyebrow. "Wait, how are we going to stay in contact with the twins during this time?"

Liz turned the dial on a walkie-talkie she'd found in a thrift shop on the way to Sean's. She shook the thing once or twice, then spoke into the microphone. "Hey, you both pick up on this?"

"Loud and clear!" Quincy's voice came through the device. It was clearer than it had ever been through Sean's setup.

Liz threw the little black box into Sean's hands and smirked. "What? You really think that this particularly *genius* combination of out-of-date electronics is the only way to tune in to the ghost dimension? Any type of analog frequency will work. Hell, even more than that, actually. But we don't have time to explain the semantics right now, we need to go!"

"Where are we going, anyway?"

"To the ruins of the Swansong family estate on Eldritch Island, just off the coast of Massachusetts." Liz grimaced as the ground underneath them shook again.

"So anyway, as we were saying, Sean," Lilly's voice merrily continued. "There was this broadcast tower, but I was having like, an existential crisis at the same time…"

House of the Night

Chapter 9

DO you want to know what used to scare me the most about death?

The absolute nothingness of it all.

To think that after we die, there would be nothing at all except for a never-ending existence, or non-existence of pure void. It was terrifying.

I never tried to dwell on it much, but in my head, I had always hoped for some kind of afterlife. Anything would do, really. Pearly gates. A big wide-open field where your bygone loved ones would stand to greet you. An eternal palace to dance away the ages...

Even the most obscure or esoteric thoughts I preferred more than to think there'd be nothing at all. I liked the idea of sinking away into the ground and becoming one again with the grand cosmos. For all the tiny, microscopic beings that make us who we are sleep and stir deep within nature's soil until one day a big tree or beautiful flower blooms in place. Then I would be a silent sentinel marking the life and death of Lilly Swansong, a name forgotten through the eons of time that had passed.

I liked that.

And this...this certainly wasn't what I had expected. Anything that used to scare the wits out of me about an empty void after we die kind of pales in comparison to the thought of drifting in between the fissures of life for all eternity.

What punishment could be more severe than to be denied an ending?

The poor souls we see around here, the shadows flittering in and out of the broken and fractured manifestations of what could've been cozy family homes and beautiful parks in the real world...I pity them. I feel a profound sadness every time I see the ghostly outline of a child hiding in a corner of some bizarrely shaped living room.

No way back and no way to the light.

Perhaps this is hell, and hell isn't some kind of fiery pit where sinners roast in eternal flames. Perhaps the desperation and pain of forever drifting in a space where you do not belong is true damnation.

That, and public transport...

"Fifteen men on a dead man's——"

Quincy put his hand over Lilly mouth stopping her from singing more. "Please don't. Just...don't."

The bus ride was going fairly smoothly, but something about an undead driver whose lower jaw kept falling off and the fact that the twins were the only 'sentient' bodies among a host of skeletal passengers just didn't sit well with Quincy.

Before their bus ride began, they had visited the strange broadcasting tower standing atop the peculiarly manifested hills surrounding the ghostly version of Darkness Falls—which had only been a short hike. However, it proved to be less useful than the twins had initially thought.

Prying open the big metal door of the shack next to

the tower was easy enough, but getting the complicated machinery working was a different beast altogether. It took them several hours of messing about with wires, tuning dials, tone generators, and all that good stuff, until eventually they got the job done.

Quincy had softly spoken into the microphone, announcing that they were two new arrivals looking for Samuel Hain by order of *some grey old geezer in a cloak.*

Initially, there was no response.

A few minutes later, one of the bulky printing machines groaned to life and started to spit some ink on the yellowed paper that had been stuck in its gears for what could've been centuries. It was a bus schedule and the north-line at 1:30 a.m. off of Darkness Falls Main street was encircled. Having no other options, Lilly ripped the paper off and headed back for the door.

Quincy had tried to protest at first. He wanted to try a different frequency, possibly find some kind of afterlife radio station to contact. But he knew that his sister was immovable once she set her mind to something. He knew she'd be all over that bus schedule—she loved stuff like that. It was like a scavenger hunt to her.

Looking out of the bus window, Quincy now stared at the peculiar streaks of pink and blue neon high up in the sky. He thought dawn was approaching by the glowing rim of light peeking at the edge of the horizon. But that was hours ago. It appeared that the place they were in was cast in a permanent twilight of sorts.

The air outside seemed to change then.

The twins could see a cloud of black vapor trailing the bus. Quincy could swear he saw ripples of places other than the stretch of road on which the bus was grinding along. It was as if they were glimpses into other worlds, most of them mundane like with brick walls or a random garden toolshed. There was one with a wooden fence and a curious cat staring up at the moon. Another that had a lonely high lantern on the edge of a busy street in a sprawling metropolis. The lantern was different, however, and Quincy couldn't look away.

The more enamored he became with the sights of that unknown street, the more of the shadowy city around it became visible. Tall spires of brick and steel and monolithic skyscrapers loomed over the lonely little street-light. Quincy could feel fear and claustrophobia. There was a panic rising within him as he felt engorged by this strange city. He tried to look away, but the gnashing teeth and grinding gears of the urban jungle were holding—

"Sunshine! *Helloooooo?*" Lilly snapped her fingers and he blinked. "Hey, he's back! There you go. Thought I had to drop you off at the scary, Nearly Departed mental asylum there for a minute." She waved her journal in his face like a fan blowing cool air. "Man, you're sweating a lot." Her smile slowly faded as she noticed the look in Quincy's eyes. "Hey, you okay? I was only joking. You know about the asylum... Is this about the singing? I'm sorry."

"No, it's alright, Lil," he sighed, trying to rub the exhaustion from his eyes. "I just think this place is getting to me already." He gave Hewie a pat. The little dog was sitting in his lap, rubbing his small see-through ears against Quincy's hands and looking worried.

He looked around at the glowing skeletal passengers sharing their public transportation ride. *See-through* skeletons felt like a bit of an exaggeration to him, but he and

Lilly were strangers in a strange land, and these guys and gals seemed friendly enough—surely, it could've been much worse.

"Seen the *abyss,* have ya?" the old prospector apparition in the seat in front of them asked. His lower jaw clicked every time it bobbed up and down. It sounded like the clashing of balls on a pool table and reminded Quincy of that ultimate dream: a sweet and boring life.

"What?" Lilly replied before Quincy could speak. "What's he talking about?" She turned to her brother.

"Young feller here, had been gone for a good few minutes there," the skeleton clicked. "I reckoned he gone and took a good glimpse of the abyss. You've got to watch out for that, sonny. Don't let it swallow you whole, now. There's still a chance of a good life here in between the shadows, hmm. But if the darkness between the curtains of reality claims your soul, you'd be left a mindless husk. No ways of returning here, or wherever you think you might end up at."

"WOOF!" Hewie barked with enthusiasm.

"That's it, lil' feller. You give your owner a good old bite now whenever you see him drifting off like that now, you hear?" The skeleton ghost man waved his hand to pet Hewie—it went right through the spectral dog. Though Hewie tried his best to catch the luscious bony ghost fingers coming down at him, it was no use. He wagged his tail happily nonetheless.

"Thanks," Quincy answered. "I guess."

The speakers above their seats stopped playing Van Halen's *Eruption,* and the bus came to a grinding halt. The gravelly voice of the driver sounded through the speakers. "Next stop..." The driver stopped for a moment to snap his jaw back in place. "Next stop, the Hollows."

Lilly shot up from their seat. "That's us, let's go. You can fill me in on your little brain fart on the way to"—she looked at the torn off piece of printing paper—"*the Nebulous Nest.*"

The shoddy riverboat lay still at the edge of the bayou. It was little more than a rusty bucket floating haphazardly in the muddy waters. The motor appeared to be almost literally eaten by the humidity and, much to Liz's dismay, the most trustworthy way of maneuvering this thing appeared to be the two long paddles laying on the inside. She imaged they were used either to push the thing forward or get it out of constricting shrubbery. The colored tiki patio lights, however, *were* actually a pleasant addition. Liz thought they added some flair and coziness to an otherwise tetanus-filled death trap.

Moira hopped on board and went right to working on the motor.

"I know it's a shitty way to travel, but I kind of consider it my baby, and it'll take us as close to New Orleans as we can get without risking interference." She beckoned Liz onto the wobbling watercraft before batting off a mosquito. "It's either this or the roads teeming with Haven. Your choice."

They were extremely lucky to have escaped Darkness Falls at all. Moira's little trick of lending a little hand in making sure the twins were not blasted off into eternity forever was yet unknown. But her absence, together with that of the now fugitive Lizbeth Borden, would've absolutely not gone unnoticed. Therefore, it was in the best of both their interests to lay as low as they could.

After teleporting to the nearby library, the pair had a significant enough head start to get out quickly and quietly. Unfortunately, especially for Lilly and Quincy, they couldn't drive the compromised grey Ford Fiesta, and had left it behind. So, they took out all necessities from the Fiesta's trunk and sped off with a nearby car that Liz had managed to open and get running with what she called *rogue witch* tactics—Moira regarded it as *thievery*. The rest of the way was uneventful.

However, an increasing number of Haven agents popping up everywhere as they got closer to their goal led them to the backroads and sticks in the swampy outlands near the world-famous Crescent City itself, New Orleans.

Liz stepped into the boat, lifting the cracked oar and eying it suspiciously. "Tell me again what it is we're looking for, exactly."

The engine sputtered to life and Moira raised her head up from the machinery and gears in triumph. "Yes!" She wiped her forehead with the top she had taken off more than an hour ago. "I told you, this old piece of junk has still got it!" She noticed Liz's inquiring eyes. "I'm sorry, what did you say?"

"I asked what we are looking for in New Orleans?" Liz scratched feverously at all the fresh mosquito bites she had managed to collect in a mere hour and a half of fun in the swamp.

Moira carefully wobbled toward the other side of the boat. She rummaged through a locker for a bit, then pulled out a map. Sitting next to Liz, she spread the map wide open over their knees. "Here." She pointed at a district just east of the mid-city center and a tad northeast of the French Quarter. "It's an old library that holds a vast array of occult and magical tomes in a secret room said to be accessible only by those who share the esoteric gift."

"Shit, that's Bywater," Liz said. "But Bywater was destroyed and taken over by Ningens and stuff years ago, right? It's said to be crawling with aquatic cryptids."

Moira shuffled uncomfortably in her seat. Her eyes narrowed, and for a moment, she drifted off slightly, looking hypnotized by the wavering willow trees hanging low and dipping into the murky waters. "That is exactly right," she conceded. "It's not ideal, I know, but trust me when I say that this is our best shot at getting into contact with the Swansong twins and figuring out how to get them back."

"And you can't get some voodoo necromancy recipe from one of your evil LaGrande aunts?" Liz remained skeptical. "There must be an easier way. Bywater is, from what I've heard, a deathtrap."

"It's the only collection of works I know of that are in the possession of a voodoo priestess or corrupted witch or janky warlock that would evaporate us on the spot if they found out what we were planning on using it for." She shook her head. "There is no other way."

"Well pardon me for keeping a healthy dose of doubt anyway. It's not like I can trust you or anything; you still had a hand in killing my friends," Liz spat.

"I get that, but you're going to have to start trusting me anyway. If I wanted you dead, I could've killed you ten times over already." She sighed. "Like 'by accident' when teleporting you over to the library. Or I could've handed you over to Haven no questions asked." Moira started grinning. "I also could've pushed you into the swamp an hour ago and made sure nobody ever found your sad bones again."

"But you didn't."

"But I didn't," Moira agreed. "Cheer up, Borden." Her grin turned into a sincere, warm smile. "We're on the same team, I promise." She sat up straighter and coughed. "Tell you what, ask me anything. Anything at all. I'll answer with the absolute truth." She then waved a spoon in Liz's face for some reason.

"Okay, why'd you do it?" Liz's face was rock hard and emotionless.

"I knew that was coming," Moira said, sighing sadly. "I really did *not* want to. I'm serious. I never wanted to associate with Haven at all. I was forced to do it, by my family. They've had their doubts about my…commitment for a while now. It was their way to pressure me into their evil fold or to face the consequences. If I didn't play ball and take up this contract with their newfound allies, Haven, they would've killed me on the spot."

Liz's eyes grew wide. "Your own family would kill you?"

"To hell with them!" Moira clenched her fist. "I don't want to be associated with such…monsters. I had heard of the Swansong twins and their antics before, so I needed to make sure I had a plan to get them out of this mess safely. Because this is important, Liz, believe me…" She paused and took a deep breath.

"With or without my interference, they *would* have died either way. So yeah, I kind of made a deal with a corrupt voodoo entity from beyond the living world. But I trust everything will work out. We just need the tools now to make them aware of their ability to communicate with us. We need them to know we can help them from here, help to get them back, and help to get revenge." Moira was now tapping the spoon against the rusty side of the boat.

"Sounds like one hell of a dangerous and convoluted plan. You couldn't send a text or anything?" Liz huffed. "Either way, Haven and the LaGrandes in allegiance is bad news for everyone."

"Anything else than feigning my loyalty up to the very end would've surely ended up in misery, death, and hopelessness."

"You are a real somber person, aren't you?" Liz blurted out. She didn't mean to insult Moira, but it kind of slipped out nonetheless.

"Not really. Thing is, I was raised by Alina LaGrande, aka the Voodoo Queen of the South, as an aspirant priestess in all things dark and esoteric. Death is a companion. So, I am not somber, it's just a normal part of me."

"You're weird. But considering the people I hang out with, I'm sure you'll fit right in," Liz joked, smiling weakly. "Okay, LaGrande, thanks for sharing. I believe you, but I'm just a careful person, so bear with me."

"I get it, *Borden*, it's okay. But by all means, call me Moira, so I can call you Lizbeth."

"Liz."

Moira laughed heartily. "Fine, Liz. I'm glad we're making progress. Go ahead, ask me another question."

The shiny metal spoon in Moira's hand shone in the

light of the setting Louisiana sun. Liz couldn't help it—she had to know: "So, what's with the spoon?"

"Seriously? That's the second thing you want to know? This?" She held up the spoon in front of Liz.

"Yes, I'm dying to know. You've been gripping that thing as if your life depended on it."

Moira grunted. "It's a curse. This stupid thing appears every time I'm near water or thinking about being thirsty or something like that. It's not always there, but when it is, I can't get rid of it physically. It's *super* annoying."

Liz nearly fell over from laughing. "Are you serious? That's like the stupidest curse I've ever heard of. It's so...*not sinister.*"

"Laugh all you want. But have you ever tried to do some power training in the summer when you're constantly in need of hydrating? Or tried lifting some weights with a spoon in hand? *Hell,* how about just sitting behind a computer and typing something up while holding a spoon? Good luck hitting three keystrokes at once with this...*food utensil* constantly mucking shit up." With her free hand, Moira gently pushed the tiller to turn the rudder and keep the boat from bumping the shoreline.

Liz snorted. "Surely it must have its positives as well, right?"

"Yeah, it's really funny, Liz. You must think it's a perfect thing. With all of our southern cuisine, Cajun cooking, and the like. Always lots of stews and soups going on, always having a spoon on hand." Moira rolled her eyes.

"I'm sorry." Liz subdued her giggling a little bit. "No,

I really am. In fact, I might have a thing for it. As long as you're ready to be possibly rid of it right away."

"I would marry you on the spot," Moira replied. Dead serious.

Liz laughed. "Wow, you can hold the marriage." She rummaged through her knapsack of magical doodads for a bit. "Okay, let's try this." She took a bit of sparkling powder from the bag and gently blew it across the entire spread of her hand. "Ready?"

Moira nodded.

"Three…two…one…*adversum malificara.*" Liz whispered the incantation and blew the powder, now glowing bright white, over the spoon and Moira's hand.

Moira's entire arm flew back over the railing of the boat, and the spoon shot toward the bushes along the riverbed on the other side. Her eyes lit up with giddiness. "Damn, Borden! You actually did it. I don't know how to—"

Both Moira and Liz blinked.

The spoon was back in Moira's right hand.

"Dammit!" they both exclaimed.

"Well, that's one possible way down, but I've got like *thirteen* more possible solutions if you're up for it." Liz nervously played with the piercing in her nose. "How did you get cursed in the first place, anyway?"

"If none of your methods result in blowing up us or this boat, then by all means, let's go," Moira replied. "And as far as how I got this thing…let's just say a lot of bad things can happen with a case of lukewarm beers, some fireworks, and an aunt who wants to teach you a lesson. Oh, and the only crossroads demon that apparently didn't have a shred of humor in him."

"You're not going to tell me the full story now? Boo!"

"Calm down, calm down. We've still got a lot of hours to kill on this thing, and the only deck of cards I had sank into the swamp long ago. There's plenty of jabbering to be had in time."

There certainly were worse places to spend eternity than the *Nebulous Nest*. Lilly was sure of it. Then again, she was also sure of the fact that there were a lot of better places as well.

The 'bar,' if you could call it that, was a dreary den filled to the brim with ghastly-looking apparitions and sinister skeletal manifestations sitting around small wooden tables in all of the dusty corners and shadowy nooks the shack could supply. A honky-tonk piano was playing a slightly out-of-tune melody on its own next to the bar. The ceiling was low, and its rotten wood was constantly creaking from the wind outside. An eerie green glow filled most of the space. It looked like a fog bank had rolled across the cramped room from outside; however, it might've just been the copious amount of smoke rising from the hundreds of candles scattered around, the occasional burning stick of incense, and a pungent cigar here and there.

Quincy and Lilly felt all the eyes in the building sweeping over to them the minute they had set a foot inside. However, it was only a few seconds after the door slammed shut behind them that most of the patrons turned back around and went back to their night-to-night business. Hewie barked in satisfaction of this new temporary hangout and scooted off toward the doggy drink bowl already provided by the barkeep for the *Nest*'s four-legged visitors.

"You're glowing," Quincy whispered to his sister. His eyes darted around looking for a place to sit while hoping desperately not to offend any old dead person by simply existing.

Lilly raised an eyebrow. "Weird time for a compliment, but okay, thanks."

"No, I mean…" Quincy shook his head and stretched out his arms. "Look. I'm—*We're* glowing."

A faint blue streak of light perfectly traced around the twins' arms, hands, and fingers. Upon closer inspection, the blue glow appeared to emanate around them entirely.

"Holy crap!" Lilly gasped. "Quince, don't freak out, but I can kind of see…your bones. I can see your bones. You're…"

"See-through," Quincy finished. He hated the stereotype that twins always knew how to finish each other's sentences. Yet he couldn't deny the power that came with the closest blood bond of all. This all flashed through his head in a millisecond, because twin-powers aside, they were see-through.

Lilly stared at the phalanx bones in her hand with awe. "This is freakin' *awesome*." She gasped. "Look at those!"

"I'm wonder if it has anything to do with how long we've been here so far," Quincy pondered aloud. "Look around you at all the…people." He ran his hand through his hair. "Some of them look like spirits, real people, just slightly transparent."

They arrived at a small table in a dim-lit corner all the way in the back and sat down.

"Uh-uh. Go on," Lilly told him.

"Others are literally just bones. They have this same neon glow as everyone else, but they're indistinguishable save for the shape of their skeletal anatomy. In this place, having a deformity or other remarkable *boney* trait will save you from a lifetime of being *nobody*. Well, the word *life* is to be taken with a grain of salt; still, it's a very interesting theory to explore, perhaps…"

His sister waited a minute for him to catch his breath before snorting. "Yo, keep it real, Mister Brainiac. This is probably us finally starting to fit into society here. Perhaps it's a personal preference thing. Or perhaps…"

"Or perhaps we're only half-skeletal and half-transparent because we're only halfway there?" Quincy said. "Of course!" he yelled, full of enthusiasm. "You're a genius, sis."

"I am?"

"Yes! The afterlife is undecided on how we're to look just yet because we have one of these!" Quincy triumphantly held the glowing string he and his sister both had—their *tethers* as the old hermit had put it—in the air.

The music abruptly stopped playing and once again all eyes seemed to be fixed on the twins.

"Crap." Quincy broke out in sweat. "Was it something I said?"

"Rather, it was something else you couldn't keep to yourself," came a new voice from the dark corners just behind the twins.

"Yikes," Lilly peeped.

Where there were once just cobwebs and patches of darkness, the shadows now moved and reshaped themselves into a new form—the silhouette of a crooked man with a top hat who spoke with a slight Caribbean accent. Fortunately, the rather remarkable happenstance had the bar patrons spooked enough to go right back to their furtive whisperings as before. It was the twins' problem now, to figure out if this had been a blessing or a curse.

"Where do you go around, flashing about your tethers like that, huh?" the strange off-pitch voice spoke again.

Three smoky black fingers draped over Quincy's shoulder: Quincy was acutely aware of a presence speaking very closely to his ear, but from the naked eye, there appeared to be just a casted shadow on the wall… accompanied with a very real sense of dread.

"What you have in your pocket there, dear Sir Swansong, is something that the majority of souls around would *kill* to have, were it not that killing something that is already died is perhaps a bit unnecessary?"

"You mean it would be overkill?" Lilly hesitantly interjected.

The voice slithered over to Lilly's ear and whispered, "I like this one!"

It was now back in Quincy's, saying, "She's got *moxy*!"

Lilly laughed nervously, starting to tap her foot against Quincy's shin. "What a hoot, huh, bro? Tell me, who's our new friend?"

"Sshh," the shadow whispered now to them both in hushed tone. "The girl is anxious and easily startled," it mumbled just to Quincy. "But you two, do not fear. You will get to know me quite well, take it from me—he-he-he. Allow me to introduce myself. My name is Nibo. I am a Loa, a caretaker of souls. You might be familiar with the term, hmm?"

"Familiar enough." Quincy wiped the sweat droplets off his forehead. This *thing* gave him the absolute creeps. "What can we do for you, Nibo?" he stammered.

The shadow jittered in the corner. "I prefer the title *Master Loa*," it hissed. "But I forgive your transgression, my newly-awoken-to-the-afterlife friends."

Quincy could swear he saw a row of shiny white teeth appear against the wall for just a few seconds. Hewie growled from under the table. Even he appeared flustered and shaken up—unusual for the happy-go-lucky critter.

"What you can do for me," the voice continued, "is keep that thing in your pocket where it belongs. Out of sight of so many…hungry…needy…weary souls."

Quincy gulped, audibly.

"For you see," Nibo said, casually, "I was the one who provided this *boon*, this life-preserver, this…second chance…and I would hate to see it go to waste, hmm? Deals were made, Swansongs, and I tend to get my rewards, so I am going to need you two to hold up your ends of the bargain and hold onto that tether of life long enough for you to step back into your waking world as soon as your duties here have ended."

"Wait, what? Duties?" Quincy asked. "*You* got us here? What does that even mean? What bargain? I don't know anything about a deal—what deal?"

"Tsk-tsk. So many questions, so little time for answers." Nibo's silhouette shook from laughter. "The one that holds the other end of your tethers is Samuel Hain. Once you do whatever it is you need to do for him,

I will find you, and we'll see if we can strike a deal for ourselves now, huh?"

"Another deal? For what?"

"You think you can simply walk out of the Realm of the Nearly Departed with your completed tethers without a care for the world? You need a guide!"

"We have a guide," Quincy said and pointed to Hewie who, for the third time in a row, knocked his little spectral skull against the side of the bar, chasing tiny ghost-rats that *just* managed to squeeze in between the creases.

"A proper *crossroads* guide, Swansong! You'll never make it without help from the outsi—" The silhouette's forehead disappeared in its palms. "*C'est la mort.* I said too much, all in good time." The silhouette appeared to take a bow, even going so far as to remove the top hat in good etiquette, and then disappeared.

"Well, this is nice." Lilly's voice dripped with sarcasm as she spoke. "As far as Liz told me, we could be chumming it up with Christina Ricci right now. Drinking a few beers, burning some incense, gossiping with the girls. You know, witchy stuff? Normal stuff."

Quincy said nothing.

"But nope! '*We have to find the source of that strange infection, Lilly!*'" she mimicked in Quincy's voice. "Gotta pull through and all of that stuff. Nobody else who'll do it yada, yada, yada…"

"Yada, yada, yada?" Quincy's eyebrow twitched, then he chuckled.

"You know what it means." Lilly sighed. "Or is the expression simply too *boorish* for you?" She raised her hands and shook them in exaggeration.

A man coughed—a man now sitting across them at the same table. He tapped his bony finger loudly against the cork coaster on which a blood-red cocktail drink appeared. The glass had one of those fancy little umbrellas in it.

"Who—" Lily started, but the man shook his head.

He was dark-skinned and had frizzy black dreadlocks. Outside of the familiar Nearly Departed Realm complimentary outer glow, the man appeared quite mortal, save for the white face paint in the shape of a skull on his face.

"Are we going to do this all night?" He scowled. "My name is Samuel. You've called on me, and I believe I have something of yours. So, are we going to talk business?"

Quincy and Lilly stared at each other.

"Boy, are we popular in the afterlife tonight or what..." Quincy laughed nervously. Hewie curled up between his and Lilly's legs.

Lilly waved. "Yeah, the phrase *dead men tell no tales* really is a load of bull." She paused. "Hi. I'm Lilly."

Chapter 10

NO MATTER how interesting and wonderful the realms of the afterlife are, the history of the living world is likewise *just* as fascinating.

When the first bits of nefarious chitin started to writhe around deep beneath the sands of Egypt and the Elder Giants rose to power soon after the God obelisk appeared, New Orleans was one of the first places to go through the change. Not entirely unsurprising, you may say, for the Crescent City's roots in occultism and vague hoodoo mysticism are very deep and very wide. Louisiana and its bordering southern states had always been particularly dark places. But the God affair changed it like never before.

It started in the city at first. The dead started to rise from their graves. The city's world-famous cemeteries were suddenly full of the shambling things. But these were not any malicious zombies or lumbering monsters hungry for flesh.

They were the literal living dead.

The poor souls wandered around aimlessly looking for loved ones, not understanding why they would not visit *now*, now that they were right there instead of under the ground. But the families stayed at home, boarded up their windows, and prayed to whomever they hoped was listening.

But this was New Orleans. And New Orleans's ties with the dead and the restless went back hundreds of years. It did not take long for the local voodoo community to take the situation under their wing and take control of it. They would help the wandering souls, both rotting, animated corpses and disembodied spirits, find their place in this quickly altering world. It was, moreover, pretty much their specialty and what they had always done just a little differently now.

Now, more so than ever before, the community was hand in hand with their magical, and sometimes strange, past.

Where in London, England the Highgate Cemetery vampire was terrorizing the locals at full force and with horrific results, the French Quarter in New Orleans was home to no less than three outstanding vampiric private detective agencies. Where so-called *ghost hunting* companies started to pop up across the entire globe, the local spirit populace of Louisiana was revered for their help in solving unresolved crime, traffic regulation, and even scavenger hunts.

Elsewhere, folks were stockpiling weaponry to fight the monsters they had only heard of in legend and never laid eyes upon except for in nightmares, but in *NOLA*, all kinds of awe-striking monstrosities willfully subjected themselves to questionnaires made up by students at the

Dillard University. The prestigious college was also proud to offer the number one course in Occult Sciences in the world, a course that even Quincy Swansong dabbled in for a semester or two.

In spite of these developments, let's not forget that the city of New Orleans and more so the entire state of Louisiana, was becoming even more dangerous: Bywater happened, and was not forgotten. And even though the rest of the city hosted mostly kindhearted spirits and friendly ghouls—perhaps a particular trickster here or there, but nothing earthshattering—in the swamps surrounding it, it was a different story altogether.

There were tales of evil things lurking about in old forgotten Creole shacks or hiding in the foggy black morass of the deepest parts of the bayous. These things, whatever they were, be it creatures, monsters, or malicious spirits, took on wholly unknown forms. There were tales of strange amalgamations of beast, metal, and blood; of slithering things with thousands of teeth and millions of eyes; of humanoids without faces, just bright red eyes piercing through the reed, ready to snatch away unsuspecting young children.

Never before was it this easy just to walk into the swamps and never be seen ever again.

Nevertheless, New Orleans was the purest example of perfect adaptation to these strange new times, while simultaneously being more aware than ever about all of the consequences. Whatever the state of the world was, there had always been that balance to keep. The balance between life and death, natural and unnatural, faith and rationality.

Liz watched the dock they were approaching, reflecting on the surrounding area as they neared.

The city looked fairly beautiful in the crimson and dark blue shimmering of early twilight. The pink sky fading into the rolling black of the night reflected gorgeously in the water of the Mississippi. It was something Liz could not help but be enamored by.

"Please keep hands, feet, and other appendages on the inside of the boat at all times," Moira stated. She tapped the spoon (the de-cursing didn't take, unfortunately) on the side of her head, which Liz took to mean to keep her wits about her.

"Gators, right?"

Moira scoffed. "No. Sea Devils, Deep Ones, Aharikogari…you know, the *actual* dangerous stuff? I know you Night Lights are all about living in harmony and respecting every living, breathing thing out there, but these aren't your run of the mill beasties, you get me?"

"So, what's the difference, then? Lions are dangerous, but what makes them less so than a…Deep One?" Liz asked.

"Well, for one, a lion kills for food or to protect its territory or its pride. A Deep One will kill you to trap your screaming soul in a box for all eternity in the hopes of one day amassing this huge, big lot of screaming soul boxes that'll wake their supposed ancient sea god."

A bubble popped up on the water's surface just a few yards shy of the boat. Liz swore she heard a little yelp rise up among the roar of their boat's engine. "I…" She fell silent. "Do I really want to know?"

"Probably not."

"Noted." Liz stared at the long belt of flickering lights that started to appear along the shore of New Orleans. "The city looks beautiful at nightfall. I wonder what it's like to explore there nowadays."

"Don't think we'll be seeing much of the city proper, I'm afraid," Moira said sadly. "Probably just be a quick in 'n out of the shittiest part of town. Nothing to do or see anywhere else at the moment. Besides, once word gets out that we're still alive and probably in cahoots with each other, our faces will be plastered on every street corner and on every digital screen imaginable anywhere Haven has a presence. You can thank our Swansong friends for that."

"They're not *your* friends," Liz retorted.

The loud hissing of a steam whistle shrieked over the sounds of the river flow. The strange brass tones echoed from one side of the riverbank to the other. An enormous steamboat appeared out of thin air. Every few seconds, spurts of hot air shot up into the sky from one of its two gigantic exhausts, followed by the iconic and piercing noise of the air-pump.

Moira instinctively ducked down. She pulled Liz down with her after observing her just sitting, looking flabbergasted. "Sit down," she whispered, "and don't make a sound!"

The boat started playing *Down by the Riverside*.

"What the hell is that?" Liz whispered. "Why is it making that horrible noise?"

"That's Natchez, our steamboat," Moira answered. "Kinda been going around and leading its own damn spooky life ever since the big event, ya know."

Liz sighed. "What is up with this weird city?"

"Good grief, Borden. Have some respect. By the blessing of Lady Laveau, New Orleans is probably the best damn city on Earth." Moira smiled. "And if you don't want to end up being snatched up by that thing over there and be forced to listen to some mediocre dixie band playing and eating stale, cold jambalaya for the rest of your life… I suggest you *shut up*."

"So, we'll be stuck here listening to this ghost monkey's crappy piano playing and eating these stale bar-room peanuts for the rest of our *un-lives* if we don't *shut up* right now?" Lilly asked.

"I don't think I can make it any clearer than that, Ms. Swansong," the man with the frizzy dreadlocks and skull face-paint named Samuel replied. "I believe you were directed to me by a certain cloaked individual back in the reflection of the town they call Darkness Falls in the living world? Stop me if I'm incorrect."

Quincy's lip twitched. "That's correct."

Samuel grinned wide and revealed his sharpened pearly white teeth, even brighter than the markings on his face. "Ha! Good old Mortimer, eh?" He stirred his drink with the somewhat oversized complimentary umbrella sticking in the glass. "He hates change, you know? Wants things to go back to the way they belong as soon as possible, ha!"

"And what's that? What's the correct way of how things should be?" Lilly asked.

"An afterlife in which Quincy and Lilly Swansong do not exist, and a living world where they do."

Hewie barked approvingly.

Samuel laughed. "You see, friends? This little one gets it. And a good boy he is, too. He knew exactly how to get you here as soon as possible. Didn't you, little one?" Samuel hand went right through Hewie, but the little spectral corgi yelped and rolled over. He was less afraid now—even enthusiastic, you could say. Perhaps it was a sign that Samuel really didn't have malicious intent. At least not with the twins, or poor Hewie himself.

"I can help you get back," Samuel continued. "Don't think I didn't overhear your conversation with Nibo just now." He shrugged. "It's how things go here. We make deals."

An eerie wind blew through the dusty corner and three candles snuffed out instantly;

the twins shivered.

"What kind of deals?" Quincy asked. "We've been hearing all about *deals* this entire time we've been here. But to be honest, all we know is that we're dead and have no clue how to get back except for something called a—"

"A tether," Samuel interjected. "Those bright sparkling ropes you both keep in your coat pockets. *I* have the other ends and thus a way to get you out. I got it from Nibo himself, who bartered to preserve your souls with some kind of mortal girl."

"Liz?" Lilly panicked. "Are you talking about her? What kind of deal did she make?"

Samuel waggled his finger and took a sip of his drink. "I don't know about that deal, and frankly, I don't care.

Just know that I bartered with Nibo for your tethers, and thus believe I hold all the cards in this exchange."

"Seems that way." Lilly fell back into her chair, frowning. "What happens once we get our tethers back from you?"

A cigarette appeared in Samuel's hand as one of the candles on the table flickered back to life. The light bouncing off the painted skull was unsettling.

Samuel lit the cigarette and took a deep drag. He blew out the smoke, and in the air it formed the images of a lock and a key. Hewie stared at the display, his eyes big and full of wonder. "Look at it this way, mon," Samuel began. "Your complete tethers will serve as a key to get out of here, but you need the lock, yes?"

The twins glanced at each other, then nodded.

"That lock is for you to find. Only yourselves or the ones you trust the most in life can help you find it, got it?" His eyes narrowed and his voice shrank to a whisper. "You get this one for free, little Swans: Do not trust Nibo. He will claim to be able to do anything for a price, but he can't do *that*, okay?"

The twins were leaning across the table, mesmerized by the serious tone Samuel managed to take in a matter of moments. By the time either of them had a response ready, the strange fellow went right on with his story.

"But let's not get ahead of ourselves here, okay?" He smiled. "So, first things first, are you willing to help me with a little ordeal I have?"

"Well…" Lilly raised an eyebrow, and Quincy saw it slink back into her slightly transparent forehead—he found it fascinating. "It's not like we really have a choice here."

"Unless you like stale bar food, eh?" Samuel smirked at Quincy.

Quincy waved at the skeleton lady with a perm coming by on roller skates. "Could we have some drinks, please? Make it something strong; we'll probably need it," he requested before turning back to Samuel. "All strange things we don't understand aside, you've got our attention, Mr. Hain. Let's make a deal, okay?"

Samuel's eyes lit up. "How did you know my last name?"

"The old, cloaked man told us," Lilly said, but then searched for acknowledgment in her brother's eyes. "Right?"

Samuel laughed. "Mortimer, you old bastard. Ha! But yes, friends, yes. A deal! You are starting to learn the ways of how we roll around here, hmm?" He took another drag of the cigarette. "Let's hear it."

Lilly clenched her fists.

"You tell us your favor you'd have us do, which we will probably accept, and in return, you'll answer some of our burning questions so we won't go out and end up doing dangerous and probably horrifying thing without beings prepared. Sound good?" Quincy told him with confidence.

Lilly unwound a little bit; Quincy's approach sounded pretty reasonable.

"I accept." Samuel nodded.

Quincy noticed his eyes darting from him to Lilly to him again. He'd been doing that for almost the entire time they'd been sitting at this table having this conversation. He also hadn't blinked once.

Samuel pressed the cigarette on the edge of the table

and the last few flecks of ember fell to the ground and disappeared before making contact. "It's all about territory down here. You have turf, you have leverage, you have power. Sound clear?"

"Sounds a lot like the living world," Lilly scoffed. "What's your currency? Damned souls?" She giggled.

Samuel did not seem to grasp the joke. "Yes, how did you know?" he responded, to which Lilly only gulped in discomfort. "Anyway, I've been having a particular thorn in my side lately going by the name of Ludwig LaGrande." He paused, his lips twitching. "I'm going to make this really easy for you, my little Swans. Go down into New Orleans and get rid of LaGrande for me in any way you see fit. You do this, you get your tethers back, easy." He sat back with a grin. "Now, do we have a deal?"

Agent Dutch slammed the door of the barn closed. From inside, the muffled cries of the grotesque being known as *Mother* could still be heard, although they sounded more distorted than ever. The gibbering was vague and distant. He began nervously pulling hairs from his chin stubble, not fond of the situation in which he now found himself.

The call came just a few minutes earlier: One of the LaGrande elders or, *terrifying voodoo fuckers*, as he liked to call them in his head, had made her presence known on accounts of their missing fledgling, not to mention the presence of witches in their territory.

Alina LaGrande, like most of her flock, scared the absolute pants off of Dutch. Giant, slimy atrocities or unholy amalgamations of pain and suffering were more his thing. The kind of thing that screams a lot and rips off a head or two in the process, but still bleeds and dies no less than just a regular man like him. These black magic queens and kings of the South were a different story altogether in his book.

There was something about them. Like when they were whispering to unseen entities hiding just beyond a normal human's peripheral vision, and soon afterwards, four people turn edup with simultaneous heart attacks… It was just plain wrong. Agent Dutch held no love for the ethereal plane and likewise, as furtive whispers among the initiates of extraplanar studies at Haven go, neither did the arcane world hold any love for him.

It was just his luck then that he got the job offer of a lifetime, keeping a giant blubbering mess happy and contained, while having others keeping track on whatever the hell it was that that *thing*—that *Mother* did to melt those people's brains to mush. And yet, the *one* time he got orders to work together with a LaGrande girl, things went absolutely wrong.

The orders had been clear enough: Spring the trap on some wanted scum they'd been following around for months and get information from them. Then make sure that the voodoo girl does the ritual thing that makes sure that those infamous Swansong twins could never, ever set foot on their, literal, forsaken Earth anymore. *But then there was a witch amongst them, and then the LaGrande girl went AWOL and then the bodies in the field and—*

"Miss LaGrande!" Agent Dutch's eyes were ridden with terror upon seeing the imposing figure of the voodoo priestess appear around the corner of the barn wall.

Alina LaGrande was a tall, dark-skinned beauty in a

vivid purple and green robe. She wore dreadlocks adorned with loops, jewelry, and other bijous tied back into a big bundle. She also had long, razor-sharp nails that looked as if they could gut a pig if need-be. The scariest thing about her, Agent Dutch thought, were her penetrating, bright green eyes. They were filled with contempt, perhaps even hatred, for just about anyone that crossed her path outside of her own congregation.

"Agent Dutch…" Her strong southern accent was almost warm were in not for the snarling tone. "I believe you are aware of the nature of my visit, are you not?"

Dutch silently invited Alina to walk with him across the farm grounds by waving his hand. With a simple, almost non-existent nod, she accepted.

"I am aware," Dutch confessed as they started to walk. "We had not taken into account the possible presence of a witch amongst the targets, not with one of you *folks* around. Figured she could pick up on that kind of thing."

"Thank you for your faith, Agent Dutch, but I'm afraid it does not work that way. Have you managed to identify the witch?"

"Not yet, but believe me, we're trying to figure out the pieces ourselves as best as we can. Your protégé is gone as well, as you will undoubtedly know."

"I do. Moira is my niece," she said grimly.

Dutch cleared his throat. "Well, I suspect we may have a traitor in our midst. Someone who led the witch to the Swansong twins in order to give them a fighting chance. But most importantly, someone who would uh, *indispose*, your niece long enough for the ritual to be, uh, not handled correctly."

Alina face soured quickly. "What happened here?" She squatted down and traced her fingers over the loose sand and dirt.

"This is where we found them—Agents Gibbous and Pickman—bloated to hell and purple to boot. We're trying to track down who sent the order for them to go down here. It was obvious the witch had ambushed them from inside the field."

Alina shook her head. "Your hunches may be on to something, Agent Dutch, but your logic is far from sound, unfortunately."

Dutch swallowed hard. "What do you mean, Miss LaGrande?"

Alina dipped her finger into the blood-soaked bit of earth in front of her and licked it. Sighing, she stood up and took a few steps back. There was a look of sheer anger now taking over her features, but underneath there was a hint of utter disappointment, maybe even sadness too.

"I noticed something wrong a few days ago. There were two soul jars missing from my collection. I thought little of it at first, thinking the children might've taken them for their games of creating living voodoo puppets from the rats around town. But things are starting to make sense now."

"They are?"

"The Swansong twins' bodies, I take it you had no luck disposing of them yet?"

"Nothing seems to take so far, but we thought it might be a part of the half-finished ritual." His eyes narrowed. "Where are you going with this?"

"This was no *white witch* spell." Alina spat on the

ground. "This was one of ours, one of *mine*. There was a traitor in your midst, Agent Dutch, but it is none of *your* concern anymore. It is *mine*."

"You want us to go to New Orleans and get rid of an undead crime lord so you can stake claim on his territory? Holy shit, am I hearing this correctly?" Lilly rubbed her temples. "And how are we supposed to do that, exactly?"

Samuel smiled at her, then at Quincy. "Come now, you are an inquisitive pair, aren't you? Perhaps find a way to send him off to the afterlife for good? Perhaps talk your way into his ranks, spy on him, and figure out his weakness in order to blackmail him… Perhaps you can strike up a deal of your very own? I don't really care, my little swans, but get the job done, and get your ticket out of this place. Get a fighting chance to go back where you belong."

"This all sounds really fishy," Quincy admitted. "How are we supposed to get to New Orleans, anyway? We have no clue where we are or how anything in this world works."

"Walk with me," Samuel ordered. He stood up and slid over toward the front door of the barn. Hewie hobbled after him, glancing back once or twice to make sure his friends followed.

Outside, countless stars formed unknown patterns across the inky black curtain of darkness. In the lower atmospheres, the colorful, pulsating ribbons of bright neon shone dazzlingly. The street in front of the bar was empty; it felt cold and abandoned. It was as if everyone in town simply went and vanished all at once, never to be seen again. Even the odd shadowy figure here and there did not diverge from the fact that this very moment in space and time felt like the loneliest place the twins had ever experienced.

It was mortifying. Lilly grasped her brother's hand tight. It was a small reassurance that, at the very least, they had Hewie and each other.

"A reflection through a broken mirror," Samuel said, grabbing their attention. "That's what old Mortimer likes to call this place, yes? A distorted version of reality, where the spirits of all things linger freely."

"Something like that," Quincy answered. "Is this philosophical spiel going anywhere?"

Ignoring him, Samuel rummaged through his cloak and produced a small hand mirror. "Ah yes, lovely." He grinned at his reflection before punching the glass and letting the pieces trickle onto the ground. "A reflection of the real world, but with endless possibilities in the realms of the metaphysical."

He picked up a shard of glass from the ground, examining it. "One cannot go from one side of the world to the other in the realm of the living, at least not without consequence," he said. "But here, in a world *fractured*, it might be possible to travel from shard to shard—if you know the way."

"Sounds complicated," Lilly admitted. "But you're telling us we can get to New Orleans this way? Er, *what* way, exactly?"

Samuel crept closer to the twins, his face eerily illuminated by a little candle that simply appeared in his hands out of nowhere. Lilly thought he was quite the showman.

"This world is old, my little swans," he whispered. "Unlike your real world that keeps renewing and improving and learning from the past, here it all congregates into one. It's all layered on top of each other, and the surface you see here is merely the latest snapshot taken of the living world." His gaze flicked to their feet. "Beneath us, you'll find the *Underworld Railroad*, a series of countless dark passages through countless periods in time and space. Through there, you will find the shortcut you need in order to reach New Orleans, or rather the distorted reflection of New Orleans."

"Cool…" Lilly's eyes lit up. "So, what's this, then? You said something about a snapshot in time." She waved her arms around. "What time was this 'picture' taken?"

Samuel grunted. "There will always be discrepancies between the living world and the hinterland, but if you were to put a year on it, we'd be looking at the reflection of 1985."

"Oooooh, that explains all the neon!" Lilly laughed and jabbed Quincy's side. "Hey, Quincy, imagine being stuck in a world where it's *always 1985!*" Her eyes sparkled.

Hewie yapped approvingly while

Quincy rolled his eyes. "Yeah, *imagine* that…" He turned to Samuel, asking, "How'd you know so much about this place, anyway?"

Samuel snuffed the candle between his fingers and chuckled. "Oh, Mister Swansong, if you had been here as long as I have, maybe then you'd learn to understand. Knowledge comes slowly, like peeling away layer after layer of an onion, just to find out what's in the center of it all. Power comes even slower, but it's worth every bit of the wait." He lit another one of his funky smelling ciga-rettes and stepped back. He tossed the snuffed candle to the side of the street. "Any other questions?"

The twins exchanged looks. Lilly shrugged and Quincy ran a hand through his quaff.

"I can't believe all this stuff that keeps happening to us, can't even rest in peace," Quincy complained. "But okay, you've got yourself a deal. Where do we start?"

Samuel, having pulled a dashing cane out of his coat pocket for some reason, pointed to the last house on the north-east side of the empty street. "That house has a basement with an old trapdoor leading to a second, much older, basement beneath it. In there, you will find a crummy painting with a faded bronze frame sitting against a wall—there's a button on the left upper side of the frame. Push it and a door will open on the southern wall. Then there's a stairwell going down that will lead you to the *Hall of Petrified Somethings*. From there... Ehh, you'll find your way."

"Wait, how will we know where to go?"

Samuel looked down at the corgi wagging his tail near Lilly's feet. "You have your guide, have you not?"

Hewie barked and tiptoed between Lilly's ankles. As if by instinct, he sniffed out the spot on her ankle where Lilly had hurt herself before she, well died, and licked it carefully.

"One last thing," Lilly started. "Why...why us?"

A burst of laughter came from Samuel, his pearly white grin wider than ever before. "You have a drive, my little swans. You feel your purpose is not here, but in the living world, yes? You get the job done, to the best of your abilities." He got up really close to their faces and his dead eyes, like a doll, stared at them for a good few seconds each, making them squirm. "And you are absolutely *expendable*."

"You mean we can *die*?" Lilly was flabbergasted. "Wait, how does that even work? We *are* dead, right?"

"You lead a half-life: There is the living world or the cold vacuum of death's eternal void. But a middle ground? You're on it. Tread lightly, lest the scales will tip out of your favor."

"Right, well—"

"He's gone, Lil," Quincy interrupted. "I blinked for a nanosecond and he up and left."

"I hate it when they keep doing that!"

Chapter 11

THE DINGY BOAT, held together by rust and the sheer determination of Liz and Moira combined, rolled into the dilapidated and abandoned district of Bywater. Once, it had been a flourishing community and a beautiful, picturesque collection of colorful Creole cottages and lavish green gardens by the quiet waterside. Now, it was a flooded ghost town, a drenched tumor of drifting wood and waterlogged homes along the mighty Mississippi river.

Liz's fists clenched upon seeing dozens of aquatic carcasses strung by clumps of moldy rope. Spears were jabbed through their open mouths, gills, and blowholes; the expression of those that did not yet have their eyes rotten or eaten away: sheer terror. It seemed an equal amount of normal 'old world' creatures as well as unknown cryptozoological, supernatural, and 'undiscovered' species. None of them looked the least bit menacing, not to Liz.

"Do not mourn for them, Liz." Moira said. "They

were here at the wrong place at the wrong time—something that is not quite uncommon in nature. You know that."

Liz shook her head. "If we're talking predator and prey, then yes, it's the circle of life and nature's way of keeping balance. But this…" She averted her eyes. "Disgusting, monstrous acts by low-life scum."

The boat hummed in the quiet moment that followed. Moira pointed her spoon at the half-sunken gazebo that at one time had probably adorned a beautiful garden. Now there were several unidentifiable gelatinous *somethings* pierced on the spike ridges along the top. "That there, you see it?" She didn't wait for the confirmation. "It's fear, Liz. Look more closely around you, and you'll find the answer as to *why*."

Upon closer inspection, the morbid truth of abandoned Bywater came to life. All around them, Liz could see faint traces of death and decay—*human* death and decay. Lifeless skeletons stuck in nets or grasping hopelessly at some form of flotation device, some missing appendages or entire undersides of their bodies. There were also the 'fresher' ones. Bloated carcasses, blue and pale with eyes rolled in the back of their heads cursed forever to this watery grave in which no sane person would dare to venture and reclaim what was theirs.

"Humanity is cruel," Moira continued, her voice soft. "You know that, I know that. It's no secret. But don't forget that humans do not just act out of sick pleasure. They fear what they don't understand, and they lash out to try and conquer it, lest it consumes them."

Moira stopped the little boat motor and threw a line out

at a nearby huge French colonial building sticking out halfway from the surface. She started, very carefully, to pull the rope to inch the boat closer to the building's second floor balustrade railing, which was equal with the water level. She gestured for Liz to keep sitting down for the moment.

"Thing is, Liz, there's a reason why folk aren't here every damn day trying to hunt every damn monster down and reclaim their beloved district back. You want to know why?"

Liz shrugged, but relented. "Of course."

"They understood. They understood and they backed down." Moira helped Liz up the balustrade and tied the boat to a half-rotten wooden pole. "Look." She pointed. "The water just dissipates to the north and west. The people backed down because they found out that there was no grand plan to flood the entire city. Whatever swims through these waters nowadays, just wants to be left alone. Well, except for the Deep Ones, but fuck them. They're a problem everywhere." She sighed. "You see, Borden? Balance. Give and take."

From the murky depths of the water arose the gaping maw of a giant, shark-like fish. Within a split second, the enormous, terrifying beast snapped their boat in half, flew several feet up in the air, with just inches to spare from Liz and Moira's face, then plunged back down. It all happened extremely fast and way too close for comfort for either of them.

"Holy fucking *shit*, dude!" Liz's face was void of all color. She clutched Moira's denim jacket and noticed she was shaking; they both were shaking.

"Yup, circle of life and all that jazz," Moira gulped

with a forced laugh. "I suggest we get our asses inside…*right now!*"

"Who knew being half dead meant giving off a soft hue like a natural light source?" Quincy reached over the picture frame of the ghastly renaissance painting and felt around for a button—sure enough, there it was. He pressed it. "Do you think I could write a book about this when it's all over? Something like, *Mysteries of the Afterlife, Partially Revealed!*" He snickered, but quickly felt back in a gloomy state of mind. "That is, *if* we ever get back."

In response to Hewie's barking, Quincy softly patted the corgi on the head and looked toward Lilly, who was waiting for the staircase in the wall of the basement's basement to appear. She seemed lost in thought. "Hey," he called, "anything on your mind?"

Before she could answer, the bricks on the wall softly hummed as they sank into the ground, revealing yet another staircase. Lilly looked kind of mesmerized by it. "Yeah," she called back, sounding a bit distant. "I was thinking about what that Haven agent said, you know. Or what he asked about, rather."

"The last Celestian tomb in North America?" Quincy nodded. "Yeah, I thought that was a bit strange too."

The hole in the wall was complete and a flight of stairs going down appeared from the thin musky air with a loud *bang.*

"Strange?" Lilly's eyebrow twitched. "You thought it was a bit strange?"

Quincy sighed. "Lilly—"

"Just a teensy-weensy bit strange, hmm? *Very* strange indeed, yes. Strange enough for some random dude to kill us over? Even though we have no clue what he was on about…"

"Well, to be fair, Haven agents aren't random dudes. Any one agent could've killed us regardless. And we have a little bit of an idea what he's talking about. We know what the Celestians are——"

"But we know jack about some forgotten tomb in which another one of them is apparently buried. Do you think he was just messing with us?"

Quincy shook his head. "If his agents really were trailing us for weeks beforehand, I don't see why they couldn't just nab us at any given moment when our guard was down. This guy, this Agent Dutch, he really thought we knew something. I just don't see why else he would go through all of the trouble to get us. It's disconcerting to think Haven might know more about the Celestians than us. It's just as troubling as the fact that they managed to get some sort of extraterrestrial being on Earth after we turned the Deus computer back on. Lots of unanswered questions."

"Do you think Mom and Dad would've known something more?"

"Maybe…maybe we should go back home when we get out of here. You know, back up north, *home*?"

"Eldritch Island."

The name brought with it a pang of warm, fuzzy nostalgia and sadness for both of them.

"There's a place I never thought to revisit." She sniffed. "Do you think the old mansion still stands?"

"I don't know. Might be a bit run-down, might be

completely destroyed by the floods. But I don't think a lot of people even know the island exists anymore."

Quincy paused for a moment, and Lilly recognized the painstaking expression on his face—he was in deep thought. After a few seconds, he snapped out of it.

"We would surely have heard something if anything happened, but it's been such a while since we've been home, back in New Orleans I mean, and our landlord must've been sending back all our mail under the impression that we're either missing or presumably very much dead."

"New Orleans." Lilly sighed. "We always said it was our hometown even though it wasn't—sure felt like it, though. Now we've got two places to call home, and none to go back to. Not with any conventional means, anyway." She stared at her transparent wrists. She was amazed how the muscles in her arms and hands wrapped perfectly around her joints, a perfect machine. "There's no reason to be discussing any of this while we're still in this little pickle." She waved her see-through hands in front of her face. "Let's not think too hard about any of this yet. We need to get out of here."

"Agreed."

Lilly turned and stared down the hole leading into darkness; leading into a place apparently called the *Hall of Petrified Somethings*. "If only Tim was here. I'm sure he'd have some sound advice to give us." She chuckled.

Quincy scoffed. "Yeah, I'm sure turning our skin and intestines inside out to hail the coming cosmic overlords of Xeenz is really sound advice," he said, his voice dripping with sarcasm.

They both laughed.

Hewie barked, and Lilly quickly kneeled down to comfort him. "Now, now, little man. We're both very glad that you *are* here." She stood and looked down the staircase again, reminded of something she had stashed away in the far reaches of her memory, kind of wishing she'd never have to think about it ever again. "I tell you one thing," she said as her foot touched the first step. "Whatever happens, I'm *not* going down another inverted pyramid thing. Calling it right now."

"None of *my* concern?" Agent Dutch protested. He had repeated the sentence three times already, four if you count the time he half incorporated it in the lackluster order he had blabbered into the walkie-talkie to his men.

"I'm very sorry, but so long as there's a shrivel of doubt that the Swansong twins are permanently disposed of, this is very much a concern of mine." His face was red with anger when Alina ignored him. "Now, you listen here, dammit. Haven assured me they had explicitly partnered with the LaGrandes for their unrelenting longing to be part of Haven's master plan. I was assured of the unwavering belief in the righteous cause of both of our organizations, I was—"

Alina LaGrande snapped, reaching out to wrap her right hand tightly around Agent Dutch's neck. She squeezed hard, ignoring his sputtering and pleading. Her eyes flashed and for a moment, they appeared inhuman: tiny black slits like those of a cat or snake against an orange and yellow iris.

Alina hissed, and copious amounts of spit splattered

in Agent Dutch's face. "We are no organization, *lick*. The LaGrandes are family, and we take care of our own. The good seeds and the rotten." She released the tension from Dutch's neck just a little. "Now, you and your little parade may assist in tracking my niece and that witch down in order to find out if your *plan* worked." Alina was burning with passion and rage; she pitched her voice lower. "But if you ever disrespect me or my family again, I will melt you on the spot and feed your runny carcass to the swamp dwellers, Haven be damned."

Agent Dutch nodded in panic, fighting for air.

During the whole spectacle, one of the field agents working the project had walked up to the pair and stopped, gaping. He was just about to walk off when Alina dropped Dutch onto the ground and turned to the lone soldier—he started sweating profusely. Meanwhile, Agent Dutch just laid there coughing.

"Report," Alina LaGrande commanded.

The soldier gulped and looked at Agent Dutch for a moment. Dutch shot him a look that could only be described as saying, *'Talk to her, you idiot; she'll* delete *you from existence otherwise!'* The soldier began stammering: "Uh, about the voodoo girl, miss. One of the men a few towns back reported seeing her doing some ritual with a chicken and cigars right before she was stationed at Darkness Falls."

"Cigars?" Alina's eyes grew wide.

"That's all I know," the man said, wiping the sweat off his brow. "Truly."

Alina waved him away. Thankful and relieved, the soldier disappeared back toward the basecamp near the barn.

"Nibo."

Agent Dutch was back on his feet, still clutching his throat. He looked at Alina expectantly at hearing her whispered word. "You think of something?" he grunted, his voice raw. Talking hurt, but that's what a nearly crushed windpipe does… It hurts.

"We're going to need livestock, a lot of candles, some cigars, and a Bordeaux red, preferably old world. I'll be having a chat with a…friend."

The *Hall of Petrified Somethings* sure was…something. After a brisk ten-minute descent, the downward staircase ended up in a wide space that resembled a grotto more than it did a hall. A clear view of an unknown starry night sky, complete with an enormous full moon stretched out in front of them. Even though the moonlight was bright, the cavern they stood in was still dark, as if some kind of forcefield held back the light reflecting off that strange moon hanging in the impossible sky. Just out of plain sight, the twins could see figures shambling around aimlessly.

At least, they looked like figures to Quincy—humans. He got an unnerving flashback to the ancient Celestian pyramid a few years back when they'd encountered the living shadows. Every fiber in Quincy's being hoped and prayed that they did not have to go through that ordeal a second time, although he was quite curious if there would even been such entities around here, a place where everyone is pretty much a shade of their former, living selves.

Lilly's head spun around as the shapes of whatever they were appeared to reach out to her. She clenched her jaw and anticipated something jumping out of the darkness ahead—nothing did.

The twins slowly made their way forward until they reached what appeared to be a train cart. But upon closer inspection, it was not. It was an old New Orleans streetcar. Its paint was peeling off the damp wood, and Lilly was reminded of the fact that it felt extremely humid and warm down here despite the fact that it appeared to be night, as well as the whole being dead thing. The folding doors of the car stood half open, inviting anyone with the ability to move half a pound of anything inside.

"I don't like this," Lilly admitted. She turned her head back to where they had originally come from—the stairs were gone. "I think we're being surrounded," she whispered, watching as the peculiar outlines of semi-humanoid figures darted closer.

Quincy opened the streetcar door wider. "Everything is weird here, Lil. I think the best course of action is to run with it." He looked at Hewie expectantly, asking, "Hey, buddy, is this where we need to go?"

The corgi stayed put right next to Lilly's legs and sneezed, possibly in disagreement.

Quincy threw a quick look into the car and stilled. He could've sworn he saw a cloaked figure sitting in one of the seats. It looked small and was jittering, not to mention its mask (or was it a face?) was that of a bird's skull. Quincy shook his head and looked again—there was nothing or no one sitting there. He sighed in relief.

"Where to?" a low baritone voice rang out from the

driver's seat. Quincy and Lilly both jumped up from the unexpected breach of silence: Lilly hopped in the streetcar quickly, Quincy and Hewie following not far behind.

"What was that?" she exclaimed. Her eyes were fixated on Quincy as he slid closer to her on the seat.

Quincy pointed at the apparition sitting at the front of the car. It was the ghostly image of a tall streetcar operator; his face was all messed up and melting away.

"Where to?" the specter repeated.

The whole scene felt phantasmagorical.

Everything up to this point had been a rollercoaster ride for sure, but somehow still felt expected. The Hall of Petrified Somethings was the first time since dying that the twins felt truly unnerved.

"Uhm… E-esplanade Av-venue?" Quincy stammered.

"Really?" Lilly whispered. "You'd think it be that easy?" She frowned. "I don't know about this, Quincy. There's something wrong here." She glanced inside the car. "I-Is someone…? Yikes!" She nearly fell out of the open door.

The ghostly driver turned his head to Lilly. "Watch. Your. Step," he grumbled. His gaze shifted to Quincy. "Not on my route. Can take you to…" He paused for a while as if he were trying to fish out something deeply lodged in his memory. "Death Knell Drive."

The twins looked at each other and the car jerked into motion.

Suddenly, Quincy yelled, as if he was terrified. For a brief moment, it was not Lilly sitting beside him, but someone, some*thing* else entirely: A man, who had long black hair, all broken, split, and burned. The man's face was pale, and his eyes were bloodshot.

"*In or out! Make your move,* now!" Quincy heard him mutter. It was as if the man was speaking directly in both his ears, but he wasn't near them. He was beside Quincy, and then again he wasn't—it was Lilly all along. Wasn't it?

Lilly reached for him, seeing the absolute terror imprinted on his face. "Whoa! Hey, what happened?"

Quincy wheezed.

Lilly dragged her brother out of the streetcar as it came to a stop.

He blinked, slumping forward.

The grotto was once again empty save for the glowing aura of light emanating from the twins and the sky above them, which was now hued in a pink and purple twilight. There was a rustling sound, and soon it appeared as if new strange shadowy beings had arrived, circling around them, but Lilly paid them no mind at the moment.

Hewie started barking toward a specific direction.

"Ssh. Hewie, one second!" Lilly kneeled down besides Quincy, who had slumped completely to lay on the ground. "What happened?" She touched his shoulder. "Hey! Quincy, talk to me, please."

Quincy pulled his knees to his chest and rubbed his temples. "Oh, man, I feel like shit." He chuckled.

"Unsatisfactory answer!" she snapped, grinding her teeth. "You need any—" He sat up, wobbling. "Oh, okay, easy." She helped him stand up and took a good look at him. "You look less dead than you did just now, but still as dead as you did earlier—sorry!" She laughed through gritted teeth. She grasped his upper arms tight between her hands, worried he'd slump over a second time. "Now, last time I'm asking, what did you see?"

The occasional unidentifiable foot or hand still appeared, distracting them.

"I think I saw a ghost," Quincy sputtered. "Just for a brief moment."

Lilly opened her mouth to say something, hesitated, then shook her head. Quincy thought she looked funny— a mixture of confusion and contempt.

"Look, it wasn't just a normal ghost, okay?"

"It better not have been," she replied, almost insulted. "You just gave a yelp as if you had hit the *destroy all living things in the known universe*-button by accident… Looked the part, too!"

Quincy poked her in the side. "Listen, it wasn't just that he startled me. It was just a flash. I don't know, but I recall one thing very clearly. Everything was dark, and *you* disappeared. You were gone, and I had no idea why or what the hell happened, so that *yelp*, as you so gently put it, was me being in sheer panic over my sister vanishing."

Lilly flushed. "Okay…thanks, I guess."

"What? For caring about you?" Quincy huffed. "Don't be silly; I just figured out I had a better chance of escaping this place with a teammate around." He winked and was almost sure Lilly didn't not appreciate the joke.

At their feet, Hewie let out three short barks, and Quincy looked down. "What's going on with him? He's been real adamant about *that* way, hasn't he? Think it's best to follow his lead, right? He's supposed to be our guide, and apparently he wants to guide us very much." Quincy scratched the now-wiggling dog behind the ears. "Hush now, Hewie, it's okay. We'll go and take a look."

"Are we?" Lilly folded her arms. "I don't know, Quincy. Things are looking fishy all around us. I don't know what these things are, but considering what your reaction was to just one of them…" She hesitated. "I just don't know."

Quincy tried his best to concentrate and closed his eyes. Slowly but surely, a picture started to form in his mind. Travelers: lost, abandoned, afraid. He felt their fear and sorrow. It was intense and almost suffocating to behold. "I don't think they will give us any trouble."

"Why is that?"

Quincy opened his eyes. "They're just like us. Trying to get away from whatever place they felt trapped in. They're terrified, I can feel it. This…underworld railroad, as Samuel put it, is just like the real underground railroad at home. We can't see these souls wandering about because *they don't want to be seen*. They just want to get on with it as quickly as possible."

"Perhaps this place is called the Hall of Petrified Somethings because you'll freeze in place and crap your pants if you stand still long enough to behold the scary stuff around you," Lilly joked, smiling.

"I'm going to pretend I didn't hear that."

Another bark from Hewie had the twins slowly starting to pace after the impatient corgi. And as Quincy had suspected, whatever or whomever was wandering at the edge of their peripheral vision minded their own business and left the twins alone.

Soon enough the strange twilight grotto gave way into a smaller labyrinth of tunnels, which Hewie had no trouble navigating through. The twins tried to keep up as best as they could. They were thankful for their guide, but glad nonetheless when he stopped for a brief moment to sniff the air around him before focusing on a thick wooden door in the marlstone wall.

"Do you want us to open this door, Hewie?" Lilly grabbed the handle and tried it. "It's open," she called to her brother. Quincy was checking out a different tunnel altogether, but it smelled kind of funny. Hewie wandered over as well, took one whiff, and immediately started nudging Quincy back toward the door in front of Lilly. "Maybe this'll lead to a less damp place; my hair's a mess." She giggled softly.

As soon as Lilly opened the door Hewie started sniffing the old moldy doorposts—they probably hadn't been opened in centuries. He suddenly growled then barked.

"Hewie…" Lily started.

The little corgi yelped really loud.

"Hewie," Quincy said, reaching for the dog. "Hewie, look, there's nothing there, it's okay."

But it was too late. Whatever Hewie had sensed behind the wooden door scared him so much that he bolted out of the cavern and ran off in a random direction.

"Shit!" Lilly exclaimed. "Hewie! Come back!" She started running after him.

Quincy glanced back at the passageway through the door behind him. There was *something* there. He could feel it.

But it would have to wait.

Chapter 12

WANDERERS, rogues, vagabonds. Aren't we all lost spirits our entire lives until we end where we think we need to be? We walk around with our hands up in the air and wonder what the hell we're supposed to do.

When you're a child, you look to you parents for guidance. As young adults, you try to learn as much from each other as you can; ignoring pretty much everything and everyone else. When you get even older, everything around you changes so much that you feel entirely overwhelmed by it all. When you die, apparently, you still have no clue as to what to do and where to go.

Oh, and you end up following a corgi around that was once part of your life long ago—you haven't forgotten him, you'd never entirely forget him, but you certainly haven't thought about him for a while.

That corgi is now your lifeline, your only hope, your salvation. Because leading a half-life between two shades of reality is no way of 'living,' you're better off just…never mind.

In this world, where everything is just a slight shade darker and more sinister, nobody can be happy. Because everybody here is lost.

Every single one.

Whether they seek fortune or meaning, or they're running from something different altogether—no one wants to be found. They don't want to be seen. They're old souls, having wandered for years, if not decades: that is, if such a thing even exists in this world. And where would they go once they've reached what they think is their final destination? Would they be happy there? Or would that 'pang' of panic come again, once they realize they've ended up exactly where they left off, only with different species of drab trees and slightly different shades of vague lights in the skies?

I think I'm slowly coming to the realization that purpose, meaning, and happiness can be found in places sure, but true purpose, a true feeling of home, comes from the company you keep. I couldn't do this without my brother, never in a million years. He gives me purpose, he gives meaning, he is my rock.

But then why do I still feel lost and anxious when I think about escaping this place and coming back to life and being right there beside him?

Am I supposed to be somewhere else?

"There's something in here with us," Liz whispered just as the orb of light she conjured floated effortlessly off the palm of her hand. It was a stark contrast to the more primitive homemade torch and cursed spoon combo that Moira was wielding. "You feel that too, right?"

The library was dark, extremely humid, and the smell of fish and rot protruded from just about every crack and orifice of the unstable structure that was not flooded. The entire ground floor was underwater, nothing to do about that. Any books that were once down there were now part of the exclusive papier-mâché collection. No exceptions.

Luckily, Moira had already figured out days ago that the restricted and occult sections were located on the top floor. The book they'd been looking for in order to learn how to speak with people across the veil of death had to be there. If it wasn't, then they could be sure it had been long-since taken.

The only thing they had to do currently was not to fall through any broken boards of moldy wood into the water… They'd be just fine. Except for the countless of possible dangers that might lurk inside the library on dry ground.

Moira laughed. "Well, whatever's in here, it's not going to be one of those giant sharks that ate up the boat."

"Oh?"

"I didn't see any legs on that thing, did you?" Moira smirked. "So as long as we steer clear of the flooded lower levels, at least those beasties won't bother us." She shrugged.

"You know, for a black magic practitioner, you seem pretty optimistic." Liz stopped for a moment and sniffed the thick humid air. "There's magic dripping from every crevice in this building, and it's old. Very old."

Moira stopped in her stride, turned around and poked Liz on the chest. "First of all, voodoo and black magic are not the same thing at *all*, and I don't do black magic. I know it's hard, but you've got to start looking at me and the rest of my family as entirely separate entities." She frowned. "And as far as what you saw me doing to those two Haven agents back in Darkness Falls, 'cause I'm pretty sure that was going to be your next remark, it was a means to an end. It was survival—them or us. Surely you can understand. You must've used hostile magic before to save someone, or defuse a situation?"

Liz thought back at the hunters in the diner who had dragged the Jersey Devil young inside. A brief memory flashed before her eyes as she remembered what she had done to the local men. She saw their pleading eyes, the terror on their faces, the realization of the finality of their existence as it arrived.

At first, she said nothing. Then she finally admitted in furtive whisper, "Okay, yeah. I know what it's like to be misunderstood."

Seeing the look on Liz's face, Moira gave her a nod, then continued: "Secondly… Yeah, I feel it too. There's something here that's out of place. Not just figuratively, but more so…"

Liz stretched her hand in front of Moira to stop her from walking on as something caught her eye.

"What—"

Ignoring Moira's confusion, Liz plucked the golden leaf hanging in front of her face from the dark brown chestnut branch sticking out from between the two book-cases in front of them. The branch swayed effortlessly without the help of wind, and the bark sparkled now and again as if reflecting an invisible miniature sun hanging in the corner of the unbroken roof. "Metaphysical?"

"That's it," Moira admitted, having had trouble defining what had just manifested itself in front of them. "Your instincts have not failed you, Liz. This is not the work of your current-day Bywater dweller, monstrous or otherwise."

The two women rounded the upper floor balcony corner and found what could've only been described as an entire forest of trees. They were all of different types of trees, but all of them oozed that faint spark of magic. The damp wooden floor felt more and more like dirt and grass the further into the room they walked. Rocks and smaller shrubberies began littering the fertile ground, which smelled like a meadow in the early spring. The bookcases and other identifiable parts of the library became lost in the created tapestry of lush brilliance.

The weeping willow that appeared in front of Liz and Moira felt like it was a curtain hiding an even more beautiful place behind it. Both Liz and Moira felt the urge to sweep the hanging branches aside and indulge in the fantastical place that beckoned them. But they also felt hesitation—logic crept back.

"Initial thoughts?" Liz whispered. She tried to trace a couple of magical symbols into the dirt in front of her as quietly and as inconspicuously as she could; searching for a hidden trap.

Moira briefly touched the willow's stem, but her hand jolted back as if receiving a shock. "I've never seen such a thing before," Moira answered, carefully putting her hand between some bushes that obscured a still-present part of a bookcase that stood nearby. "Not even during my very brief time with the Global Defense Force when I was sent out to the Black Forest in the southern regions of Germany."

Liz's eyes grew wide. "You were with GDF? A LaGrande?"

"It was but one of many things that led my family to keep a constant eye on my activity—of which planted the roots of mistrust deep between their opinion of me. Truth be told, I didn't last very long. Pretty sure my mental state had less to do with it than the huge influence a family like mine had on the fragile upper echelons of such important but fresh organizations…but I digress."

Moira reached further within the bushes, back toward a little book cabinet she'd spotted and pulled out a torn-off tag: *Shelf of living fiction—DO NOT OPEN WITHOUT LIBRARIAN PRESENT.*

Moira passed it onto Liz and her hand disappeared back into the bush. "You think you've seen a lot of things around here. But Europe, man, there's things there like you wouldn't believe. Ancient things, legends, and myths that predate even primitive scripture or symbolism." Her eyes took on a glaze. "From when the world was young, and a chaotic vortex of all kinds of blasphemous and terrifying things was a constant feeling. A reality we only glimpsed briefly those few years ago when Egypt happened, and a reality whose coming to fruition was ultimately delayed, thanks to the Swansong twins."

Liz nodded. "The old world has many roots, many of which also come from a place of good. My coven was first established in what is now Poland, millennia ago. I've always wanted to visit Europe someday."

"Do not be surprised when that day comes closer than you think. You have a knack for pathfinding, I think." Moira smiled. "As for now…" She pulled her hand back again and produced an old, tattered book: *Myths and Fairytales of the Old Woods.* Moira carefully flipped through it and landed on chapter eight, which was entitled: *The Wicked Crone & the Enchanted Glade.*

On the yellowed page was an empty frame where an illustration used to be. Below it something was written: "*Beware the evil hag that dwells where the magical forest grows, lest you wander her gloomy maze forever and ever,*" Moira read aloud, then passed the book to Liz. "We have a problem. One that we both couldn't foresee."

Liz took the book with shaking hands and stared at the empty square on the half-torn page. "An ancient problem, by the looks of it."

For a short-legged corgi, Hewie ran as if the Devil himself was chasing him through the narrow corridors of the Underworld Railroad. Granted, the little dog did not need to use such mundane things as lungs or muscle really, but neither did Quincy and Lilly—both of whom still found it a challenge to keep up with him.

The twins were dumbstruck by the situation, but the true unnerving reality hit them when they realized they had no idea where they were going, nor where they had come from.

The narrow underground passages that had led from the Hall of Petrified Somethings, or as Lilly thought of it as, *The Night People Place*, had given way for broader hallways of marlstone at first, and then wet jagged rock and silt. The walls dripping with seawater led them through passages that ended up back outside, to a field of reed and marshland watched over by a black sun hanging low in a bright red sky.

In the field, everything felt like a blur, and it literally was, for most of the surrounding area was vague and unsharp. Not like a fog bank or rainy day, but rather like a smudge on the lens of an old, broken camera. The place had that distinct feeling of something being horribly awry, but the twins did not plan on sticking around long enough to find out whatever that was.

Whichever direction Hewie decided to run toward, Lilly and Quincy could feel eyes staring at them, burning into the back of their heads: A light brush of the reeds, a footstep in the mud, the cracking of a branch. Again, the souls of people were all around them. But they felt different this time: angry or jealous, disapproving, perhaps even scornful. Quincy could feel them breathing down his neck like they were either really close, or his brain was getting the better of him. But did his brain even work down here?

He could tell Lilly felt it too. Yet, she never gave whatever hateful souls the satisfaction of looking back. She kept her eyes on Hewie.

Meanwhile, Hewie ran like the wind down a slope and caught the momentum of a mudslide to propel himself into a sewer drainage pipe. The pipe was broad enough for the twins to run through without ducking their heads too much. Lilly actually counted this as a win, despite the loathsome smell.

For a brief second, Hewie turned his head and looked back toward his old friends. Lilly saw the terror in his eyes.

"Hewie!" she panted. "Stop for a second, little guy. Hey! C'mon, what's going on?"

Quincy pointed ahead of them to an especially dark corner in the, he now realized, unusually brightly lit sewage pipe. "Lilly, look!"

It was as if the shadow itself moved and lashed out toward the dog—Hewie yelped and jumped away from the darkness as the shape of a many-limbed human torso disappeared back in its black lair.

Lilly gasped. "What? What was that?"

Still running, the twins passed the black patch of deep shadow with as much circumvention as possible.

Quincy made the mistake of looking over his shoulder, and what he saw was once again trivialized by what he felt. The only thing worse now was the fact that not long after, Lilly too rounded her head, and for the first time stared down that deep, never-ending pit of sorrow and despair.

It was the void.

It was the feeling of infinite guilt, absolute nothingness, and the worst pain and suffering anyone had ever known all congealed into a single, solitary point of focus.

It was jagged rocks and unlit otherworldly caverns countless fathoms below the deepest ocean.

It was the murder of innocence and the suicide of happiness.

It was a splintering wooden fence with a black cat sitting atop of it staring at a moon that was grinning like a mad jester.

It was a grey field filled with the ghostly apparitions of family, friends, and ancestors with twisted, inhuman faces.

It was a sprawling metropolis filled with dark monolithic skyscrapers piercing up into the sky as if stabbing the heart of the world itself.

It was a harvest of souls.

It was the absence of everything where never again could they be happy, never again would they be together.

Nothing. It was nothing: cold-hearted abyss. An eternity of mental torture without the sweet embrace of sleep.

Nothing.

Lilly cried.

Quincy fell to his knees.

Hewie barked, growled, peeped. Then nothing.

Nothing.

Chapter 13

"BY THE WHIP, snap, cracking of my age-old thighs, something wicked is about to occur, I surmise!" the eerie, high-pitched voice shrieked through the enchanted library's forest glade.

Liz and Moira, hidden in a thick blackberry bush, heard the brushing of leaves close to them and the pounding of a something—someone—stomping around even closer.

The hag's voice cackled. They heard it all around them. "Come out, come out, little birdies and play. I have long foreseen your arrival, so just enjoy your stay. Teehee-heeeeeh!" She trailed off somewhat, but her words were soon replaced by labored, heavy breathing. It sounded as if she was hunting, angrily so.

"Well, so much for the stealthy, *in and out* approach, I suppose," Liz remarked in a nervous whisper. "Looking around, I might be able to cook up some spell to buy us time. But I don't know if it'll work… I'm not sure what

I'm dealing with except that it's old, ancient even, and according to the book, it loves to eat children."

Moira wiped the sweat from her brow and blew softly as if whistling without noise. "Man, European folklore is hardcore. We got nothing like it in the States, do we? Ghostly confederate soldier here, Chupacabra there…"

"Have you been outside lately? Like in the past couple of years?" Liz rolled her eyes.

"I didn't mean it like that," Moira countered. "I mean in the old days, you know?"

As they bantered,

they stealthily snuck from the bush across a small dirt path and behind a gigantic oak tree towering over the glade. Books were stuck inside the tree here and there, and both Liz and Moira had to refrain from making jokes about paper going back to its *roots*.

"Skinwalkers, Wendigo, Sasquatch, Lizardmen…the list goes on. We're *just* as hardcore as Europe! That's all before—"

Moira shushed her and put her hands on Liz's mouth. "Okay, you made your point," she whispered with nearly no sound at all. "Quiet."

The heavy breathing sound came back, hovering again all around them. The stench of sulfur, like rotten eggs, penetrated their noses; they nearly gagged.

The noise came even closer.

The branches of the huge oak cracked and groaned from the onset of an eerie, unexplainable wind. Fervent whispers of voices speaking strange, dead languages emanated from the faraway walls of the library. Somehow, some way, this was still just a building, Moira thought. There had to be a safe way through this mess—

"Pretty little birdies hiding behind the big tree, the voices may not find you, but that doesn't mean me!"

A terrible moaning came from right above them. Moira and Liz looked up in shock and saw a small wrinkled old woman sitting on branch right above them.

The sharp talons that stuck out from her tattered clothing had clawed themselves into the tree branch. The old woman had extremely long and frizzy grey hair which drooped all the way down to the dirt floor. Her features were nearly indistinguishable due to the abundance of creases in her face and neck. Layers and layers of skin overlapped, the only recognizable feature being the horrific red piercing eyes staring down directly at them. She was also very short…and smelled of death.

Above her hung all kinds of magical trinkets made from hemp-rope, small branches, and little animal bones.

"And now I have you here in this lair of mine. I want to have a proper introduction. Let's have a friendly chat, and it's got to rhyme." She scowled and bared what seemed to be silvery fangs.

Moira and Liz exchanged quick glances. "Yeah, I'm going to stop you real quick there, freak show," Liz answered, shaking but determined.

"We don't do the haggle with old-ass bitches that eat children. Why don't you pick on someone your own size…" Moira eyed the tiny little wicked witch above them. *Did she have a hunchback as well?* she wondered.

Clearly offended, the woman started shrieking. Her mouth, now visible and stretching out far wider than humanly possible, showed rows upon rows of silver, pointy fangs. The mouth became a gaping maw of shining little razors. Some of them had blood already (or still?) dripping from them, and more than once, Liz and Moira spotted the remains of what was once human tissue or viscera stuck between the deathly gnashers.

The terrible hag jumped and plunged down headfirst toward them.

Moira saw the shapeless maw of razor-sharp fangs coming toward her and braced for impact. Liz, on the other hand, clapped her hands together and closed her eyes. At the very last moment, she pushed her hands away from her chest and yelled something unintelligible. A violent primal force emanated from Liz and blew the sinister old hag back up in the air.

It was like the sudden impact of a wave crashing ashore, or a gust of wind hitting a window at over a hundred miles per hour—the hag crashed into the tree branch, which broke off and took all of the little talismans and tokens with her as well. She disappeared from view, flying up toward the magical night above them.

Soon after, hundreds of books started falling down from an invisible ceiling. The old giant oak tree morphed back into a huge bookcase stranding crooked among a big pile of torn pages and desecrated leather book covers— the case looked ready to tip over. Liz and Moira, not eager for it to squash them, stepped back.

"Holy crap, Borden," Moira panted. "You…you blew her sky high, like pushed her away, with sheer magical energy. You're like a Jedi! Force. Push. You know, blam!" Moira pushed one of her palms in the air.

Liz laughed. "You're not the first one to make that comparison. But unlike with the Jedi, this took a tremendous amount of energy from me, and I don't know if I have another one of those in me for a while." As soon as she finished speaking, she grunted and quickly sat down. Moira noticed that one of Liz's hands was pretty messed up and bloody. "Give me a minute."

Moira sat next to her and pulled out a roll of bandages from her backpack. She also plucked out two pins from her braids. "She nabbed you on the way down, huh?"

Liz said nothing, simply nodded.

"I heard stories about the powers you witches hold," Moira said as she started to clean the wound. "Our magic is different, you know. We mostly work with artifacts, reagents, rituals, and spirits communion. I see you white witches tear the essence needed for such mystical sorceries right from your own hearts. That's it, isn't it?"

"We…need to channel energy from living things to do huge spells, but…ouch!" Liz gritted her teeth as Moira threw the disinfectant alcohol on. "We try to…refrain from draining energy from living beings around us. Usually I use ingredients too, just like you. Powders, stones of power, stuff like that. I didn't really have the time nor the luxury to do that now."

Moira shook her head. "You all are killing yourself to preserve what little time this shithole planet has left before being ground up into space-dust by whatever cosmic force figures out the formula to circumvent the barrier."

"It's not like that," Liz groaned. She brushed one of her few dreadlocks out of her face. "Careless magic will end up killing things that do not deserve it. It's a matter of balance, as it is with so many things. It's give and take. We never take more than we need, and if we need more, we take it from our own essence, because we cannot give life back to things that've already died. That's necromancy, black magic. We leave such horrid things to your LaGrande circles, or the Edinburgh warlock order, or any other such wastes of magical talent." Liz spat. "No offense."

Moira shrugged. "None taken. Fuck 'em." She shoved both pins through the bandage and helped Liz stand up. "Just keep in mind that getting Lilly and Quincy back is all thanks to a little bit of necromantic magic, but done in the name good, not evil." She winked. "I try to avoid draining my own soul to cast. I just keep a hex-bag or two handy at all times. Like when I saved you back in Darkness Falls. I prepared that serpent spell days before." Moira wiped some of the dust from Liz's shoulders and back. "Anyway, speaking of things dead or alive, what do you think about this witch?"

"She's...definitely still kicking." Liz nodded at the edges of the room where branches and tree roots still covered the walls and floor. They could even still hear the strange whispers coming from the direction of the magical trees: They were very faint, but sounded more erratic than before, and neither Liz nor Moira had a clue what they were saying... It sounded pretty wild nonetheless.

Liz picked up one of the books scattered about and eyeballed it for a second. She then looked around properly. Except for all of the books fallen from their places and the one big bookcase ready to topple over, the library room looked, well, normal. "I think I have an idea how she operates, though." She pointed at the tree branches creeping around the edges of the doorframe leading to the back corridor that went all the way to the main hall.

Moira nodded. "Yup, I think we're on the same level here—it's territory, right?"

"Exactly!" Liz lit up. She looked around for a bit and soon enough found the old fairytale book they had been reading earlier. "There has to be something that we overlooked earlier... Hey, look, the illustration is back like, halfway?"

"Looks more like a third to me," Moira remarked.

"That could be important." Liz's head bobbed. "Anyway, look here: '*The wicked crone's territory is marked by the bijou's hanging from trees along the borders of her domain. Though their purpose is unclear, some might say they are a totem of the hag's evil power. Although,* some *also went into the woods never to return again, so who knows for sure anyw—*' Yeah, okay." She shrugged. "But hey, we just whacked that old bat so hard in the meat-grinder that she flew off into her precious baubles and took half the garden of *unearthly* delights with her."

"A third," Moira corrected again.

"Eh, semantics." Liz waved a hand. "We might have something here. We're not quite sure yet what else she can do. But we know how to decrease her hold on this place."

When Moira didn't answer, Liz looked up from the book to see she was standing to the side, looking at what appeared to be a floorplan for the building.

"Well, I'll be damned. I don't know how exactly, but we're on the top floor. The restricted and occult section is right next door."

"No kidding?" Liz sounded genuinely surprised. "That's the first bit of good news since..."

Both of them stood silent for a bit before Moira laughed.

"Yeah, we had a run of shitty luck, huh? But this is good, though; we evade the wicked crone long enough until we find and destroy her toys, then we're home free to nab the book we need to learn how to communicate with the other side and get the hell out of here."

Liz clapped her hands. "Let's do it! We're already halfway there."

"A third," Moira mumbled.

Cold-hearted abyss.

If the void was so lifeless, if the abyss so desolate and empty with life, then why was there no rest? The answer?

Absolute nothingness was the absence of everything —even sleep.

Then why did it nag so deep? Why did it pull one back? And back toward what?

The abyss was for those lost, wandering, without purpose.

But…there was purpose. Purpose brings hope. Hope is light. Light drives away the dark. Could it drive away this dark? Or was the dark too strong? Too sinister. If the abyss was the absence of everything, then why was there sound?

Was…was that a dog?

"On your right! Watch it!" Moira dove back into the bushes just in time for the insanely fast old crone to fly past her up the trunk of the big willow tree that stood in the middle of the forest that was once the library's restricted section. "She's heading back your way!" she yelled, flustered, plucking thorns from her arms and legs.

"I see her!" Liz called back. She fumbled with something in her hand. "Past the willow and over the babbling brook toward that pink smoke! Haven't been there yet!"

"Don't give away our plan!" Moira groaned.

The so-called Wicked Old Crone of the Enchanted Forest came running up to Liz with literal breakneck speed. She was on all fours, and her limbs and neck were contorted in a way that no mortal person could ever survive. "Liiiiitle birdieeeees, aaaagggggghhhh!!"

The moment she was right up next to Liz, Liz blew powder she had been collecting in her purse right up into the wide gaping mouth. Pieces of excess skin and blood flubbed all around as the hag's terrifying red eyes blinked uncontrollably. She screamed and then started to heave.

Liz covered her mouth and ears as best she could as all the bile, blood, and stomach contents of the witch started to pour out onto the ground. Among them were the remains of a child: Liz recognized the young girl's half-digested clothing from a missing person's article she'd read weeks earlier—she looked away in absolute anger and disgust.

Just when the retching and sounds of streaming liquid stopped, Moira yelled, "Ha! Gotcha now. You wrinkled, old-ass, bone-collecting skank."

Liz averted her eyes to the blinding puff of light in which the crone disappeared, and the library section started to return to normal. Everything left behind by the wicked witch, including the liquid nastiness on the floor, disappeared. Liz and Moira could hear the little old woman moaning as she scurried about.

"This will buy us some time," Liz panted. "But...I don't want to just make a run for it after we find the book." She was still shaken up from what she had just witnessed. This ancient thing, a true monster, did not just hole up here in Bywater. She actively hunted innocents and had to be stopped. "I saw what she's capable of. I want her gone."

Moira sighed loudly. "We're going to risk our asses... but okay, I trust your judgement. Don't you forget this, Night Light. Let it be a token of trust, okay?"

Liz nodded.

Moira had been sifting through the bookcases of the restricted and occult section for at least an hour now and hadn't found anything yet. She couldn't quite explain what to look for exactly, and since *communing with the dead* was not exactly being Liz's expertise, she decided to sit out the majority of the search.

Instead, she kept watch on their surroundings near the edge of the top floor railing where she could see the grim illusion of the magical forest that still loomed. Now and again, the cold breeze of the unnatural winds flowed across Liz's hair. They carried the strange whispers, which were now in full-blown panic mode—or so Liz guessed, because there was a certain desperation in their tone.

Were they pleading to leave the old hag alone? Perhaps they were unseen servants deathly afraid to lose their master? Or were they the voices of the crone's victims, trapped forever in the entangled roots of her domain? Maybe they were, and they were begging for Liz and Moira to finish the job. Liz liked that last explanation a lot—the more people she could help, the better.

She smiled at that, realizing she was starting to think like Lilly and Quincy. Even though they had not been together for long, she had felt a kinship with them (especially Lilly) that she hadn't felt since her Night Lights communion.

The aching in her knees told Liz it was time to stand back up before her legs went to sleep. She kept a close eye on the creeping roots that wrapped around and through the balustrade. Further down the path going into the forest, in which a fog bank had now rolled in, was the outline of a wooden totem. For a moment, Liz was ready to make a dash for it and end the crone's reign, quickly and painlessly, but something stopped her.

The totem was different than the ones before. It was made of bundles of sticks wrapped together and held by rope or ribbons of purple and blue velvet. But it had limbs this time… It was the vague shape of a humanoid creature. It even had sticks going all the way down to its straw-like hands, making it appear as if it had thin, elongated fingers. Its head was the skull of a large horned animal, and the lower jaw was missing.

The thick fog obscured the trees around it so well, it made Liz panic. She suddenly wondered how she could see the stick figure so clearly. In fact, she couldn't look away. It was as if her gaze was ensnared by the force imbued in the wooden mockery. The animal skull twisted around and looked straight at her with glowing red eyes—*you!*

Liz was sweating profusely; she tried to say something, but it was no use. No air could escape her lungs. The voices came back in full-force, louder than ever, clearer than ever. More familiar. Still, she couldn't quite place them. It took all of her power to avert her eyes from the mesmerizing figure.

But eventually, she did.

"Yes! I think I found it."

"Aaah…wha-what?" Liz felt as if her head had just split open. She looked across the balustrade. The forest was still there, but the figure had disappeared.

Moira peeked over the top of the gigantic tome she was perusing. "I said, I think I've found what we're looking for. But it's kinda vague and inconclusive. Shit." She waited for a response, but next to the crone's thrashing about in another part of the building and the ever-present whispering voices, she could only hear Liz's labored breathing. "Hey, are you okay? Something happen just now, or…?"

The wooden floorboards creaked as Liz steadied herself and cast a reassuring glance toward Moira. "It's good. I'm good." Her voice was like gravel. "Place is getting to me, that's all." She rooted around in her purse for the water bottle and took a big swig. "What did you find?"

Frowning, Moira plopped the heavy book down on the antique marble library table in the center of the dusty and moldy backroom. She tapped the spoon that just appeared in her right hand to a faded yellow page filled with esoteric imagery and hard to decipher Latin. "Hey, I —" she tried, but started to cough. With her left hand, she reached out for Liz's water bottle. Liz handed it over without question.

The thirst had left Moira with a half-broken voice and kitchen apparel she really didn't care for at the moment. She downed the remainder of the water. "I believe I have found the fabled, *Voces Mortuorum*: a book explaining the history and practice of speaking with the recently departed." She paused. "How recently? It doesn't explain, so keep your fingers crossed. I've uncovered a couple of rituals here, but nothing easily obtainable. The reagents are simply too…exotic."

Liz snuck a peek at one of the pages. "Liver of a white wolf? Shavings of a heart-tree? Talk about impossible. It would take years to get some of these."

"That's right, but there's one page here, look…" Moira pointed at the paragraph beneath the image of a perfectly detailed anatomical heart—very surprising considering the book's age was rumored to be over a thousand years old. "This here explains a sort of meditation state by which the dead can be contacted through sheer force of will. It's supposed to require a strong emotional connection to the departed. The closer you are, the better it would work."

"That's it?" Liz said, frustrated. "Not really the clear-cut way we were hoping for. Ugh, just take the book and we'll figure it out later."

"Yeah, that's not going to happen." Moira scoffed. "Have you seen the size of this thing? And I've already decided to pack that relatively heavy fairy tale book since I figured out if that old witch got here by escaping it, we could probably use it to trap it back in there." She glanced at the enormous tome again. Several pages stuck out at the top and bottom, the cover leather was flaking, and the spine seemed like it was just about to fall apart.

"There's no way. The book would never survive, and it would slow us down too much." She sighed. "A double-edged sword this is, either way. There are secrets in here that could possibly change everything, but it could likewise spell unmitigated disaster in the wrong hands." She shook her head in dismissal. "No. Even if we *could* take it, the book should stay here and rot. It's too dangerous."

"Okay, we're just going to have to find another way to…oh no. *Moira.*" Liz sucked in her breath. The rolling fog she had seen at the edge of the magical woods further out in the library had made its way into the backroom somehow. In an instant, it managed to fill up the entirety of the room. Everything vanished, save for the one or two feet in front of them.

"Two birdies trapped in my cage…I have uses for ones such as you. Did you really think to trick me at my age? Your shambling corpses I will command as they rise, rise from my cauldron's brew."

The writhing tree roots Liz had seen coiled around the balcony grabbed them by the ankles and pulled, hard —Liz and Moira slammed onto the ground. Liz's head throbbed as her vision blurred. The roots pulled again, and they got dragged across the room over toward the forest. Splinters and rusty nails cut deep in their skin as they slid across the library's upper floor into the abnormally brightly colored shrubberies of that damned enchanted glade.

Moira's head was swirling. She reached out for Liz when she came into view for a brief second, but one of the roots nabbed her wrist and snapped it with ghastly precision. Moira, screaming in pain, saw a bone was sticking out of the flesh and the muscle was torn asunder.

The fog cleared for a bit, and Liz could see the familiar shape of the beast skull totem looming ahead of her. Red eyes pierced the darkness and mist like the headlights of a truck ready to erase you from existence, leaving nothing more than a red stain and hazy memories of people who have long forgotten your name.

Then the crone appeared in front of it.

She was more terrifying than ever. A primitive headdress with large antlers splattered with blood adorned her head. A crown of sharp brown and golden leaves accompanied it, thorns buried its razored edges deep within her forehead. Her enormous gaping maw was an instrument of death, ready to strike. Blood and mucus seeped from it onto the floorboards and passed right through them like acid.

She shrieked.

The forest rumbled with her, and the voices roared as if in triumph. There was no indication of any building here anymore. There was only the forest: Just that enchanted wood in which children wander in search of golden apples and stories of adventures to tell, never to be seen again. That cursed, ancient glade which had no place here, another one of the countless unfortunate side-effects of a world bursting at the seams.

"Moira! *Moira!*" Liz cried desperately toward her friend lying motionless to the right of her, but she got no response. The living totem planted one of its long, spindling legs right next to Liz's head and loomed over her like a predator ready to toy with its prey before devouring it whole. Liz closed her eyes and wished it would be over soon—her power was drained and there was nothing she could do.

She thought back to the scene in the diner when she first met the Swansong twins. The hicks that had mortally wounded the young, defenseless Jersey Devil were standing over it like they were immortal gods, acting on divine right to slay an innocent creature for the sport of it. She damned them all to hell. And just when she was wondering whether or not she had done the right thing, whether or not she went too far, it was Lilly Swansong who had her back. Lilly…

"Lilly!" she yelped aloud. The nasty, bloodstained hands of the crone grabbed her by the throat and stared at her with malice. "Lilly…" She could barely breathe, let alone speak. Still, she went on: "Lil… Quin-Quince…"

Liz slowly watched the world fade from existence around her. The last thing she heard before losing consciousness was, weirdly enough, the barking of a dog.

"Cold-hearted abyss," Lilly whispered.

She saw nothing. Not nothing as in being blind, but simply nothing as in, the absence of anything. But that wasn't right, she surmised. There was the barking again. She recognized it earlier, but the relentless pressure of the void proved to be too strong. Now it seemed clearer. There was a message to it, one she could not decipher (for obvious reasons), but a message she heard, nonetheless. It called to her specifically.

"Cold-hearted…" She opened her eye. Not her physical eye, because that would be pointless. There was nothing to see here except for the absence of anything. No, she opened her *mind's eye*, a simple trick thought to her by... Did anyone actually teach her? Her memory was unclear, but images started to form in the ever-present darkness that was now her consciousness.

Lilly!

A voice in the darkness had Lilly gasping. She did not gasp physically, for that would be impossible, but in her mind, she did. Did someone really just call out to her? Did a voice ring true from those formless shapes she saw rising up from the grey and vague distances of a far horizon?

Shapes. She could *see* shapes taking form in her head. But was it in her head, or was something happening? How could something happen in the absolute nothingness that was the absence of anything? Did a light, far away and miniscule, just enter that cold-hearted abyss of her restless soul?

Lilly... She heard it again. This time it was weaker, but definitely not lacking for passion.

The barking became louder still. She heard it coming from her right. *My right. That's correct, directions exist*, she thought. She looked over her shoulder (*Limbs! Neat!*) and there he was—Quincy. Her brother. He was lying on the hard cobblestones of a deep cellar floor, twitching like he was enduring an everlasting seizure. The room had manifested itself from the shapeless void. It was the grasp on reality Lilly needed to pull herself and her brother back toward a conscious, albeit half-dead, existence. Lilly kneeled down beside Quincy and rested her palm gently on his brow.

Lil… Quin… The voice, weaker still but closer than ever, came again.

Quince…

"Quince…" Lilly said simultaneously.

And Quincy opened his eyes. His expression betrayed numerous things: fear, confusion, anger, pain, and suffering.

Lilly grabbed his hand and spun around quickly. The barking had returned, now right under their noses. Sure enough, Hewie manifested in front of them as well. Behind him was an old cellar door.

Lilly… the voice echoed.

"Come on, Hewie. Let's go find that voice, okay?" Lilly exclaimed after making sure Quincy could stand alright on his own.

Hewie barked in agreement.

Together, the twins turned the knob on the cellar door in front of them. The room shimmered for a very brief moment. It was as if it fell out of reality for a few nanoseconds, or as if something, a darker force, had left and taken all the pressure and anguish with it.

The door opened and Hewie sped off, but this time, he made sure his friends could keep up.

Lilly… Quincy… The voice returned every ten seconds or so. And every time it did, the twins noticed it becoming more desperate, but also closer.

They ran through brick hallways dripping with copper-colored water, made their way through musky old crawlspaces as fast as they could, and ascended wooden ladders and iron industrial scaffolds heaped on top of each other.

The underworld railroad proved as strange as ever.

Lilly! It sounded like a last-ditch effort to call for help before something inevitably horrific would happen.

They were in a library now. The rows upon rows of bookcases seemed larger than life, stretching out toward an infinitely high ceiling. All of the books inside were the same, perfect copies of each other and none of them had anything written on the outside.

There was one bookcase that stood out against the right wall. It was of normal size and had normal books in them, but it was surrounded by fog and a peculiar sense of dread and oppression. The voice came from right behind it—the twins were both entirely convinced of that.

Together they pushed, and with all of their might, the bookcase cracked loose from the grey plastered walls and fell right through the hole and hit the ground on the other side, hard.

Without hesitation the twins stepped through the hole, which revealed a very similar library hall like the one they had just come from. The difference was that everything was in an appropriate size and perspective here, although judging by the deep shadows and cold, lonely atmosphere, it was still very much a manifestation of the Nearly Departed Realm. The twins wandered around the row of books for a moment, not entirely sure what to do next.

Lilly? The voice was right next to her, and Lilly turned to look—

The inconspicuous elm tree hovering over her, and next to the living totem, cracked aloud as the roots loosened and the ground began to spat dirt—Liz came to. Her vision was blurry, and she felt like everything was very distant and distorted. She scrambled back as the tree turned into a bookcase before her very eyes, utterly destroying the living totem that was caught underneath. The familiar surroundings of a dilapidated building full of moldy books slowly came back into focus.

"Nooooooo!" the old crone shrieked right before she started to shrivel up. "Return you shall, little miss, to my mystical maze." She cackled as her dead organs regurgitated in her throat. "I will be with you, haunt you to the end of your day—"

"Rhyme this…bitch." Liz panted and made some obscene gestures. She shuffled over to Moira, checked her pulse, and put her ear to Moira's mouth—she was still breathing.

Relieved and disoriented, Liz sat on the ground and grabbed Moira's hand.

For the first time in a while, the library appeared entirely silent. No creaking, no wood settling, no voices, and no scary ancient witches hanging from the ceiling among a conjured woodland. She sighed a breath of relief and enjoyed the bliss of silence, which unfortunately only lasted a few seconds—ten at the most.

Footsteps, almost imperceptible, came from the direction of the wall from which the bookcase had exploded out of.

Liz could not shake the feeling of security, of happiness and calm that emanated from the soft scuffle. "Lilly?"

<hr>

Chapter 14

<hr>

"I CAN'T BELIEVE this is really happening!" Quincy's voice echoed through the abandoned and mercifully empty, void of life library hall.

Quincy genuinely sounded relieved and in good spirits. Upbeat even, Lilly thought. Meanwhile, she couldn't believe they were talking to Liz.

Pleasantries were exchanged, briefly and to the point. But only between the twins and Liz; Moira had kept quiet the whole way through. She did not feel the need to speak up until she had room to say her piece. Mostly, the conversation was simply repeating over and over again how wonderful it was to be able to speak to each other: The twins were relieved that Liz had come out of the whole ordeal in Darkness Falls generally unscathed. And Liz was relieved that the twins were *available* to talk at all.

At one point, Liz and Moira simply stood there, their eyes wide open and gasping at the realization that what they had come here to find, their entire goal for which they risked their hides in this perilous place, had been worth it.

Likewise, Lilly and Quincy breathed a sigh of relief, insofar they were actually *breathing*, and they both felt that burden of insecurity and hopelessness lift up from their shoulders, if only for a little while.

It was so, so good to hear a friendly and trustworthy voice, Quincy thought, between all of the sinister deal-brokers, the lost and aimless wandering souls, and the strange figures knowing more about the twins than they were comfortable with—this was more than a welcome change of pace. This was a little light at the end of a dark, twisted tunnel filled with all sorts of unspeakable devils.

It was hope. Something to hold onto. Trust and famil-iarity. It was…

"A way to escape this forsaken place!" Quincy sput-tered aloud.

Lilly turned, seeing how his sunken eyes sparked with excitement and mirth.

Yet, Liz and Moira couldn't see a thing. They weren't around. And yet they were. It was a thing of beauty and madness, speaking with someone in the same place, but at a different place altogether. Two realities bouncing off each other, little snippets slithering through the cracks here and there.

It was all very exciting, and would have continued to be, if it were not for the fact that everyone's main concern was to have Quincy and Lilly be returned to life as soon as possible. And so, while Liz and Moira did not see Quincy get all excited, they certainly heard his *eureka* moment loud and clear. And that was enough to warrant further questioning.

"A way out how?" Liz asked him; Lilly pretty much echoed back the same question.

Quincy turned to his sister. "Think about it, Lil. Both Nibo and that strange hermit character were talking about having to find our way home after we get our full tethers restored. But we would need help from the outside. What if Liz is that help? She could guide us back to—"

"What's this about tethers?" Liz asked, interrupting.

"Nibo? What did he tell you? When did he contact you?" Moira asked. She had stayed entirely silent up until this point. She still thought it wasn't her place to speak up —it was Liz that made contact, not her. It was Liz that was their friend, not her. And it certainly wasn't Liz's partial fault that they were in this mess to begin with; that *was* all her. But hearing the name Nibo immediately pulled her out of her vow of silence.

The new voice emanating from whatever general direction that Lilly and Quincy found themselves on in the Realm of the Nearly Departed came as a bit of a surprise to them. "Who is *that*?" Lilly asked, contempt in her voice. She did not expect anyone else to be around.

"I'm Moira. You have met me before. Briefly..." Moira's voice trailed off. "I was with Haven when you two were...when you were..."

"You *murdered* us!" Quincy exclaimed. "Liz, what the hell is going on?"

"I swear," Lilly hissed, the echo of her disembodied voice bouncing from wall to wall in Liz and Moira's living reality, "if you did something to Liz..."

Liz waved her hands in the air. She was pretty sure the twins couldn't see it, but she couldn't help it. "Stop! No! Time out!" she yelped. She didn't want to spoil the bittersweet moment she had reuniting, at least in some form of capacity, with the twins, but she also didn't want things to run rampant with misinformation.

"Lilly, Quincy I need you to listen really carefully to what I'm going to say, okay?" Liz breathed in slowly and let out an elongated sigh. "Moira is with us," she stated firmly. "She was part of a scheme set up by her family, the LaGrandes, to gain them influence within the ranks of Haven. All of it, however, was against her will. She served in the GDF, Lilly. Just like you. She knows how this wretched world works, and she knows better than to put her eggs in the same basket as Haven, or even her own dysfunctional family." She paused.

"Less than an hour ago, Moira risked her life just for the opportunity to *maybe* find a way for us to communicate with you two. She risked everything she has ever had or known because she believes in the same things we do and wants to see the world change for the better."

Moira stood there, staring at Liz in admiration and gratuity. She was so thankful that her intentions were finally clear. It was a relief. She really did believe in a change for the better, a world without Haven to start, but she never felt like she belonged. Up until now.

"Are you two-thousand percent sure on this?" Lilly asked. Her tone was still skeptical, but she had all the reason in the world to be mistrusting. Moira knew and understood this as well.

"We haven't known each other very long either, Liz," Quincy admitted. "But if I know anything about how to place my trust in people, it's that I follow my sister's instincts to a tee because she's never, ever wrong. It was clear as day when we first met you, that we could put our faith in you. Now, lo and behold, we're talking to you from pretty much beyond the grave, all because you've made it possible to do so." He chuckled.

"You might not realize now, but we were in a very bad place just now. I dare even say that we might've been lost forever were it not for your voice guiding us back to the path we needed to walk in order to return home."

On the other side of the living world, a small corgi barked in protest. Liz glanced over to Moira with questioning eyes after the faint sound, as she was unsure what she heard. It was very far away. Moira shrugged.

Quincy continued. "Liz, I feel the same aura of trust emanating from you whenever we speak that I do when I'm with Lilly, and for that I trust you completely when you tell us that this woman, Moira, has the best intentions at heart."

Lilly nodded along with her brother. She felt an emotional pang upon hearing him speak of her so highly. She never really felt that special, but whenever Quincy made one of his speeches, she went all soft inside, and her cheeks would burn red.

"Okay," Lilly admitted, quietly. "I agree with Quincy. It hasn't really been a secret how quickly we hit it off, Liz. I've told you before how you make me feel; I trust you completely."

It was silent for a moment before Moira spoke.

"Thanks. For giving me a chance, I mean. I can imagine how it all must sound like from your perspective, and believe me, I don't blame you at all for reacting the way you did." She looked down at her wrist and finally noticed the damage that had been done. She broke out in a sweat and started to feel very woozy. There was still a lot of blood and…bone.

Noticing how pale she got, Liz pulled one of the wooden seats, the one that looked the least like it was going to break in half, toward Moira and motioned for her to sit down. "Okay, perhaps it's best if we just pause for a moment and break down what has happened to us ever since we got separated that day in the fields near Darkness Falls. It'll give us a bit of time to get updated, and in the meantime, I can tend to Moira's wrist." She pulled her bag toward her and gestured again for Moira to sit down since she was still standing, staring at her wrist. "Let me show you how we *white witches* really do healing magic," she teased.

Lilly sat down on the floor while Quincy wandered over to look for a seat of his own to claim. Although neither Liz nor Moira could see or sense anything happening, Liz could swear she heard the distinct creaking of the floorboards betraying a presence amongst them. She could distinguish two pairs of footsteps and a pattern of smaller patters. She wondered for a moment how thin the veil between their two worlds were before returning her attention back to the discussion. "Okay, who's going to start? *I*, for one, am really curious to hear what dying is really like?"

"Oh, it's great!" Quincy replied sarcastically. "Let us tell you all about it."

And so, the twins told their story on what had happened, where they ended up exactly, and what being *nearly departed* felt and looked like. They told of the strange characters they had met on the way, the deals and bargains that were struck, and the quest for their tethers that followed.

They spoke of Hewie, who barked a hello, and mentioned how glad they were to have a small token of warmth and familiarity in a cold and sad monochrome world. Next they spoke about the strange series of tunnels, passageways, and maze-like shortcuts that ran underneath that strange world. And they told them of the void—the black abyss that almost swallowed them with hopelessness and misery were it not for Liz's voice, and Hewie's reaction to it, that pulled them back out of that place of eternal agony.

In turn, Liz and Moira told of their adventures searching for knowledge on the *Mother* monstrosity, as well as looking for a way to speak with the dead. They told of their escape from Darkness Falls and the numerous Haven agents sporting questioning eyes they had seen on their way.

Moira told them of the soul jars she had stolen to secure the twins' essence inside and the deal she had made with the Loa Nibo to secure their tethers; although she refrained to go into detail on what the deal actually entailed.

The two women went on to speak of their boat trip in the bayous of Northern Louisiana, and the ensuing journey to New Orleans. And finally they talked about confronting the abandoned Bywater district, the run-down library, and its hidden ancient denizen that had thrown a wrench in their plans for a bit.

It was quiet for a while after that. Both parties took

their respective times to let all the information sink in for a bit and process it on their own.

"Quincy?" Moira asked, sounding unsure. "Quincy, you told us you might've figured out what the next step could be *after* you've collected the other half of your tethers, right?"

"That's right, yes." Quincy nodded, glancing at Lilly. "I think now that you have figured out how to call upon us, due to needing a highly personal and emotional connection, I might know the missing link to navigate the crossroads and the Underworld Railroad for when we get tethered back. Lilly and I talked earlier about our home, our true home in Massachusetts, and how we longed to be back there during one of our darker moments down here. It's also the place where Hewie grew up as a pup. I think that might be the place where you need to be to call on us and we will let Hewie guide us back from here."

Hewie barked in agreement, his tail wagging in excitement.

"That's a lot of speculation for…well, speculation," Liz said, folding her arms. "We need to head all the way up to Massachusetts? Are you sure about this?"

"It sounds like the best chance we got," Lilly admitted. "It adds up, though. Even when I was trapped in that cold and dark abyss in which nothing was allowed to exist, there was one thing that flashed in front of me on occasion: Eldritch Island."

"Okay, so what's the plan?" Liz asked. "What do you want us to help with?"

"The best course of action is for you to collect our soul jars from where you hid them and make your way to Eldritch Island. We don't know if the house still stands or if it's absolutely ruined by the tsunamis that followed the Daemonic Depths rising up, but it's our best shot," Quincy replied.

"Try and pick up Sean too. I know it's not really on the way, but I get the feeling that we're going to need his help in this," Lilly added.

"What about the *Mother* entity? How are we going to defeat it when we're hundreds of miles away?" Liz asked.

Moira took the flaky brown tome out of her backpack and sifted through it. "*Sticky things on Infinite Plains* hasn't yet revealed any solutions we may have hoped for. Nothing conclusive. Only thing I can say is judging on what Agent Dutch told me, I'm deathly afraid that *Mother*," she said with disgust and contempt, "is not the only entity responsible for what's happening on the outside world."

"As much as I would love to see that thing explode in a million green and gooey pieces, we're just going to have to cross that bridge when we get to it," Quincy admitted.

When Liz sighed, Moira cleared her throat. "So, how are you going to get the other halves of your tethers back? From what I've heard about the infamous Ludwig LaGrande, he was a loose cannon during his living days, mad like a hatter and incredibly dangerous. I don't suppose dying has done him any good on that front. Especially since he's running a, as you call it, near-afterlife mafia."

"Let us worry about getting our tethers back. We already concluded wit and cunning would be the way to go here; we're just going to need to hammer out the kinks and fill in the details and stuff, easy," Lilly boasted.

Hewie yapped in agreement. It was loud. Especially

for Liz and Moira, who for the first time heard the little dog's exact barks and whines clear as day ever since they had been talking with the twins.

"Oh, my Earth Goddess, was that Hewie? Were those strange noises actually his cute little barks before? Hewie, hiiii, I'm Liz and this is Moira. We're Lilly and Quincy's friends." Liz was happily waving at a pile of waterlogged religious texts next to an empty bookcase.

"WOOF," Hewie yelped. Even though he was technically on the other side of where Liz was waving.

Lilly laughed. "Okay, we've got a plan cooking now, yeah? Anything happens, you know how to contact us…I think."

"Man, can I just say *again* how much of a relief it is just to be able to talk to you two like this," Liz admitted. She was blushing. "I can't wait to see you again."

Lilly's heart skipped a beat. She suddenly felt a sense of urgency to get on with the plan. "I—*We* can't either. Okay, I think we better get a move on then." She sighed and looked over to Quincy, who nodded. "We'll see you very soon, okay?"

"Okay," Liz said, blushing. "See you soon." Again she could swear she heard little bibs and bobs of noise which she was certain of were the twins closely weaving in out and out of the veil between their respective realities. Moira concurred that it did feel like a presence had left the room when the conversation had concluded.

Once any and all supernatural phenomena had abandoned the library, the library went back to what it had once been before all of the mayhem: a creaky old building with a severe danger of collapsing.

The raft floated inconspicuously a couple of hundred feet away from the façade of the half-sunken library.

Agent Gloom was happy with the giant shark repellant spray the organization had so *graciously* provided, but her disguise, consisting of actual rotting human body parts, had left more than a little desire for more comfortable circumstances. The smell alone tested her stamina and usual iron stomach to the limit. Just so, she knew she had to deal with it if she'd ever hoped to gain enough influence to climb the ladder all the way to the upper echelons of the Haven pyramid.

"C'mon," she impatiently whispered to herself. "Show yourself and say something useful so I can get the *hell* out of here."

As if it was a kind of divine intervention, (or rather a spell of good, coincidental luck), she saw two lone figures carefully climb out of one of the upper windows. Agent Gloom's eyes were glued to her binoculars as she followed the two women clambering down the rickety building. With her free hand, she turned the dial of the wireless radio and held it to her ear. The little satellite dish atop of the radio whirred.

"So, what do you think we'll find when we reach Eldritch Island?" Agent Gloom heard one of the women say.

"I don't know," the other responded. "But we need to move quickly and stealthily."

Agent Gloom watched the two figures disappear from view, then immediately shoved the gross, stinking guts off her shoulders and brought the burner phone to her ear after blindly tapping the familiar sequence of numbers that would connect her to the Louisiana Haven HQ.

"Yeah," she said to the recipient on the phone. "Tell the boss the intel was correct. Mr. Greenwood can have his wife and ch—er...his leverage back in one piece." Agent Gloom nodded. "Yes. Yeah, I got a location." She paused. "Wh—really? LaGrande herself? Yeah, I'm on my way. Ciao!"

In the realm of the Inbetween, the Hinterland, the Shadow, *Purgatory* (if you're into that sort of biblical thing), or as Lilly and Quincy now most commonly referred to it, the Realm of the Nearly Departed, the New Orleans district of Bywater was empty, quiet and surprisingly void of water. In fact, the entirety of the city with its stagnant humid air and empty grey streets was very much out of place in contrast to the rowdy city, full of music and life that they were used to.

New Orleans didn't feel all that much different from the rest of the places they had been so far, generally speaking at least. The lights in the sky were a tad less green and blue and added now was a very pretty golden hue next to a strongly emphasized royal purple. Considering its cultural and historical background, pertaining especially to voodoo and the close-knit bond the practitioners (and the city as a whole) had with the afterlife, why wouldn't they have expected the city to be a bustling metropolis of nearly departed souls looking to find their place in the world? But as the twins crossed through the Marigny district by way of Royal Street, and stepped onto

Esplanade Avenue, they got what they expected and then some.

Just like in the living world, everything and everyone collided together in the French Quarter. It was a huge mashup of widely different cultures and people, now with the added bonus that all of them were dead. Hewie barked with excitement upon seeing all of the strange apparitions appear and disappear on a whim. The main difference, Quincy could surmise, was that all of these spirits, souls, or whatever they were here, appeared to have a purpose in mind.

They saw the spirits of men and women greeting each other heartily as they went in and out of little bakeries, chocolatiers, grocers, and whatnot.

Two skeletal men were playing a friendly game of chess on the curb, and an old woman was happily sweeping the sidewalk, then waved at the driver of a coach that came rolling by with skeletal horses and all. A see-through girl sat on the sidewalk, wearing traditional Mexican *Dia de los Muertos* sugar skull face paint and a lot of denim. She had a boombox with her, and from it blasted Cindi Lauper's '*Girls Just Want to Have Fun.*' The girl flashed a knife, which blinked in the glow of the streetlight above her.

On the edge of the street stood a man dressed in a pitch-black suit and huge top hat. He had no skin to speak of, and by definition no lips. Still, he could play the saxophone like an absolute pro. On one of the empty lots across from the French Market a group of young-looking girls were practicing a dance routine to the beat of '*Tarzan Boy.*'

A smile appeared across Lilly's face. "Quince…" She giggled. "Look at all of this. It's…It's amazing."

"It's like a shadow out of time." He chuckled. "It's literally 1985 here, just like Hain said. I didn't know what to expect, but…it certainly is something." He raised an eyebrow. "It's almost…pleasant?"

Lilly nodded as she took in the sights and sounds around her.

After what felt like an eternity of depressing, downtrodden, and lonely places, quiet backwater town streets full of nothing, and strange shadows whirling around in empty and forgotten corridors, this place was truly something else. The city was busy, the spirits or souls of its inhabitants seemed content, perhaps even happy. It was the closest thing the twins had felt to a place feeling *alive*. Hewie basked in the upbeat music and the warm glow of the neon lights. He also happily barked at anyone that greeted him with a friendly face. He seemed to be in his element somewhat.

Both twins felt the shroud of darkness lift from their shoulders just a little bit more. They didn't want to say it aloud, but both of them figured that if push came to shove and things wouldn't work out with getting back to the world of the living, this place didn't feel *that* bad.

Somewhere in the back of her mind, Lilly still remembered the black void the abyss showed her. It would stick with her forever, and slowly but surely, she was convinced that even this bastion of light and bustling crowds would not last forever. Everything would end someday—that was inevitable.

To defy it, however, was to know there was still hope left.

The twins wandered the French Quarter for a while. They had no real clue on how or where to proceed. New Orleans was a huge city, and they didn't have any leads to where Ludwig LaGrande might be holed up. As far as asking around where a possible crime-lord might reside, Quincy figured that would usually count as a very bad idea.

They eventually stumbled upon the historic St. Louis Cemetery No.1 just across the Basin Street station. At first, the twins didn't really pay the weatherworn graves much heed, as they figured that not much about some old crypts could surprise them wandering around a literal necropolis like New Orleans. But a little black figure darting between two of the white 19th century tombs caught Lilly's eye just as she passed the rusty gate. She stopped and rubbed her eyes. She saw the shape coming closer, but somehow it didn't become much clearer.

It was then right in front of her on the other side of the gate.

"You two still here? I've got multiple records stating you're pretty late with all your business," the shape stated.

The voice was familiar, Lilly thought. She'd never forget the first 'friendly' voice they'd heard when they'd arrived in the Nearly Departed Realm. "Little hermit man? Is that you?" she asked, rather bluntly.

The shape in front of them sharpened, and it was indeed the crooked old man with the long beard and bald head. "I take offense to that," he muttered, and waved his cane around in frustration. "But yes, it's me." He unlocked the cemetery gate and opened it—the twins went in without giving it much thought.

"What did you mean by us being late?" Quincy asked. "Is there something you know that you're keeping from us?" He leaned against the gate casually.

Now, in the eleventh hour, Quincy too felt like he was getting *comfortable* for lack of a better term at being here in the Inbetween. Whether that was a good thing or not was still to be seen.

The stillness of the cemetery was interrupted only by the occasional soft synthesizer droning on the breeze and Hewie shuffling about chasing bugs and small birds among the age-old slabs and tombstones.

"Oh, this and that," the old hermit responded distantly. "Excuse me for being vague—a friend of mine once told me it's not a good idea to know too much about your own future."

"You can see into our future? But that means we still *have* a future, right?"

The old man scratched his beard, making little flakes of dandruff fall to the ground. He then pulled out a small silver pocket watch and held it in front of his dark, empty eye cavities for a few seconds. "All I can tell you," he started without taking the black holes off the ticking dials, "is that things aren't the way they are supposed to be. I can see you two in different places still. The old country, high gothic spires in times of utter darkness…deep cellars beneath the earth, not those of any afterlife traversal system, but somewhere where the living still roam. A place of hope, creativity…and smelly canals…"

"The old country?" Quincy perked up. "Do you mean Europe?"

"I said enough," the man told them. "Please do not ask me for anything more, I implore you. I will vanish this instant and you will be stuck here forever!"

"We'll live after all of this *and* we'll go on a holiday? Rad!" Lilly laughed.

The little crooked man raised his cane. "Stop!" He sunk his hand into the dust cloak he wore and rummaged around until he took out two objects. One was a fairly large book filled with snot green and otherwise smudged papers. The other was a leather handle like that of a knife with a button on it. The button was engraved with the image of a skull.

The man handed the tome to Quincy. "That should *just* be able to fit in that fancy jacket of yours," he said. The handle he gave to Lilly, but before she could pull her hand away, he gasped it and squeezed. "Do *not* press it! Not just yet. You'll know when you'll need to. I promise."

A little uneasy, Lilly took the handle and started to stash it away in her back pocket. An image flashed through her head of her sitting down and accidentally pressing the button, unleashing heaven knows what on her bum and everything around it. She thought about it for a moment and tucked the handle safely in her inner jacket pocket. "Okay, since you seem to know exactly what we're supposed to do, what *are* we doing?"

"Here's an address." His creepy, bony hand stretched out again, holding a piece of paper. "It's on Bourbon Street. I reckon you've been there once or twice before. Well, not *this* place exactly—it was bought up and changed into a souvenir shop somewhere in the mid-90s, but you get my point. It's Ludwig LaGrande's base of operations, so to speak. A friend of yours, at least he claims to be, will meet you in front of there: Aleister Crowley, heard of him?"

"Oh, lord." Quincy scoffed. "I kind of figured out he was going to show up sometime sooner or later."

Lilly gave a snort of contempt. "Why him? Why are we only encountering shady strange types instead of people we can genuinely connect with, like our parents?" There was a tremble in her voice. The thought hadn't occurred to her until now, but it was a legit question nonetheless, she figured. Hewie's head popped up from behind a gravestone. He whined at hearing Lilly mentioning their parents.

The old man chuckled. "You should be happy, Miss Swansong. Your parents are resting in peace and tranquility, with no troubles aching their still hearts. They are not here because they aren't the type of, as you describe it, shady individuals that just *have* to cling onto a shred of their former lives, such as it is with the likes of Ludwig LaGrande."

"What will Crowley do for us?" Lilly asked, ignoring the possible jab the hermit made at the twins' inability to accept death themselves.

"You will go with him and introduce yourselves to LaGrande. He's mostly responsible for getting you in there, but I'm sure he has some kind of plan already in mind. I can already see a different possible future forming from the tiniest grains of the sands of time."

"Oh, I'm sure it will be lovely," Quincy retorted.

"Fine." Lilly sighed. "But if this all goes to hell and we're stuck here, I'm getting the Cindi Lauper makeover." She squatted down and stretched out her hands at Hewie, who came running straight into her arms. "That's a *good boy*, Hewie! Did you get all the bugs, did you?"

Quincy did not take his eyes off the little grey figure. "Tell me, little old man, what's your angle in all of this? You know so much about us, but we know nothing about you."

"My name's Mortimer and my sources tell me *someone* told you that already. As for the rest, hmph, *you* figure it out."

Quincy blinked.

The man was gone.

Lilly shook her head and Quincy saw her eyes roll up into their sockets. "Really, again with the disappearing?" she exclaimed. "Why do they keep doing that? Seriously, I really, *really* hate it when they do that."

———————————

Chapter 15
BOURBON STREET.

———————————

IF OVERALL DEPRAVITY and debauchery had to be given an illustration for it to fit in a dictionary or something similar, it would probably be a picture of Bourbon Street at, well, any moment in time. The wild reputation of arguably New Orleans's most famous street was almost always based in absolute truth.

The typical Creole architecture so distinct across the French Quarter was here merely a colorful façade of the streets' many shady bars, dives, and strip clubs. It was the perfect place for an *afterlife mafia* to hold out. It was typical in the living world that petty crime and pickpocketing were ever-present on Bourbon Street; so here in the shadowy world between the living and the dead, that petty crime was probably manifested tenfold.

Drunk specters littered the streets at all hours. Although the twins had several questions burning in their minds: How do you get drunk if technically your insides don't work? How come everything a soul swallows here turns green and can be seen swirling around in their transparent belly? How in the *hell* is that one guy pooping in the gutter over there? They soon realized it was best just not to bother with questions.

Another man with the Mexican sugar skull face paint and wearing a tinfoil hat stood outside of a sort of multi-plex movie theater, ushering folks in with the promise of free popcorn and a two-for-one deal on any seats in the first ten rows. Seeing the billboard announce movies like *Back to the Future*, *The Breakfast Club*, *The Goonies*, and *Re-Animator*, Quincy could certainly understand Lilly's innate urge to go inside immediately.

But they were on a strict deadline—at least, that's what he thought. He had no idea how time worked here, if at all. Everything he saw or experienced worked actively against the laws of nature as he was used to, and yes, that included everything that happened over the last couple of years. Thus, the twins metaphorically strapped in and braced for impact as they headed straight to the address old Mortimer had provided for them.

Without knowing what to expect or to encounter at all, Quincy felt a kind of finality kick in. He felt a *now or never* scenario was coming up, and it made him very nervous. He fiddled with the deck of cards he always forgot he carried in his pocket and kept quiet.

During the walk, he let his sister do the talking for the both of them as she proposed a three-tier system of argu-ments on why exactly *Back to the Future* could be, and should be, regarded as the best movie ever made. Quincy, in his quiet and increasingly nervous state, saw no reason to argue. He loved it as much as Lilly did, and she knew.

The horizon stretched out across the vast plains of the desert and with the setting sun the air was colored a beautiful orange, pink, and purple. The roadside café was just at the edge, the threshold if you will, of a civilized, urban society and the mysteries and emptiness of the Chihuahuan beyond it. There was nobody inside except for a waitress that Liz thought looked eerily familiar, like the one she had encountered at the diner way back in Georgia with Lilly and Quincy, and a single patron drinking black coffee and eating a slice of cherry pie very slowly.

The place overall wasn't too shabby, but it looked as if general maintenance was more of an exception than a rule. One of the lights was buzzing and flickered on and off every few seconds, the jukebox made a sound as if there was a meat grinder hidden away inside somewhere, and most, if not all, of the tables and chair were chipped or broken in some way. The only noises except the buzzing of the lights and the man slurping his coffee were the creaking *whooshing* of a single fan on the ceiling that looked just about ready to fall off, and the radio blasting a never-ending weird combination of jazz and surf rock. And that was excluding all of the static.

Liz and Moira sat in the back booth. They said nothing for a while, simply taking in the ambience of the place until they heard the waitress speak up.

"I see you eyeballing this here collection of *unsolved mysteries* photographs, Mister Horne." She nodded at the man drinking his coffee.

He didn't respond much as at all, simply stared wide-eyed at the wall of pictures, newspaper snippets, and prints from questionable websites. He shoved another forkful of pie in his mouth and took the photo the wait-ress handed to him. Moira could just make out the blurry image of what seemed like a naked human squatting in a piece of desert shrubbery.

"That there is the best picture you'll find of a Skin-walker just about anywhere. Old Navajo legend, you see. Turns out, they really exist," she told the man and pointed back at the wall. "Got a whole load of evidence of the paranormal here if you want to see."

The man handed the picture back to the waitress. "Peculiar. Unnerving possibly, but I'm sure there's a logical explanation for everything. Ghosts, monsters, and aliens simply do not exist, I think—well, except in our own unlimited imaginations, of course."

Liz and Moira exchanged glances.

"Shit," Liz whispered. "This is the kind of stuff I was telling you about. Lady could have a literal pack of ghouls living around her café, yet here she is showing vague pictures of some naked dude shitting in the woods." She fiddled with her necklace. "I don't like this. People are becoming oblivious—like literal zombies unable to think."

"Like lambs to the slaughter," Moira agreed and shook her head. "You're right, this is serious."

The man downed the rest of his coffee in one fell swoop and put his jacket on. "Now, those strange govern-ment men, I did see." He pointed at a newspaper article dating back to the late forties. The header said: *Mysterious 'Men in Black' Spotted at Roswell Incident Site. Government Cover-up?*

Squinting, Liz saw another newspaper article next to it was talking about how the newspaper company that had published the aforementioned article had suspiciously gone bankrupt not long after that particular article had been published. And an article next to that covered a massive fire in the offices of the previous article's company and so on.

"Those men in their fancy black suits and shiny cars, which you can't see through… I see them more and more snooping around. Just now, I saw a pair of them eyeballing that nice modern motor vehicle those two ladies over there in the back booth have pulled up with." He waved at Moira and Liz—Liz broke out in a sweat. "Well, I best be off. See you tomorrow, Miss Mayweather." He went out of the door.

Liz and Moira scampered out of the booth as fast as they could to go after him. Moira swung open the door as Liz let out a prominent, "Hey, wait up, sir!"

But there was no one there. There was no one to be seen for what appeared to be miles around. Defeated and slightly confused, the two women went back inside.

"Who was that?" Moira asked the waitress.

"Oh, that was just Mister Horne. You must've just missed him, ladies. He's been coming here every day for over forty years. Doesn't look a day over thirty, though. I tell you, I *must* ask him what his secret is."

Liz raised an eyebrow. At least they got their answer on why the man disappeared without a trace, so she avoided that elephant in the room. "Forty years and you just now talked about all of your clippings on the wall over there?" she asked instead.

It was as if something did not quite add up in the waitress's mind. She appeared to stop for a bit, as if the gears in her head were jamming, then she blinked a few times and smiled. "Oh, these pictures over here? You're right, they *are* fascinating. I really *should* show some of them to Mister Horne when he stops by tomorrow. Like this here picture of a Skinwalker. This is probably the best picture you'll find of one in just about anywhere."

"Riiiiight," Liz said, backing away from the counter. "I think we'll be going now, c'mon, *friend*." Liz grabbed Moira by the arm and dragged her outside.

"Hey, ouch! Watch it! What's your problem?" Moira complained.

Liz walked with her around the corner off into the public toilets outside and closed the door behind her. "Sorry about that, but damn, it's worse than I initially thought. We're going to need to order out. I think we're being followed. Ever since New Orleans, maybe even since Darkness Falls."

"That's some heavy conspiratorial thinking. Is it because of what that obvious residual haunting said back there?"

"Not just that. When I asked about him, and what he had seen and discussed from newspaper clippings, it was as if I tripped a silent alarm inside that lady's head." She lowered her voice to a whisper, and her eyes darted around the parking lot. "Listen, we know Haven is basically brainwashing these poor people, yeah? What if they somehow *programmed* her into dodging our questions?"

"I wouldn't put it past them." Moira rubbed her temples. "What do you suggest we do now?"

"Except wonder where all the coffee and pie goes if it's a ghost downing it all?"

Moira couldn't help but laugh. "Yeah, except that."

Liz closed her eyes for a minute and concentrated; Moira didn't know exactly what she was up to but decided to play along anyway. She closed her eyes as well. "Lilly?" Liz called out in a soft whisper. "Lilly, are you there?"

"Hey, what's up?"

Liz and Moira heard the disembodied voice of Lilly Swansong echo through the small confinements of the public restroom. There was also a saxophone, but questioning that would just have to wait.

"Hey, we kind of have a problem. We're pretty convinced Haven is on our trail, and we need some tips on how to dodge them. Got any?"

"Well, that's not good." The voice of Quincy Swansong had joined his sister's. "Best thing to do now is to check for any audio or recording devices that may have been planted on you or your transportation."

"Did you manage to get the Fiesta back?" Lilly chimed in.

"No not yet," Liz answered. "But we did hear someone say some suspicious types were fumbling around with our car, so thanks for the tip. We'll be sure to switch it back out in Darkness Falls if we get the chance. And we'll take care to check every inch of this one."

"I think it might be better to get yourself another car altogether. If the one you're using now is better than the one you're taking, you're basically doing someone a favor. Just leave the keys," Lilly said.

"Not how that works exactly, but okay," Quincy added.

"Anything else?" Moira asked.

"Yeah, use diversion tactics," Lilly answered. "If people saw you, talk to them again and make it explicitly known you're heading into the exact opposite direction you want to go."

Liz jiggled the keys in her pocket. "Okay, sounds like a plan. We'll get to work on it," she said, turning to Moira. "I think it might be best if we leave Sean for now, drive back to pick up the soul jars first, then return."

Moira let out a big sigh. "That's like taking five big risks to negate just one."

"It's risking five *possible problems* to negate one problem you *definitely* have," Quincy chimed in.

"Eh, when you put it like that," Moira conceded. "You really are smart. Liz wasn't bullshitting."

Quincy laughed. "Thanks, Liz."

"Yeah, yeah." Liz was a bit absent, perhaps lost in thought as she calculated every possible risk in her mind. She could really use the help of her fellow Night Lights witches and warlocks right about now, but they were too far off to lend any assistance. "How about you two? How are you doing?"

"Just about ready to head into the den of a gangster, notorious across all spectrums of life and un-life, not really knowing at all what to expect or do."

Moira began pacing. "Listen, Ludwig LaGrande was a terrible, ruthless, and murderous asshole. But from the stories I heard from him, he had one weakness: games."

"Games? What, like *Monopoly* or something?" Lilly asked.

Moira shook her head. "No, think of it like a game of playing with your food before you eat it. Like a cat does."

"Eh, somehow that's not encouraging at all, Moira," Quincy said.

"No, no, listen. Ludwig LaGrande may look and

speak as a scary, scheming weasel, but actually, he's quite dumb. You've got to come up with something that makes *him* believe he's got the upper hand, but it's actually you two that will pull the rug from under him. Does that make sense?"

"Eh…"

"Good. Just remember he loves situations in which he thinks he can't lose. He's a sucker for them. Use it to your advantage."

Crowley was leaning against the outside of the scrappy looking bar. A very intoxicated looking skeletal man hung over the porch railing. It cracked and broke just as the twins arrived, and the poor soul fell and rolled down the steps. The despicable bald man with the hollow dead eyes cackled and inched down the porch. He saw them and grinned. "Ha! Ever the bringers of good fortune, aren't we?" he said.

"Spare us the insincere formalities, Crowley. Why are you here?" Quincy asked.

Aleister Crowley huffed and bloated his chest. "I am sworn to protect you two Swansong heirs from all harm that may befall you on your quest to—"

"Nope, no way," Lilly interrupted. "We're done with that, remember? Technically, your whole solemn duty or whatever is over. So…cough it up."

"Why all of the mistrust? Can't I do something out of the goodness of my heart?"

"I'm pretty sure you once had a reputation of being one of the most evil men in the entirety of the continental

United States. And considering you've fulfilled your previous task, we remain skeptical, especially with the whole us being dead thing and you conveniently showing up at the very end, even though we could really have used your help a lot the past couple of…days? I can't even tell when it's night forever." Quincy huffed. "This sucks. Anyway, we needed help a lot earlier. And only *now* you're here. So, what's really up?"

Lilly chuckled.

"Fine," Crowley conceded. "I've got a bet riding on you two."

"Oh, come on!" Lilly threw her hands in the air.

"Let me finish, let me finish," he countered. "It's only because I believe in the full capacity of what you two are able to do. And because I still don't want to see the world ending in the flames of the apocalypse just yet, dead or not."

"Apocalypse?" Quincy asked.

Crowley coughed. "Never mind that. Shouldn't have said that. Ignorance is bliss, etcetera. Just know that I am here to help."

"Help how?" Lilly raised an eyebrow.

"I'm here to keep an eye on you two and make sure this all goes as smoothly as possible. I'm here to make sure you don't do anything stupid to get yourself into an even bigger mess with the biggest, baddest, scariest mobster soul this side of the Mississippi." At their looks of surprise, he scoffed. "What, you thought you'd get the surprise on him? He already knows you two are coming. He's known it all along."

A big-boned skeletal fellow burst through the front door of the bar and flung himself over the railing into the wilting rose bushes below. Crowley smiled at the sight. "After you." He beckoned the twins inside.

The inside of the bar was cramped. A blanket of smoke hung across the interior like a hazy fogbank. A jukebox played light jazz in the corner. The spirit of a tough looking man with an impressive moustache was cleaning glasses behind the bar counter. He eyed the trio of strangers suspiciously when they entered. The other patrons kept mostly to their own, conducting their no-doubt shady dealings below earshot so as not to attract unwanted attention from outsiders, like the kind that just walked in.

The entire place seemed lost in time somewhat. With the Inbetween's tension of rendering places nearly always in a monochrome fashion, the place had a real *noir* vibe to it. It was as if they were stepping into a real 1940s bar, or possibly even earlier, like a 20s or 30s speakeasy. But that wasn't the case, Quincy realized. He noticed distinct differences in what he had learned in his history classes.

It wasn't some place that had been stuck in time for nearly eighty years or more. It was very much a recreation of a bygone era seen through the lens of a contempo-rary's vision on what it must've been like. Thinking about how he was in a place that was modeled after what someone from the 1980s thought the 40s looked like while hailing from the 21st century himself made Quincy's head spin. He figured it was probably better to concentrate on other things.

The twins saw Crowley head over to the bar and start to chat up the man behind it. The barkeep pointed angrily at Hewie, who cowered beneath a table at the gesture. Crowley, however, held up his hand and nodded. The barkeep looked annoyed.

Once in a while, the twins felt eyes burning at the back of their heads and saw individuals quickly dash back behind their newspapers or averting their gaze back out of the windows whenever they spun around to catch them in the act. It wasn't before long that Crowley returned to them.

"We're expected downstairs. You're to leave any weapon you may have on you with this fine gentlemen over here." Crowley pointed at the bartender.

"Weapons? What good could weapons possibly do in this place?"

A vein crawled over Crowley's bald head and started to throb—a feat and a half, especially with being dead and all. He leaned in closer. "Oh, my little Swansongs, you do not want to know the many fates that are worse than to simply be dead and buried or to be lost in the Realm of the Nearly Departed. Believe me when I say, even if you two never find your way back out of this place, you should count your lucky stars."

His eyes darted to Lilly playing with the leather handle old man Mortimer had given her. "You do not need to give up that one, Lilly." He winked at her from his dead black holes that were once eyes. "*A lighter will be a fine thing to keep*," he said extra loudly so the angry bartender would hear. "*At least one of us will need some extra tobacco before we're through, ha!*"

"What are you d—" Lilly started. But Crowley shushed her and gently pushed the twins forward.

"Down we go now, children. Into the lion's den," he

whispered. Hewie tiptoed after them; he was as cautious as he was curious.

The basement room of the establishment was somehow even more claustrophobic than upstairs. The air was stale, and there was a constant blanket of *something* hanging around. It wasn't just smoke, it was as if the building itself kept many secrets it did not want to be found, and so it obscured whatever it could, whenever it could. Hewie and the twins were careful to maneuver the broad stairs going down.

Weaving through the strangely sentient-feeling vapor, they finally arrived at the back, where three very rough looking souls sat in anticipation. They were dressed to kill, in fancy, tailor-made suits and fedora hats with enough room to hide *solutions* when at a disadvantage. All of them shared the same condition everyone suffered from in the Inbetween, but what everyone else lacked was this particular aura of menace and superiority. If Samuel Hain (their 'contractor') or Nibo (their 'instructor') possessed any similar traits, they did not show them, which was perhaps for the best. Although they themselves surely knew how to make someone feel uncomfortable.

"Please, sit," the middle man said. He was dark-skinned, had curly hair, a scar across his right eye, and at their silence threw a wicked, unsettling smile. "My name is LaGrande, Ludwig LaGrande." He took a sip of whatever brown liquid he had floating in his tumbler glass.

"These are my two associates. Mister Nightshade"—he

gestured at the tall, slithery looking fellow sporting a long, thin moustache—"and Mister Saffron." He in turn gestured to the incredibly broad fellow sitting to the right of him. Mister Saffron was sweaty, appeared partially blind, and could likely keel over any minute. Yet, he still looked like he could snap necks as if they were twigs. Neither Crowley nor the twins were eager to find out if that turned out to be true.

"Aleister Crowley. A name so notorious and wicked that the man attached definitely needs no further introduction, I'm sure," Ludwig said. "And these must be the *famous* Swansong twins. Offspring of old Will himself. Tell me, did you perhaps find your uncle wandering around these parts over the past couple of whatever you've been here? He hasn't been seen for a while now; makes me wonder if he finally had the gall to move on. Oh, but don't let me take up all the room in this here conversation."

Ludwig sat up straighter and lit a cigar. The twins could see the smoke travel all the way through his throat to his trachea and down to what would probably be his non-functioning, dried-up lungs, if they were there at all. His chest was obscured by the suit, and the twins didn't exactly take the time to have checked on their own inner organs yet. The smoke came climbing back up through every orifice Ludwig had in his head. "Why are you here, Swansongs?"

Lilly and Quincy each took a deep breath and tried not to look directly in LaGrande's intimidating yellow eyes. Instead, they looked at Crowley, of all souls, for guidance. "Go ahead, just tell him exactly why you're here," he instructed.

Quincy cleared his throat and nodded. "Okay, we've

been sent here by Samuel Hain to get rid of you, any way we see fit, so he can claim this territory for his own."

Ludwig exchanged quick glances with his compatriots Mister Nightshade and Mister Saffron before all three of them exploded in laughter. "And why, pray tell, would I ever agree to give my beloved city away? You've had a good look around, haven't you? This town is the best—I'd never give it up!" Ludwig cackled.

"Who said anything about you giving it up willingly? He said to get *rid of you*, not to secure it ourselves," Lilly countered. If she were still alive, she'd been sweating like crazy.

"And this one!" Ludwig howled as he waved his cigar in Lilly's face. "Is she serious right now? Mister Nightshade, do you think she's serious?"

"I don't think she's serious, boss," Mister Nightshade answered.

"And you, Mister Saffron, do you think Miss Swansong here truly has an idea who she is messing with?"

"I don't think she knows who she's messing with, boss," Mister Saffron answered.

"I'm going to give you two the benefit of the doubt since my sources tell me you are new to the whole *dead* shtick. What your deal is, Crowley, I have no clue, but you better come up with a good explanation, else nobody gets out of here the same way they got in."

Hewie barked then before growling at Ludwig. The little corgi was fierce, but he somewhat lacked the viciousness to look truly terrifying.

"Who the hell let this mutt inside?" Ludwig yelled.

"He's with us," Lilly answered. "And he's not going anywhere."

Ludwig straightened himself out, and slowly his harshness disappeared. Well, somewhat. "You…" He pointed again at Lilly. "You got moxie; I'll give you that." Ludwig grinned in a way that reminded the twins of Nibo and Samuel Hain. Did every evil guy around here come with a wide mouth of sharp teeth? "Tell me again, now. Why are you here? Why Hain?"

"We already told you why we're here," Quincy answered. "It's the truth; there's no double-cross going on here or anything. It's a long story, but this is kind of our only shot at getting our tethers to the living world completely back. That's why we need to work for Hain."

"I thank you for your honesty, Mister Swansong. However, I do not see why any of this is my problem. In fact, why don't you come work for me? I'd love to have some young souls with a name notoriety such as yours in my ranks. Highly *moldable*. Offer still stands for you too, Crowley."

Crowley shook his head.

"I don't think we're up for doing your kind of business," Lilly said.

"Appears to me that you are already doing that exact type of work, Miss Swansong, but don't let me put words in your mouth. It appears we are at an impasse—a *crossroads*, if you will. Whatever will we do now?"

Quincy had been eying the card decks in the corner next to Mister Saffron ever since they arrived. He had carefully gone through the plan he came up with multiple times in his head. None of the outcomes proved particularly positive or encouraging, but he didn't really see another way out. So, he decided to let his instincts take over.

"How about we play for it? Five-card-draw, two-decks, wild cards allowed. Any combination of five-of-a-kind automatically wins. Best of three rounds. We win, you get the hell out of town, not stirring trouble, nothing," he said in the most straightforward and to-the-point way possible.

Ludwig LaGrande appeared somewhat baffled at first, but then his face contorted into a smile. There was a glint in his eye. Quincy had unearthed something deep within him. Some longing he had, some itch that hadn't been scratched for a very long time. "I accept."

"Y-you do?" Quincy responded.

"You do?" Lilly and Crowley simultaneously chimed in.

Ludwig nodded. "Now, just to discuss the *entire* terms. If *we* win, then I will personally visit Samuel Hain and rip his undead shriveled heart out of his chest and take your tethers as my own. I will destroy them, and you will work for me forever into the eternal night of this forsaken place. You too, Crowley."

"We accept," Quincy immediately answered.

"We do?" Lilly responded in panic.

"We do?" Crowley added, perhaps even more frantic than Lilly.

Ludwig spit in his transparent hand. No actual liquid came out of his mouth, but it was symbolic anyway. "So, we have a deal, then?"

Lilly sucked in her breath, and Hewie softly whined from where he was curled up between her legs.

Quincy shook it. "Yes, we have a deal. Let's get the decks out."

Chapter 16

ONE THING TO be said about any type of poker game is that the higher the stakes, the more exciting and tense the game will be. In this case, Lilly was so tense, she could tear out her ribs one by one just to give herself a figurative breather (it would be literal if she actually could draw a breath).

"This is *not* what we discussed, Quincy!" Crowley had said to him after having taken him aside for a moment right after the deal between notorious gangster and the college dropout (but one-time world savior) was struck.

"I don't really care what you think, Crowley," Quincy told him while throwing wary sideways glances toward the table in the back where Lilly still sat with three of the most dangerous souls in the entire afterlife. "You come here now, and you're strolling around giving orders to me and Lil, when we could've used your help the moment we *got* here."

"You didn't need my help to get here."

Quincy scoffed. "You're right. Turns out we didn't.

And we don't need it now. But you've made your bed and you've got to lie in it—just like you sprang a giant bomb on us through a freaking tape-recorder a little over a year ago." His eyes narrowed. "You're going to sit down and play a few hands with our friends, the scary ghost gangsters."

"I can leave whenever I want, you know, and so can you! We're not bound to places like the physical world," Crowley retorted.

"Yeah, but as far as I heard, these guys can send us from our immaterial 1980s fever dream afterlife to the absolute nothingness of the abyss with a flick of the wrist. You *know* they'll come after you if you run, right?"

"This is an outrage! I'm Aleister Crowley, for hell's sake!"

"And I'm Quincy Swansong, the last heir of you-know-who, blah-blah. And we're both screwed if at least one of us doesn't end up with a good hand or two… Let's go."

But that was all before, minutes ago. It might as well have been ages or a lifetime ago. It didn't matter now. What mattered was the fact that Quincy—holding a two of spades, a jack of hearts, a three of hearts, a seven of spades, and a five of clubs—had an absolutely terrible hand, which made him re-evaluate all of the choices he made over the last hour or so.

Lilly glanced over to him and their eyes met. Lilly made no move whatsoever, didn't even blink, but Quincy could read exactly what she was thinking merely by looking at her—it wasn't good. Crowley seemed to keep his cool a lot better, and Quincy thought he might've had a half-decent hand, but a sudden outburst of, "This is *bollocks*!" and the slam of cards on the table betrayed the opposite.

Mister Saffron huffed and dropped down a full house: two twos and three queens. "I win," he grunted.

"Ah, not so fast, Mister Saffron," Ludwig interrupted. "A pair of tens and three kings, high card wins." He turned to Mister Nightshade. "Or do we have anything to add, Mister Nightshade?"

Mister Nightshade dropped the cards face down on the table. "No, nothing, boss," he said nervously.

"Well, then. It appears me and my associates are in the lead. Two more rounds to go. Only one, if you're *very unlucky*." He smirked. "Your turn to deal the cards, Crowley. Better not keep us waiting…"

Crowley took the two combined decks and shuffled them. Then he did a butterfly cut, then shuffled them one-handedly, then he…

"Get the damn cards on the table, now!" Ludwig yelled.

Crowley nervously obliged and dealt five cards to each of the players.

Quincy separated the cards in his hand and his heart sank to the bottom of his cold, dead, non-corporeal manifestation. He didn't even get a pair. Frustrated, he threw every one of his cards on the discard pile and took five new ones. Queen of diamonds, jack of spades, *a pair of sevens*—spades and clubs. Not bad. And a five of diamonds. Quincy bit the inside of his mouth, then realized that everyone could *see* him doing that and stopped. Either way, there wasn't much use to bluffing.

The stakes were the highest they could get; there was no folding here. Folding meant losing forever.

"All right, boys and girl. Show me the goods," Crowley said cockily, then dropped three eights on the table. "Read 'em and weep. Oh, I always wanted to say that," he added.

Mister Nightshade dropped down a pair of threes. Mister Saffron, first having chuckled upon seeing Quincy's pair of sevens, grunted in disappointment as he dropped his pair of jacks and pair of tens next to Crowley's three of a kind.

"All good," Ludwig chuckled. "But still not enough to beat a flush of hearts. So, I guess that's that then."

"Four kings," Lilly interjected, and dropped the killer hand on the table for everyone to see. "Four of a kind beats a flush, LaGrande. We're still in the game." Lilly grinned happily when Ludwig's face turned from mocking satisfaction to frustration and anger. The tenseness in her stomach area and the feeling of a vice clamping tight around her head subsided somewhat. Hewie let out an enthused yelp in support from her feet.

Quincy took a deep sigh—not a literal one, but a mental one. This was the exact outcome he had prepared and hoped for. Well, there weren't really any two ways about it. If this exact outcome of one point against and one point gained did not happen at this moment in this game of *best of three*, they'd either won fairly, or were already royally screwed. Quincy performed the card trick in his mind over and over again. He knew those classes in *basic illusionist tricks* he attended during his drama minor would pay off someday.

"I said, *hello world* to the *fucking* dealer," Ludwig hissed in annoyance. His demeanor was getting more and more irritated and vicious by the minute. Still, there was a certain slyness to him that seemed to call out, '*I can't lose, try me.*' "Swansong, I'm gonna give you five fucking seconds to cut those cards, or so help me…"

"Yeah, yeah, sorry. Lost in thought for a spell," Quincy answered, sloppily.

"Quit stalling," Ludwig mumbled.

Quincy dealt out the cards one at a time. Every time he stopped at Crowley or his sister, he attempted to shoot them some kind of look that would say, '*Hey, I got this. Trust me. I got this,*' but he didn't know if he got the message through—it didn't matter anyway.

The cards were dealt, and it was time to shine.

Quincy loudly proclaimed he was going to trade in his entire hand again, thus distracting Ludwig and his cronies just long enough to take their attention off his left hand, in which, by way of a clever sleight of hand trick, he dropped five different cards he had hidden in his sleeve back when he was speaking with Crowley.

Quincy watched the rest of the players discard and pluck new cards. "Okay, everyone ready?" He watched every hand come down one by one: Crowley's pair of eights; Mister Nightshade's three of threes; Lilly's full house of two fives and three queens; Mister Saffron's high card ten of clubs and finally, as suspected, Ludwig's LaGrande royal flush of hearts.

"It appears we have a winner, and unfortunately for you, that's not one of you three," Ludwig said smugly and began to cackle. "Mister Saffron, Mister Nightshade, time to shake these two down for their tethers and then get down to business. Seems we got a rival to kill, pronto."

"Not so fast," Quincy interjected. He laid his hand on the table and made everyone, including Lilly and Crowley, gasp. "Five of a kind," he stated coolly and dropped the cards on the table.

"What the hell is *this*?" Ludwig barked. His state bordered on the maniacal and his eyes became bloodshot —a highly improbable condition when you're basically non-corporeal. "*Five of a kind?* Of WHAT? What are these? What does that say? *Islands?*"

"Are these *magic* cards?" Crowley asked. "I was summoned to help design these," he added.

"I win, *we* win." Quincy smirked. "It's five of a kind. Five of *any* combination, wild cards allowed."

"WHAT? I'LL KILL HIM. I'LL SEND HIM TO THE VOID MYSELF!" Ludwig was fuming, consumed by pure rage. Mister Nightshade and Mister Saffron had meanwhile stood up and were reaching for their weaponry.

Lilly spun Quincy around, panic written across her face like a deer in the headlights. "Quincy? What the f—"

Oh, hello.

W.A. Swansong here, coming to you right at the climax of this incredible journey into the afterlife when you least expected me.

It's true, I agree, that my side of the story in the adventures of my heirs, Lilly and Quincy, has certainly concluded. Believe me, I have moved on. I really have!

Yes, I *was* going to let this personal and exciting tale of revenge, death, purpose, and remembrance unfold without my interruption, but considering what just happened, I simply *had* to intervene to explain the magnificence of the events that have just transpired.

You see, whenever a person dies and enters whatever particular plane of the afterlife he or she is destined for, they always take a piece of them with them from when they were alive. This can literally be anything because the object of desire, or object of remembrance if you will, is conjured on the spot when that person enters the afterlife.

It is the first thing that pops into someone's head the moment they die and thus, usually holds a true significance to the newly or nearly departed soul. For Lilly Swansong, it was surprisingly two things. Firstly, it was her personal journal, but secondly and most interestingly: her old friend, Hewie the corgi. In fact, Hewie had already been roaming the Realm of the Nearly Departed ever since he perished so he could one day be in the exact place at the exact time when his old owners arrived. Lilly calling out to him was a truly marvelous happenstance which really challenges and bends the inner workings of time and space in very exciting ways!

Now, the first thing that popped into Quincy Swansong's mind, was the word *graveyard*, which is not an abnormal concept to think of when dying, but it is also a term from the widely popular trading card game *Magic the Gathering* which, very peculiarly, was the *second* thing that popped into young Quincy's mind. Thus, in the inner pocket of Quincy's jacket manifested a sixty card *Magic the Gathering* deck, colors blue and black—his favorites.

Throughout their journey in the Inbetween, Quincy had kept this particularly strange find from his sister. Not for any malicious reason, but rather for the fact that a fantasy card game would not really do them any good here. Or at least, so he thought. For Quincy wouldn't be a Swansong without his *brilliant* mind—obviously a gift passed through the bloodline from his great uncle—conjuring up the devious plan to get Ludwig LaGrande to agree on a deal to let five identical cards automatically win in their poker game, *any* five cards.

Only a Swansong could come up with such a trick, and judging how these things tend to escalate, only a Swansong will be able to get out of this pickle.

As ever, I am so proud of these two.

What happened directly after Quincy Swansong bamboozled one of the most dangerous souls in the entire Nearly Departed afterlife, no one knows for sure. But the rage that the notorious gangster Ludwig LaGrande displayed right then and there the moment he realized he had been beaten at his own game by a couple of teenagers… Well, it could be felt far and wide.

Even in the living world, it was said that the sky above New Orleans darkened. The people felt an air of uneasiness and panic creep over them, and many rushed home to hide from something strange and invisible they didn't understand, and had forgotten was even possible. More than double the usual traffic collisions, freak home accidents, and spontaneous amputation incidents occurred as well.

It was an hour of terror and fear. Fear of the unknown, which was simultaneously fear of something that was once known but was slowly forgotten once more. No one was present on both planes of existence to link the two events to each other, so one could say it was all just a very messy coincidence. Yet, that did not take away from the fact that right after that blanket of sheer fright and horror had descended upon New Orleans, especially its French Quarter, it just as quickly lifted and made way for something else entirely: a feeling of tremendous joy and happiness. Above all, it was relief that was felt, as if an age-old dark secret was simultaneously laid bare for all of the city to see, and snuffed and destroyed the very second it had shown its true colors.

Now, it would've been a coincidence in its entirely, were it not for the fact that Lilly Swansong, ever the warrior, had at that very same moment, at the height of the dark burden's terror, struck down the fast approaching and furious apparition of Ludwig LaGrande with a large silver scythe that had manifested itself from a small leather-bound handle in her right hand. The blow that landed was so fierce, it had immediately sent Ludwig to the dark void of the eternal abyss, for twice-dead meant gone forever, and it was a spectacle so grand, it would even make the great Amazons of Themyscira flinch.

Lilly stood baffled, scythe still in hand and not entirely sure what just happened. The handle vibrated longingly between her clenched fists. Lilly's eyes darted to Mister Saffron and Mister Nightshade, who were clambering over the table, ready to avenge their fallen boss.

One strike had Mister Nightshade screaming aloud as his soul burnt up and disappeared into a tiny black hole of oblivion.

And another. There went Mister Saffron, who put up even less of a fight than Mister Nightshade did, perhaps deeming him unworthy of even tasting the blade Lilly wrought, for the gangsters had weaponry that could send a soul off to the nothing as well, albeit less accurately, and with way less style.

This all became too clear for the Swansong twins as they heard the shuffling of chairs and the unloading of guns from the bar right above their heads.

"*The Hain boys, they're right outside!*" a muffled voice cried out, right before being silenced by strangely echoing gunfire and a sense of foreboding dread.

Aleister Crowley was nowhere to be seen. As Quincy had expected, he'd taken the first possible opportunity to remove himself from his predicament—his only threat removed from the board and now enjoying an eternity of the cold-hearted abyss. But Quincy would remember this, and if he ever encountered Crowley again, he'd remind him of the boon he owed after Lilly had saved his sorry un-life.

"This was *not* how I planned that to go," Quincy yelled above the racket and Hewie, who was barking like crazy.

Lilly stood near the basement stairs and neatly evaporated the two goons she heard coming down the steps with a single swing. "Well, neither did I!"

She stared at the silver blade in her hand. In the reflection, she saw herself like she was before. Determined. Fierce. Alive. Whether it was merely a memory of what once was, or a tiny sliver of hope dangling in front of her, she took it as a sign of good fortune. "Whatever the case, we need a way to get out of here!" she yelled. "I can hold off a couple at a time, but if any of those bullets flying around hit us, we're gone."

"How do you know?" Quincy yelled back.

"Well, for one, I don't see why else two rivalling mobs would go at each other's throats without a way to permanently get rid of a problem. And secondly..." She eyed the scythe once again and felt the sparks of raw power flow through her non-corporeal self. "I just know."

"And now?" Quincy said. "I'm running low on ideas ever since my last one set off the Nearly Departed Louisianan *O.K. Corral* standoff upstairs!" A bullet flew through the basement window and hit one of the beams above him. "Oh, crap!" Quincy ducked under the poker table.

Hewie, who had taken a break from barking at the loud walls, was now actively sniffing Quincy's jacket. "Hey, no, boy," Quincy told the ghost dog and shoved him back carefully. Hewie was having none of it and dove straight back. "No! Bad dog, Hewie! This is no time to play." Hewie dragged the big black tome out—a gift from the mysterious old man Mortimer out of the jacket pocket. "Oh."

Meanwhile, Lilly had shoved a couple of chairs, a small closet, and a water cooler in front of the basement door, which was beginning to give way due to the army of angry mobsters out to avenge their fallen comrades. "We're going to have to look for a new exit, and it's going to have to be *really* soon!" Lilly gulped and looked over to see her brother and Hewie under the poker table. "What are you doing?" she asked.

Quincy reached for the black book in Hewie's mouth, but Hewie proceeded to wag his little tail and shake his head violently upon his attempt to dislodge the thing from his jaws. "Hewie! Hewie, no time for games!" Quincy told him as he pulled.

"Hewie! Give Quincy the book!" Lilly said sternly as she sped over toward the table. She had always been the best when it came to reaching an understanding with animals, domestic or otherwise, which was partially how she ended up working in an exotic pet store. "Go on," she said. "Give it to Quincy."

Hewie dropped the book and sat down on his butt with a quizzical look on his face.

"It's entirely blank," Quincy said, shaking his head as he sifted through the yellowed and stained pages of the tome. "Everything except…" He stopped and looked up, eyes wide open. "Hold my hand."

"What?"

The basement door flung open, and a horde of angry gangster souls spilled out into the room.

"There they are!" one particularly mean-looking one said, bearing the scars of burned flesh on his face. "Get them! Do not let them leave alive—uh, nearly alive!"

Lilly grabbed Quincy's hand and Hewie's paw. "What now? Wait, is that…"

"It's a picture of the cemetery," Quincy said relieved. "It's a linking book."

They disappeared right before the entire poker table was shot to pieces.

Lilly, Quincy, and Hewie quite unceremoniously plopped down in what was possibly the only pool of mud for miles around. A quick look and a glance at Nicolas Cage's stupid pyramid tomb thing confirmed the place to be St.

Louis Cemetery No.1—they had ended up exactly where they had started the night.

Everything looked to be the same as it was before: Everything was grey, depressing, and darker than it should be. And yet the pretty neon lights—the ones always glowing faintly high up in the sky—brightened just a little bit. Perhaps they resembled the tiny sliver of hope that was needed to keep a person from losing themselves to the cold abyss.

Looking at them now, just for a few seconds, the twins felt a certain energy emanating from them. They held frequencies and vibrations only perceivable by beings that achieved a greater consciousness of the cosmos. Or so it felt. Were they but silly window dressing for a copy of the living world, draped in shadows and darkness and stuck in a bygone era? Or were they something more?

A slow clapping came from between some of the older graves, and from the shadows came two figures in which Quincy and Lilly have had to put their faith: Mortimer came forward first. He calmly walked up to Lilly and took the scythe from her hand. He also took the book, which Quincy willingly held out for him, and nodded. On his face, there was a tiny, nearly inconceivable smile.

"You planned for this… You *knew* this would happen," Quincy said. "Did you know all along? Did you…?"

"I did nothing except nudge you in the right direction a teenie-tiny bit." Mortimer laughed. "These things have a tendency to work themselves out. Such it is in the near afterlife, as it is in life. No intervention needed, really." He paused. "How does that one song go? *We didn't start the fire?*" He chuckled.

"You're off by about four years on that one," Lilly told him.

"Hard to keep track," he answered, "when you're in so many places at once."

Lilly glanced around nervously. The memory of the silver scythe still lingered. Her hand tingled—so much death in one single swing. She had never felt so much power. She was glad it was gone. It would've changed her in time, she was sure of it. "Are…are you…? Am I…?"

"Oh, you don't want to think too long on what this place exactly is, what it truly means to wander the after-life. Or think of who 'lives' in it and plays its politics. It'll make your soon-to-be-working brain hurt. In good time, every answer will come to you naturally, Miss Swansong. *Seek and you shall find*." He flung his cloak around, and for a moment the tattered grey fabric turned to a deep midnight black. Mortimer's empty black skull cavity winked, *somehow*.

When he disappeared, the second figure came forward.

"You did good." The little silver skull ornaments that wrapped around Samuel Hain's dreadlocks clinked together, making a hypnotizing ringing. He smiled wickedly, and the twins saw there was fur and blood between his teeth. "I have gotten my fill tonight, little Swans. And New Orleans is once again *mine*. I relieve you of your service, Quincy and Lilly Swansong, and present you, by ways of a deal fulfilled and promises kept, your tethers to the land of the living."

Quincy and Lilly each took their respective piece of glowing string. With it, the other piece in their pockets started to become hot, burning with anticipation to reunite.

"Thank you." Quincy nodded. "Although we may never know your true intentions with the nearly departed souls of New Orleans, it should be stated that you are a man of your word, which is commendable."

Samuel Hain merely nodded and disappeared in the blink of an eye.

Mortimer reappeared, standing to the side, motionless.

Suddenly, a ghastly shadow appeared on the side of a mossy old tomb.

"Tasks completed, hmmm." The voice of Nibo resounded through the abandoned cemetery. "As my associate said, you did good. But I never doubted you for a second, Swansongs." The shadow grew larger and a long tongue emerged from its mouth; it flapped around eerily against the side of the grey stone. "Are you ready to make a final deal, to get out of this place? Hmm?"

"No," Lilly answered, steadfast. "If anything, we learned that making deals in the afterlife is a terrible idea. We also learned that we can find our own way, if we look long and hard enough. A light will always appear to show us the way. We have our tethers now; we *will* find a way home ourselves."

"Bah," Nibo answered. "Silly girl, you will be swallowed by the abyss in no time. Have you seen the souls of wanderers around you? Some of them have reclaimed their tethers may centuries ago and are still here. You will never make it back." He paused. "Never."

Hewie barked loudly in protest.

"We will," Lilly argued, sitting down and letting

Hewie's head fall into her lap. She caressed the corgi's head and scratched behind his ears. "We have a home to go to. We have true friends whose voices will act as a beacon to illuminate the darkest of night. And we have this little pup, who was always the grand winner in our hide-and-seek games. We *will* find our way home."

"There is unfinished business here; you can't be lost if I'm to reclaim what is *mine*," Nibo protested.

"Enough," Mortimer interjected. "You can't force them into a deal. Listen to them, let them create their own destiny. Now be gone."

The shadow on the tomb started to dissipate. Right before it was nearly entirely gone, they could hear it whisper, "I will return. You have yet to see the last of me." Its voice got softer as it added, *"Eldritch Island..."*

"What did he mean by reclaiming what was his? He said..." Lilly gasped in sudden realization. "The island..."

Mortimer put his wrinkled hand on his cane and straightened his grey tattered robe. "I'm sure he is referring to a deal...a deal that wasn't yours to make."

Moira nodded absentmindedly toward Liz. "Yeah, I'm sure," she said. "Just keep in touch. If anything happens to either of us, we should be aware."

"We can't risk texting, calling, anything," Liz retorted. "It's too risky; we'll have to do it blindly and just, I dunno, trust that it'll all work out."

Moira stayed silent for a moment, then smiled. "You're right. And yeah, *trust* me, it will all work out okay." She waved around the spoon in her hand. "I know what you're thinking." She laughed. "I can drive with this thing, promise."

Liz laughed too, but her eyes still betrayed the fear and insecurity she felt. "See you at the island," she said.

"See you at the island." They hugged. "And I know he doesn't know who I am, but say hi to Sean for me."

A big empty field. Eternally grey skies and nothing but wheat for miles on end. It was kind of a mocking reminder as to how the twins had ultimately ended up here. The similarities between this forsaken place and the hellish cornfields in Darkness Falls were obvious, but the twins tried not to dwell on them for too long.

"Any ideas?" Quincy asked. Even though they did not need to eat or drink in this world, he appeared parched, weakened even.

"No, I don't know," Lilly answered. She was looking over into the vague reaches beyond the horizon, trying to see if she could find anything noteworthy, anything they could grasp—anything even resembling some kind of sign or waypoint.

But there was nothing there.

Quincy patted Hewie on the head and looked at his sister. "It's been a while since we heard from Liz and Moira, and Hewie here lost any scent he had caught up with before." He sighed. "What are we going to do, Lil?"

"Seek and you shall find," Lilly whispered, mostly to herself.

"What's that now?"

Lilly closed her eyes and let the entirety of existence fall between the cracks of the proverbial floorboards beneath her feet for a moment. She could feel the pulsating lights in the in sky. They reverbed through her body, and in her mind's eye she could feel the draft leading her further into the field. But there was no draft, and she couldn't see the field. Eyes closed, she walked and Hewie followed her.

Quincy had no other choice than to follow his sister into the field. He felt compelled to ask her what she was doing or where she was going, but he refrained. She had found something with that uncanny sense of determination and hope she had, and it never failed her.

"I feel…something," Lilly whispered.

A shack appeared in the middle of the field. It was rundown and the wood appeared moldy. It had clearly seen better days, but compared with many things they had encountered in this world, it gave off a feeling of warmth and familiarity. That on its own was very strange, but the way Lilly had honed in on it made it even more bizarre.

"There is a light," Lilly said, bursting through the door. The interior of the shack was laden with radio and communications equipment. "A light that burns brightly forever."

It was all old stuff, Quincy surmised, at least by standards of the living world, but it looked to be in working order. He looked at his sister. *What is she tuned in to?* he wondered.

"Sean," Lilly said, and her eyes opened wide. "Can you feel it, Quince?" she asked, turning toward her brother. She picked up one of the microphones, brushed off the dust and cobwebs, and spoke into it: "Hello? Anybody there?"

"Hey! Lilly! Can you hear me?" And there was the familiar voice of their good friend Sean.

Relief visibly befell Quincy and Lilly. It really did feel like there always was a faint light around. A light that in their darkest hour was there—there to call them back home.

"Sean, good to hear your voice, buddy!" Quincy said, ecstatic.

Chapter 17
DISTORTION

"THIS IS a lot to take in. And by a lot I mean, really a lot." Sean paused. "So, first of all, you're telling me it was *me* that managed to contact *you* in the afterlife?" He was visibly impressed. It was a feat in and of itself, considering his general demeanor the past couple of days could best be described as dead-tired.

Lilly's voice crackled through the shoddy plastic walkie-talkie. "Yeah, I think so. And all it took was for you to feel so emotionally broken by being told we died and believing it."

"Which turned out to be true," Sean said, nodding along.

"Which turned out to be *technically* true, yeah," Lilly agreed. "But it also proved one thing, and that is that this bond we share is real and unbreakable."

Sean scoffed. "Yeah, I'm pretty sure that was established pretty firmly when Haven was torturing my ass over information about you two back in Antarctica, but okay."

"Do you always have to do this? I wasn't joking." Lilly sighed through the speaker. "We owe you, okay? We owe you big time, and after this, we owe you even more. But you don't have to constantly remind us."

"I didn't mean it like that."

Lilly grunted, but remained quiet after that.

"I've got to say, though, permanent 1985 sounds like a blast actually," Sean admitted.

"It was alright." Quincy scoffed. "Hey, ouch! Ehm, what I mean is that it's absolutely phenomenal and fantastic," he droned. Lilly's vague laughing could be heard in the background.

The ferry's horn blew loudly as, from the thick fog of the Atlantic, the vague outline of Eldritch Island came into view.

Liz took a deep breath. "We're almost there. Any idea what to expect, or what do to do?" She looked over toward the beach from the railing of the boat.

The mansion was in ruins. Moss, barnacles, and other sea-life littered the sand and rocks. The island had been submerged multiple times following the floods before the water levels had returned back to normal. Even from where she stood, she could see everything had been waterlogged and destroyed. Whatever the twins hoped to find here, there was a big chance it was gone forever.

"Damn, the place is a sodden ruin."

"I was already kind of expecting that. Furthermore, we are really not sure what to do or expect, Liz," Quincy told her, his voice was like a distant echo reverbing through the speakers. "All we know is that something is pulling us to the island. We can feel it. If there's a shot of us making it back to the living world—it all starts and ends here."

Sean pointed at the beach. "Hey, over there."

Liz squinted and saw a lone figure standing at the beach, waving. At their feet were two big, elongated jars resting in the sand. It was Moira. Liz felt as if she could finally breathe again after holding her breath for days.

"Yes," she confirmed, determined. "It all ends here."

Chapter 18

THE PREMISE of being remembered after passing away relies on two things: You have either done great things and the world has loved you for it, or you have done terrible things and you've gone down in history hated. Either way deserves remembrance, for we, as a species, learn from both.

But there is no reason for us to think so black and white any longer. For Quincy and I, we were remembered because we have friends out there that love us and cherished the times we had spent together, good and bad, even it was short.

In the end, isn't it love that makes us remember? It might've been the dealings of a shady soul keeper with a young voodoo priestess that kept our souls from floating off into the afterlife forever, but those dealings too stemmed from the love and longing for the world to become a better place. It is love that kept us going when everything went to hell, and it will be love that keeps us safe. We need love to save ourselves from barreling down toward our own destruction. Because we can't do it on our own.

Not this time.

. . .

The ferry came to an abrupt halt at about forty feet from the shoreline. The ruined foundations of the once-grand Swansong manor lay still between the rolling fog banks. In the early morning mists, the blackened walls stood like a silent guardian watching over the small island, serving as its protector against everything horrid that could rise from the deep blue sea. Strange birds had made their nests between the rotten and waterlogged planks, and from the jagged rocks at the other end of the island's shore, peculiar, vaguely humanoid, shapes peered out from the cracks out of interest and perhaps fear of the newcomers.

From the aft of the ferry, the captain descended the small flight of stairs leading to the main deck.

"This'll be as far as I'll take you. You will have to swim the rest of the way, m'afraid." His low baritone voice was barely audible over the strong currents. The wind constantly swept his ashen beard to one side. "There's a reason no one heads over to this rock anymore. Been that way since before the storms as well, aye."

"And what reason may that be?" Liz asked politely.

"The island's haunted," the captain whispered. "Always has been. But 'twas not long after the storms had come and swept the old coast away that it really started to act up. Eerie green fire—unnatural that—it swept across the house, leveling it whole. Sea devils came not long after that. Mariners 've been avoiding the place ever since they returned after the rebuilding efforts along the mainland were done. Ye lot are lucky that old captain Velaro was available to take you out to these ill-begotten shoals."

"Sea devils, huh?" Sean smirked. He appreciated the

fact that the old captain started to sound like a pirate the more he spoke about old sea legends and dangerous waters. Only he knew that there was more to these stories than mere legend, and then there was something else bugging him too.

The walkie-talkie crackled. "Green fire?" Lilly asked. "Sean, ask him about the green fire. It doesn't sound very promising at all. I'm afraid of what we'll find when we're back. Does it look really bad, Sean?"

"It's…really not very pretty," Sean answered. "If it gets you and Quincy back, then fine, but I doubt there's anything else left for you."

The captain appeared taken aback by the voices coming from the speaker. "Them's no normal person, is it?" He started sweating profusely. "It's the curse, the voices of the dead…the third sign of the coming end!"

"Oh, great. Another prophecy for us to unravel and thwart, I bet," Quincy said annoyedly.

"Aiiiee!" the captain yelled. He jumped up and a small book fell out of his coat.

Liz bent down and picked the little leather-bound volume up. "'*What Lurks Below*' and *Other Weird Tales of the Vast sea* by…oh, brother." Liz giggled. "By W.A. Swansong."

"Oh, Uncle," Lilly whispered. "What does it say?"

Liz cleared her throat. "'*When the ocean swallows up the earth, and the men of scales, descendants of old man Dagon, return to claim the shores once theirs, the ones in the stars will be signaled at last. Then, when the voices of the unnatural dead ring true back along the winds of cold Eldritch Island, the curse will manifest. Mankind will sink into ignorance once again, and with it comes subjugation to the great overlords from the sky, and the beginning of a new age not of man, but of fear incarnate.'"*

"Well, I haven't heard that one before," Quincy said. "Jeez, I was only kidding at first about the thwarting the end-times again."

"I guess it's just going to have to wait until we're back on the block again. I'd hate to miss out on all the fear incarnate," Lilly added sarcastically. There was gloom in her voice as well.

The captain, visibly reeling and shaking, snatched the book back from Liz. "Out! Now!" He pushed her toward the railing. "You bring a bad omen! I want you off this boat at once."

"Hey, okay." Sean squeezed in between Liz and the captain. "Don't panic. We'll go. Where do you keep your rowboats?"

"Rowboats?" the captain answered. "Didn't I tell you you'd swim the rest of the way?"

There was hope.

The faint glimmer of light Lilly had uncovered in the dreary no man's land that stretched on for miles and miles around any and all settlements in the Realm of the Nearly Departed became brighter with each passing minute. Quincy felt it as well. The closer Liz and Sean seemed to get to the island, their ancestral home, the closer that warm blanket of trust and comfort seemed to wash over them and take them back to a place worth living, literally.

"We're almost there," Lilly told her brother. She took

the restored string, the tether back to the living world, from her pocket and it sparkled in the light of the glowing orb in front of them—it was calling them home.

"It's beautiful," Quincy murmured, squinting. He flinched as his jacket pocket became really hot for a fleeting moment and took out his golden string and stared at it. Two halves reattached to form the token that symbolized their resurrection.

Lilly wandered toward the window of the rickety shack they had found in the middle of the lifeless empty field. She looked outside and was amazed by what appeared to be a gust of wind carrying a single green leaf up and down the abandoned dirt patch a few feet from the shack. When it finally dwindled down to the ground, a tiny circle of grey earth turned brown, and Lilly could swear she saw a few green bulbs start to poke out from the soil.

Quincy took a deep breath and startled himself. He and his sister looked at each other with glee.

A breath, there was a breath!

"Quince!" Lilly called. She took his hand and held it over her chest. "Feel," she said, and Quincy's eyes grew wide as he felt the soft beating of Lilly's heart. "We're coming back to life," she said, wiping away her tears.

There were tears again: Many times, both Lilly and Quincy felt like having a good cry about it all. But nothing ever came. It was like their emotions had been stripped the entire time they had been wandering through this strange place. Now, they started to feel literally and figuratively alive again.

The wind carried with it smells and sounds and tastes. It was like the twins could sniff the fresh sea breeze and they could hear gulls and other, less friendly, sea birds calling from somewhere just out of sight. They could taste the salty air on their tongues. They could hear Sean speaking. But it was now louder, clearer, closer. It was so close, it was as if he was standing right next to them.

"Land ho!" he sarcastically yelled.

Sean dragged his heavy combat boots through the loose sand. It was a slog. The seafloor, this close to the shore, was nevertheless turbulent and in a constant uproar through the current. Liz was straying, but not too far behind. She was holding on to Sean's hand with one arm and fiercely clutching her bag of reagents and other knick-knacks in the other.

"Dick-ish captain," Sean mumbled. "Wouldn't even lend us a stinking boat."

Liz painstakingly swiped away a cluster of pin-prick jellyfish from her face. They were called that because they were the size of a small enamel pin, and their sting kind of felt the same as being pricked by one of said pins. But in contrast to pins, these things had an 85% mortality rate. Fortunately, their tentacles proved to be useless against just about any type of clothing, or adult skin, or even toilet paper. Cheeky little things.

"To be fair," Liz called over the Sean, "you were kind of an ass to him as well. Did your best to scare that poor man."

"What? *Me*? *You* were the one reading from that book. And it was Quincy and Lilly who kept joking about it," Sean retorted.

"Yeah, but weren't you the one who said you would rather not swim because you swore you saw the Leviathan swimming beneath the boat just seconds earlier?"

"That was a joke. Cap'n had no reason to push me overboard." He brushed a hand through his wet hair.

"That poor man." Liz sighed, but she couldn't help but chuckle, if only a little.

The last few feet proved to be the hardest, but in the end, they pulled through and dropped down on the sodden shores of Eldritch Island. The beach turned out to be just as wet as the ocean had been, and the storm clouds high above them betrayed that it wasn't going to stop any time soon. The biting cold of the Atlantic was like a slap in the face, amplified a hundred times over due to their soaking clothes.

Moira came bolting down the beach and wrapped herself around Liz just when she was staggering up from the edge of the rising tide. It was an unusual hug, for sure. For one, they hadn't known each other for long, having even started out as somewhat adversaries.

Moira's spoon was tickling Liz's neck.

"You made it," she let out, relieved. "I hadn't heard from you in days. I know we decided on not contacting each other, to keep ourselves safe, but I was sure you'd figure something out." She laughed. "I guess I was scared something had happened. Hell, why wouldn't I be? I'm pretty sure I was stalked a good long time along the way as well. Got rid of them though, I think."

Liz smiled. "I totally *was* going to keep you up to date, really. But I was sidetracked when I stumbled through a strange little town on the edge of Oklahoma. They claimed to have some kind of bird problem, but it turned out that the owls were not what they seemed. But wood spirits be damned, you know? They weren't hurting anybody, and I had larger fish to fry." She looked at Sean and playfully stuck out her tongue. "Sean, this is Moira. Moira, Sean."

"A pleasure, Sean." Moira smiled. She felt a bit embarrassed with her spoon in hand. She quickly hid her right hand behind her back.

"Hey," Sean cleared his throat. "Uh, I'm all for pleasantries, but perhaps we can do this with a little more shelter?"

Soul jars in hand, Sean, Moira, and Liz climbed the cold steps, hewn from the natural rock formation, up toward the vista where the once-grand Swansong mansion stood watching over the sea. They had settled in a half-shut gazebo that stood where what once would've been the wide and elaborate backyard of the house. It was made from a peculiar stone, of which none of them could trace any origin. It looked like marble, but it felt like gravel.

Sitting beneath the little thatched roof, with a few rays of morning sunshine peeking through in-between the bouts of violent rain and thunderclouds was a humbling and peaceful experience, Liz thought. She closed her eyes and pictured the two jars, carved indentations of voodoo spells and other alchemical symbols and all, in front of her. There was no better time than now, she thought.

Grasping Sean and Moira's hands, she called out to them.

"Lilly…Quincy… Little doggo. If you can hear me, if you can hear *us*—follow our voices and become one with the living world once again."

The twins averted their eyes. A blinding light shone brighter than ever before. They could step inside; Lilly felt it as clear as day. It was a beacon of warmth and familiarity. A beloved voice called out to them. Quincy felt his knees growing weak, not from intense effort, but rather from the relief he felt. Hewie yipped happily and hopped into the bright light tunnel that was expanding ever-larger before them.

"Liz!" Lilly yelled, hopeful.

A loud *bang* shot through the air. The splatter of blood shot up as Liz dropped, hard, against the weather-beaten wood of the gazebo floor. A bullet-sized hole had appeared along her upper torso, and blood was gushing from the open wound, streaming all over her body.

Moira screamed.

Sean shot up in a fit of panic. His eyes darted around. He was speechless.

Liz lay on the planks in silence. She was unconscious, and the life was slowly draining from her face.

Darkness.

Where was the light? Why was the darkness back? The floor fell out from under the twins' and Hewie's feet. A gaping maw of pitch-black nothing opened beneath them—one ready to swallow them whole.

The abyss beckoned. Tendrils void of color reached out and wrapped themselves around Lilly and Quincy's lower legs and torso. Hewie's bark was but a distant echo, as if he was lost in another place and time entirely.

The tendrils pulled and, with no sound able to escape from their mouths, the twins were dragged down into that well of eternal despair.

From the rain-soaked underbrush of the tree line behind the gazebo came two darkly-clad soldiers, their faces obscured by black beanies and face paint. Following them was a broad-shouldered man with a neater haircut, but clothed in a similar get up like his compatriots. Next to him walked a woman dressed in purple and blue satin and wearing innumerable golden trinkets, armbands, rings, and other jewelry. She had a presence that instilled fear and awe in any who lingered at her for too long. She looked angry, disappointed, and worst of all, determined.

Moira recognized the slicker soldier of the three as Special Agent Dutch, her former boss and murderer of Lilly and Quincy Swansong. Anger and hate boiled up inside her upon laying her eyes on his disgusting grin. But it was nothing of the anger she felt compared to when she fully realized that Alina LaGrande, her one time mentor, friend, and *aunt* stood before her.

She knew immediately that Alina was the probable cause of Haven finding them on such a remote location as this. Moira also knew that Alina was the one who gave the order to shoot Liz and leave her for dead. Only she would know the power a witch of the Night Lights could harbor.

Most of all, and this was the truly terrifying part, Moira knew full-well that Alina LaGrande was out for blood…*her* blood. There was no greater sin, no greater shame than betrayal in the LaGrande Circle. Moira had been a target, someone to look after and keep in check for far too long already. But she knew she had gone too far now. She'd be sentenced to death: right here, right now.

"Did you lead them here?" Sean hissed at Moira. "Were you with them all along? Answer me, now!" His face was red with anger.

"No," Moira said, barely a whisper. "I really didn't." It was all she could muster, a tear rolling down her cheek.

"I wouldn't try anything funny now," Agent Dutch said, and kept his shining black .357 Magnum trained on Sean, who had gotten up in a flash of rage and non-existent sense of self-preservation.

"Sean *fucking* Cooper, you elusive *fuck*," Agent Dutch hissed. "I only just recognized you from the few reports we managed to salvage from the Antarctica station. Everyone died a severe death over there, and the only three people who managed to get out are the Swansong twins and you. The place is so overrun with all kinds of category-five messes, we can't even nuke it to reclaim it. Half of the shit living there just *feeds* on nuclear waste. Yet here *you* are. Something doesn't quite add up, does it? Tell me."

"Fuck you," Sean answered and spat in Dutch's general direction. He wasn't even looking at the special agent; he was only casting worried glances at Liz's unstable and frantic breathing, which became more erratic with every second that went by while Moira sat huddled beside her. It appeared she was in some kind of shock, or worse. She looked mortified.

One of the soldiers in black slammed the butt of his assault rifle hard against Sean's jaw. A sickly *crack* was heard, and Sean slammed against the wood. His face was on an even level with Liz's for a moment. Her eyes were open, and she was staring at him. She made no sound, but Sean heard her voice ringing inside his head: *Don't let them get to them. Don't let them win.*

"Let's try that again." Agent Dutch laughed. "How the hell did you three get out of there?"

Sean rose up a little. "We just like to live," he chuckled. Then he spat out blood and a couple of molars. "Why is it you Haven assholes always beat me up *so* bad, but can never finish the job?"

"Oh, just you wait, you f—"

Alina LaGrande held up her palm and somehow grabbed everyone's immediate attention. "Enough!" she spoke, and the entire world got a bit quieter because of it. "You can handle your personal vendetta in your own time, Agent Dutch. I'm here for my niece and the soul jars so unceremoniously stolen from us."

She turned to face Moira, who still did not dare to look her in the eye. "What have you to say for yourself, child?" Alina's pupils became elongated and unnatural, like a serpent's. "Explain yourself, for you have only one chance to plead your case before I cast your damned soul to the hereafter, where not even the Bawon Samdi will be able to find you and give you purpose."

Alina knelt down and grabbed Moira's chin. She snapped her head to the right and gave her the most intimidating and horrific stare that Moira had ever seen. "You made the mistake of trying to deal with the Loa, and now you have to face the consequences. *Tsk-tsk,* so amateurish. You bring so much shame to the LaGrande Circle that getting rid of you will be the biggest favor we can do for both of us. You mess with powers you don't understand, and you expect them to *not* sell you out for less than half of the price you promised?"

Alina released Moira's chin, whose head then buried itself between her knees.

"Foolish child. You don't even have the gall to speak up." Alina brushed away the strands of hair falling over her shoulder and straightened herself. "Very well." She nodded at one of the black-clad soldiers. "Let's try to make this quick."

The soldier readied his weapon. He took aim at Moira, and his finger was gradually slipping over the trigger when it suddenly appeared as if the world itself blacked out.

Twenty whole seconds of pure darkness submerged the gazebo and surrounding overgrown mansion garden. When vision finally returned somewhat, the clouds in the sky were darker than ever before, and every few seconds, lighting shot out of the sky and crashed down toward the sea and earth. It was still really dark, and the only form of true illumination were the bright flashes emanating from the lighting.

After the third flash, the silhouette of a figure appeared on one of the white stone walls of the gazebo— Moira knew instantly who it was. Her fear for her aunt and the wrath she faced made way for an entirely new form of existential dread. But there was also a voice in the back of her mind, whispering. At first it was sweet nothings, but the words became clearer with every flash of lightning that followed.

Moira pushed her head further down and smiled.

One of the soldiers screamed so loud, it made Sean's skin crawl. The man who, mere moments ago, slammed a gun to his jaw was lifted up off the ground. He hovered in place for a split-second before having his heart violently ripped from his chest. The screaming stopped soon after, and the lifeless husk of the Haven agent slumped down to the floorboards—bloodied, ribs sticking out and all.

"Holy *shit!*" Agent Dutch let out a muffled cry and fell to the floor on his back. However, his pistol was still aimed at Sean.

The remaining Haven soldier swung his gun around frantically. He was visibly shaking, but nothing appeared to want to harm him, as of yet.

Another flash of lightning.

"Your payment was due, Alina LaGrande." The distorted voice of underworld deal broker Nibo drifted on the strong eastern sea wind. "Surely, you did not mean to shortchange me, mambo?"

Alina was clearly taken aback. "Uh, I meant no such thing," she whispered. "I figured you'd come to collect as soon as you were able." She regained her composure. "We just found them, as you surmised. You have your payment, Master Loa. Now I'd like you to leave."

The sinister shadow laughed over the crashing of the thunder. "Leave? Now? You try to tell this little one how to make a deal with the Loa, yet you yourself so easily forget the terms of agreement." Nibo started to make an uneasy clicking sound, like a broken clock, but somehow still counting down. "I told you of the ones who knew about the library, and your agent stationed there discovered your little lost lamb."

Moira cast a sorrowful glance at Liz.

Sean kept quiet and his head down; this went beyond his comprehension, quite literally.

"Deal fulfilled, I'd say," Nibo continued. "And what a deal it was. A simple hint of where to find your lost flock in trade for a human soul. You are dastardly, mambo." The shadow grinned and lit up a cigar. Smoke started to appear from nowhere. It curled up at the edge of the soggy gazebo roof.

"I—" was all Alina LaGrande could muster.

Flash, and the shadow wagged his index finger as if telling a small child they had done a bad thing. "Fool me once..." He started clicking again in between sentences. "Fool me once... I keep my eyes on you. Fool me twice... You have a problem. But withhold my client from me so I cannot claim my price after the deal I made with her has nearly been fulfilled? Mmm, Miss LaGrande. I ask you to reconsider having that bag of flesh train his gun on your young protégé."

"I need my revenge." Alina cursed. "Then go ahead, finish your deal already." She nodded toward Moira. "Finish it so I can finish *her*."

Moira stood up and took two paces toward Alina. Her face held a mixture of hatred, even contempt for her aunt. "Master Loa, I am ready to give you my payment."

Alina chuckled. "Ha! Whatever it is, from what he told me, you *grossly* overpaid. I can't wait to wring the life out of you with my bare hands. Whatever was the price you named, anyway?"

"The price"—Nibo groaned with pleasure—"was her blood. One life for the possibility of saving two. A good deal. Very wholesome. A LaGrande soul is worth a lot, you know."

Alina burst out in laughter. "You stupid little bitch." She dropped her rigid facade as she grabbed her sides, still laughing. "You did all my work for me, and I didn't even know it. You are truly unworthy of bearing the LaGrande name. What insolence! What pure stupidity!" Alina was besides herself, so maddened with laughter that she failed to notice the shadowy tendril slithering hovering over her head.

"I offered my blood. A LaGrande soul, yes," Moira said, shaking and trembling. She did not plan out any of this; it was a pure coincidence, and she had no idea if it would work. But the hate she felt was possibly real enough to live with the burden of what would transpire if Nibo accepted this offer. "I did not state it would need to be my soul."

"Ooohoohooh yesssssss," Nibo hissed. "I have felt the longing coming from deep within you, young mambo. Hmmmm yes, I do graciously accept this offering you bring me."

The shadow tendrils bore down, snapping around Alina LaGrande's neck and pulling tight. Her maniacal laughter stopped just as quickly as it had come; Alina fell down the steps of the little structure and hard onto the ground. She started sputtering and her fingers dug deep in the grass and dirt as if to hold on. Her lips slowly started to turn blue right before the shadow tendrils disappeared.

Ultimately, to everyone's shock and horror, the

contorted, shivering body of Alina LaGrande was then pulled apart like an old voodoo doll. The blood and viscera painted the white gazebo in a sickly pink and purple jelly.

"Deal fulfilled," the voice of Nibo said. It was barely audible as it trailed off.

Agent Dutch snapped toward the remaining Haven soldier, whose eyes were fixed at the gory display that was once a mighty voodoo priestess. "No!" Agent Dutch exclaimed. He lowered his gun a bit. "You fool! We—"

Immediately seizing the opportunity, Sean, army-trained and having served in the Global Defense Force for several years, already had the rifle of the unfortunate, sacrificed guard in hand. Pulling the trigger, he popped off three bullets that went right through the other Haven soldier's shoulder, neck, and left eye respectively. Before Agent Dutch could even react to the shots, or even ratio-nalize any of the events that had just transpired in the past minute or two, he too caught four of Sean's assault rifle bullets straight to the pelvis, gut, chest and shoulder.

The soldier and Agent Dutch dropped to the floor within seconds.

Moira was dripping with adrenaline, and guts, and like a bucket of blood, but the adrenaline had won over the gore-riddled panic that loomed, and she raced over to check on Liz—she felt her pulse.

"She's still alive!" she exclaimed. "Put some pressure on there," she told Sean, who came to kneel beside her. "I'm going to..." Her hands hovered over the gaping wound, which was still seeping blood. "I'm going to try something. Let me concentrate... I..."

Sean ripped a side of his shirt apart and push down

on Liz's chest. "Hey…" He stopped and winced, for the pain in his jaw was inconceivable now. But he knew he had to say something. "I'm sorry if I doubted you just now. You know, I just—"

"Stop talking," Moira interrupted him. "It's okay. Really. Just…stop. I need silence."

You are nothing, the voice of the abyss said. *You are already dead. And now you are mine. You have always been mine. You are dead. Your friends will betray you, and when they die, they will also be mine. Your dog is dead, and he is also mine.*

Quincy gasped, somehow still aware of his surroundings; even though there was technically nothing.

You are weak. You have given up long ago, the demonic and off-key voice droned in his head. *You belong to the void. You long for it, you embrace it. You need it.*

Lilly opened her eyes. Even though she saw nothing but the horrid, cold abyss everywhere around her, she reached out and found her brother's hand.

But…there is no hope. There never was hope!

The distorted voice of the abyss trailed off and somehow, it did not scare her anymore as Lilly felt Quincy's embrace.

The pitter-patter of little dog feet tipped through the silent pit before a cold, wet nose pushed again their hands. The happy bark of Hewie filled them with such happiness, it was as if their hearts sun—the light returned in front of them. Without thinking, they reached out toward it and together, with Hewie, they felt solid ground beneath their feet once again.

And now, at last, after what felt like an eternity of anguished silence, there was sound. It was the steady rhythm of a heart beating strong. It coincided with the pulsating bright light at the end of the tunnel in front of them. It called out to them, and at its mercy they followed it like a beacon.

All the way home.

Liz gasped as the lifeblood returned to her arms, her hands, and the tips of her fingers. She coughed next, loudly and audibly. Sean and Moira gave her the space to do so as long as she needed.

When the coughing finally passed, her hand immediately felt for the big hole above her breast where a bullet had, not so long ago, torn up her arteries and a lot of other important bits. There was nothing there. Nothing except the torn fabric of her blood-soaked top. She looked at Moira with amazement and surprise. "Wh-white healing magic?" Liz stammered, "You…"

"Sacrificing a little bit of your own essence will go a long way for the greater good." Moira winked. "Never stop learning. I believe you told me that. Hell, I feel like I'm only now starting to learn what's truly important."

Liz struggled to sit up and gave Moira a fist bump. "Glad I'm starting to get through to you," she laughed, then coughed. "Boy, I don't envy Lil' and Quince. Dying sucks. And I didn't even go the full way." She then pointed at Moira's right hand, or rather the spoon lying on the ground beneath it. "Hey! *Shit,* man, you got rid of it without me?"

Moira rubbed her cheek with her now fully-functional right hand and laughed. "Well, it *was* Alina who cursed me in the first place. For fun… Well, okay, it was because I was messing with… Oh, never mind."

"Oh my… Oh… I…" Liz felt a bit of vomit shooting up into her mouth when she finally looked past her friends and toward the carnage in front of her. She swallowed. "What the hell happened?" She looked back to Moira, and only now noticed the dark brown stains of bodily fluids all over her clothing. "Moira… W-what…?"

"Don't worry," Moira told her. "It's done. And I *don't* regret it." She looked back at the remains of her aunt, the sacrificed agent, and the other two Haven agents and paled. "Doesn't mean I *liked* it."

Sean pushed himself up with great effort; his eyes nearly rolled to the back of his head. "You know, I make it a point to never regret anything in my life either but… But can either of you *please* do whatever it was Moira did and do the same for my jaw? Oh, man, it's *killing* me…seriously."

Liz laughed. "I'm sure we can manage. But tell me, I bet that could've been avoided, could it not?"

Sean merely groaned.

"Let's focus on getting the twins back right after. It's been long enough," Liz said. "Now, close your eyes and—"

"What the hell is that?" Moira interrupted her. She pointed at a hole in front of the gazebo that just appeared. Dirt was being kicked up into the air with ferocious determination.

"Wait…" Liz gasped. "Is that—"

The head of a corgi popped up out of the hole. He

held his head to the side a bit and barked in a friendly manner. By all means, it was a wonderful thing to behold. But the slight bit of uncanniness was that he was very much transparent.

Before anyone could properly respond to the strange sudden appearance, one of the soul jars began to shake violently. A thumping could be heard from deep within and even muffled speech, or something akin to it. Liz and Sean flinched back as the jar closest to them broke open, and a dusty, grimy size ten Doc Martens boot crashed through.

The other jar now also fell on its side, rolled down the gazebo steps, and broke open with a loud *crack* on the stones below. They heard a cry of mild discomfort upon landing and subsequently: "Oh my days, I never asked to know how a chick feels coming out an egg. Ergh." It was followed by the corgi's barking.

Next to them, someone was emerging from the jar—it was Lilly! She was caked with dirt and cobwebs and her hair was such a wild, frizzy mop, you could swear she really did hang around in a coffin for a couple of weeks.

"No one..." She coughed, and specks of dust and tiny spiders came out. "No one told us about *this* part!" she yelled bitterly. But it only took mere seconds before she conjured a wide smile. Her face was smeared with dried dirt and black soot, but she laughed. She laughed hard and merrily.

Down the steps and just out of sight, Quincy started laughing as well.

————————————————

<h1 style="text-align:center">Chapter 19</h1>

————————————————

THE EMBRACES WERE SUDDEN, quick, and frantic, but to Lilly and Quincy, they felt like an eternity. A blissful one.

Eventually, they just sat there, together with Sean, Liz, and Moira and watched the storm clouds finally parting, making way for the last glimmers of sunlight shining down from the heavens. They basked for a while in the peaceful afternoon breeze, waiting for the sun to fully set and the cold blanket of the sinister night to veil itself over their broken island in the wild, primordial Atlantic.

After the initial outcries of joy, tears, and laughter, everyone had been remarkably quiet. It was as if each of them shared the same peculiar gut feeling: a feeling of thankfulness to be there at that exact moment in time. A feeling of relief to be able to life again, breathe again for Lilly and Quincy, and relief to be able to see and embrace their friends again for Liz and Sean. Moira kept to the side at first, having only bonded with Liz during the whole ordeal. She felt a bit uncomfortable now that the twins were finally back, considering she was one of the last people they saw before being killed. But Lilly and Quincy took her in without so much as a shadow of a doubt. For she had proven herself, in their own words, an invaluable ally and friend, for risking everything she had for a mere shot at getting them back.

Later, after Quincy woke from a tiny nap caused by his extreme exhaustion, he noticed that Lilly was strangely absent from the group. They had made a fire on the beach with some of the dry sticks and wood they found churning up the sand and had been huddled around it, each of them falling in and out of sleep at random intervals.

"Do you know where Lilly has gone off to?" Quincy asked Liz.

Liz shook her head. "Nah, she just left. Said she'd be right back. I don't know where she went to; can't imagine it being very far. It's only a small island, right?"

"Right."

The evening breeze picked up momentum, and a few strands of Liz's blonde hair and dreadlocks swept in front of her face. She absentmindedly brushed them away. "She was looking a bit sad, though," she called over to Quincy, who had already stood up and was about to go look for his sister.

He nodded. "Don't worry, I'm sure everything is fine."

Quincy followed the lonesome footsteps, embedded deep within the wet sand, away from the beach and up the slope into the majestic orange and brown foliage of the hanging willow trees that lined the mansion's back-yard. He recognized the knee-high iron fence, nowadays all rusted and dirty, and followed it deeper into the over-grown garden of the once-grand estate. He remembered the three-forked road past the huge oak tree overshadowing the bench on which their mother used to sit and read all summer. The bench was still there, all flaky and crawling with plants and algae. Quincy wandered past one of the tall birches. It appeared to be dying. He could still faintly read the engravings *Q.S.* and *L.S.* marked on its white stem. He smiled softly and took a right.

Through the old, crooked gate that stood at the edge of the washed-out estate gardens, Quincy could see his sister sitting alone in the light of the setting sun, on her knees, next to the lonesome weeping willow that stood on the edge of the island's northern cliff.

"Hey, I somehow got the feeling I'd find you here." Quincy closed the broken gate behind him and wandered up to her. He saw the fading apparition of Hewie curled up against her legs. "What…What's he doing?" he asked carefully. He tried not to stare at the old weathered grave marker they had made after Hewie had passed and their father had buried him at the edge of the willow tree.

Lilly swiped away a tear and sniffled. "Well," she started, then stopped. The tears came rolling down again. "Hewie is going away now. He's done." She sniffled again and smiled. "He did what he had to do. After all this time, he can finally go. He can finally rest."

Quincy sat down besides his sister and scratched the little corgi beneath his chin. "I can't believe it." He felt happiness and sadness mixing themselves into a complex concoction deep within his gut. He felt that hankering for air, the pinching behind his eyes as they tried to keep the water from flowing. "And you sat here"—he looked at the small dog—"and you waited for me to come, before you'd go?"

Hewie peeped and yawned. He pressed his nose against Quincy's hand, then jumped on Lilly's lap and licked her nose.

"It's time to go now, Hewie." Lilly pressed the sleeve of her sweater against her cheeks to wipe the tears. "Go on."

The nearly faded image of Hewie plopped back down onto the ground. He took a few hops forwards and laid down between the tall grass of the mound. He let out a happy bark, curled up, and disappeared.

Lilly grabbed her brother's arm tight and let the tears roll down her face.

"It's okay, Lil'," Quincy told her. "He was the best dog in the world. He did everything for us, right up until the end. He deserves this. He's with Mom and Dad now."

Lilly nodded, her gaze meeting Quincy's. "What are we going to do now?"

Quincy got up. "I don't know," he said and turned around to Liz right behind the gate. She looked worried. He nodded at her and beckoned her over. "We'll figure something out, Lil'. You know we always do."

When Liz walked up, she touched his arm for a second and threw him an emphatic and warm smile before turning toward Lilly.

"You just stay a while, as long as you want. I'll need to clear my own head for a bit."

He saw Liz sit down behind Lilly and hug her tight.

Quincy backtracked through the old estate gardens, which were full of fallen leaves and vegetation grown wild. The sun was minutes from fully setting over Eldritch

Island, and soon the onset of the twilit sky would wrap the small isle in darkness. Quincy remembered his pocket flashlight, fished it out, and clicked it on to get at least a vague idea of where he was going. At the edge of the garden, across the broken wall of the destroyed mansion, something glimmered in the darkness.

"*What's that?*" Quincy murmured to himself. Carefully, he hoisted himself over the pile of rubble laden with rusty nails, glass, and other sharp objects and dropped into the ruins of the house—it was one of the old backrooms on the first floor. It could've been their father's study, he reckoned.

The flashlight beam hit the wall on the other side, and Quincy could faintly make out the remains of what was once a bookcase. He looked down and shone the light across the floor to try and find the source of the glimmer. A few feet away from him, an object sparkled in the dark —it was Hewie's collar. It was navy blue with white stitches and had a silver compass as a hanger. On the back of the compass, Hewie's name and birthday were engraved.

"Wait," Quincy said aloud. The compass was spinning wildly. "Is this thing broken?" Quincy was about to head back outside to the others when his foot scraped over the sodden carpet laying across the room and heard something akin to jingling metal. He proceeded to roll up the carpet toward the broken wall. When he shone the flashlight back to the floor, it revealed a secret trapdoor. He

chuckled.

That little rascal, Hewie. Even after getting his well-deserved final rest, he's still *guiding us to places we didn't know to look.* He hovered over the creaking, age-old floorboards and gripped the rusted handle tight, ready to pull.

The rotten wood flaked and fell apart more than what eventually would be left. A line of iron bars hewn into the vast rock below the ruined study led into darkness.

"Who's going in first?" Moira was the first to drop the question that was on everyone's mind.

Sean scoffed. "I'll probably have to go last. Jaw and back are still hurting like crazy, you know; I'd just slow you down."

"You're lying." Lilly grinned. "If the healing spells can fix a bullet wound, then your jaw should feel better than it ever had. I think you're just tired from being slapped around so much. You'd like it to *not* be you for a change."

"I'd much prefer it to be no one at all," Sean retorted. "Who knows what's down there?"

Moira shrugged. "Won't be any Haven people, at least."

"But can and probably *will* be anything else. I've got about a hundred examples of bad stuff living perfectly fine, human-eating lives never seeing any sunlight," Sean said. He rubbed his jaw in annoyance. He hated to admit that it actually *did* feel wonderful.

Lilly threw her hands up. "Ugh, *fine!*" Her hand landed on Quincy's head. "Quince will go first since he's got the best flashlight out of all of us…"

"Really?" Quincy groaned.

"Well, you always come prepared with the best stuff, so it's time to step up!" Lilly laughed.

Quincy could still see the sadness stricken on her face, but this new revelation of the strange trapdoor unveiled by Hewie—or his collar, at least—really seemed to have lifted her spirits.

"Okay," she went on, "us three fine women will make up the middle of the group, and Sean can protect our rear and be the first to get the hell out if something bad happens." She paused. "Oh, but Sean?"

"Yeah?"

"If you slip up and fall and take all four of us down with you, there will be hell to pay."

"That is if we'll live to tell the tale!" Liz chimed in.

"Yeah!" Lilly said, determined, then scratched her head and tried to figure out if that sounded all right.

For a moment, Quincy and Lilly, upon their initial descent into the darkness, were worried that the whole ordeal was starting to look very much like their misadventures in the great inverted pyramid beneath Three Rivers in New Mexico. While Sean, Liz, and Moira had heard of their exploits, and certainly weren't very keen on experiencing them for themselves, it did not directly cross their minds that this venture into an underground lair of some sorts, the depth of which was unknown, shared some very remarkable similarities to that unfortunate expedition.

In the end, it turned out that the stairs only went down about twelve to fifteen feet.

Upon reaching solid ground, Quincy clicked the flashlight on and swept it across the room. "Huh…" was the only thing that escaped his lips.

Lilly dropped down next to him and leaned against him over his shoulder. "What is this place?"

"Looks like some sort of bomb shelter." Quincy pointed at the racks of canned substances lining the left wall. The flashlight focused for a moment on the single table and sleeping cot, just enough for two, and the long defunct lightbulb hanging on the ceiling. The whole room was cramped and moist. The wet floor and moss growing in every crevice indicated that it must've flooded over and over again in the past couple of years.

Moira, Liz, and Sean descended just as Quincy rested the beam of light on a small, half-rotten, cradle against the eastern wall. It was spacious enough for two little babies.

"Did you used to sleep in there?" Liz asked carefully.

Quincy shrugged. "It doesn't look like these beds were ever used, at least there's no way to tell. Either way, I don't think we'd remember if we were."

"I can't imagine we would've been down here," Lilly added. "This is all really strange."

Sean took a look around. He took one of the cans of food and flipped it over in his hands. "It's not *that* strange, I'd say. Lots of people were anxious of a global nuclear war breaking out in the 80s. This kind of shelter—I think they might've been all over the place. Don't put too much though into it."

Lilly shook her head. "Yeah, no, I understand that. But our mom and dad? This isn't like them."

"You don't think they would do anything to keep themselves, and you two, safe from harm?" Sean asked her.

"Of course, they would." Lilly wound a strand of hair

around her finger and knelt beside the cradle. "But somehow, I get the feeling they would come up with another, more rational solution than to build something like this, something I get the feeling they would never use."

"What about the dog?" Moira's hand hovered over a patch of mold near the ceiling of the shelter. "He sensed something?"

Liz nodded. "That's right. Hewie wouldn't lead you here if there wasn't something we are overlooking."

"There *must* be something here, then." Lilly held the dog collar in the beam of the flashlight, and they all watched as the compass needle spun around like crazy, but sometimes it would jitter in place for a few seconds. When it did, it always pointed to the east, which Sean confirmed was actually incorrect. There wasn't really anything in the direction the compass was pointing—except the cradle.

"Ugh, this'll get us nowhere," Lilly groaned.

"No. We are already here." Moira looked up and down the wall before turning to face the rest of the group. "Sometimes, even in the world we live in today, we need to let rationality and natural science lead the way." She pointed at the mold against the upper corners of the walls of the shelter. "Look at how the mold travels down. It's all between the crevices and cracks. This is no concrete solid wall. It is waterlogged to hell and back. Not something you'd see normally in these types of shelters."

Sean eyeballed the weighty can of indistinguishable edibles in his hand before looking back over to the wall on the other side. "Moira's right. That wall could be fake." He threw the can as hard as he could to the other side of the shelter where it disappeared through an easily-ripped hole in the plaster.

It took about ten minutes for the group of five determined and curious truth-seekers to rip half of the wall apart. Behind the inconspicuous fake wall, that consisted of mostly plaster and wood so sodden it disintegrated in their hands, was a carved-out staircase leading down into darkness. A torch hung somberly to the side of the entrance, but that too was so drenched, it would never stand a chance of working ever again.

Now, all of a sudden, it *did* really feel like descending the ancient steps of a place once built by primordial beings, of which the age was so incomprehensible, it hurt just to think about it. The whole process was also so reminiscent of what Lilly and Quincy traversed in the Nearly Departed Realm, the so-called *Underworld Railroad*, that it seemed as if the entire ordeal was a premonition of some sorts.

They could barely remember it, they realized. Thinking back, it all felt like a blurry and faraway dream. It was something lodged in the back of their heads, a distant memory of strange occurrences that may or may not have happened as they remembered.

Lilly took her brother by the hand and took the first step down. She turned toward Liz, Sean, and Moira behind them and nodded. "It's only fair if we were the ones doing this. We know you know what this looks like. If any of you feel like you need to step aside or wait this one out above, go ahead. It's fine."

Liz, Moira, and Sean looked at each other, and then quizzically at Lilly.

Liz laughed. "I'm sorry, girl, but you're kind of stuck with us."

Lilly looked at the smiling faces of her friends: In each of their faces were the marks of somberness and fear, coupled with genuine love, courage, and determination. Quincy's hand landed on her shoulder. It startled her, but she his warmth flowed through her, and she had to fight to push back the tears welling up.

To nobody's surprise, the long slog down the roughly hewn stairs was tedious. On the flipside, it was also pretty much uneventful. Everyone knew that something huge and strange would be waiting for them on the other side of the descent. But when they arrived in the enormous, cylinder-shaped cavern and the anomalous flurries of wind blew past, they found out that regardless of their mental preparation, they did not expect to see this.

Unusual lights flickered on from right next to them and stretched up all the way to the invisible, nearly endless ceiling of the cavern. The big, bright squares faded high up into tiny little mesmerizing dots. Additionally, strange machinery buzzed and came to life the moment one of them had set foot in the cavern.

Green and grey screens flickered ominously in the glow of the yellow-ish fluorescent lights of the wall lamps. On it, lines and lines of unknown symbols crawled onto the screen and stayed for a few seconds at a time before disappearing again.

But nothing had prepared them for the enormous, nearly fossilized, body of a true-to-life Celestian that stood like a silent statue in the middle of the cave. Its wide cylinder body curved upwards to its spine from which its two elongated arms hung lifelessly. Its distinct bulbous head hung back with just about all of the scale-like skin peeled off revealing the bizarre skull within.

"It's…it's another tomb," Quincy whispered. "It's the last Celestian tomb in North America…" He gasped. "This is what Haven was looking for. It was under our noses all along. Our entire childhood. All of the strange dreams…"

"The terrible nightmares," Lilly whispered. "Paths leading down into absolute darkness. Evil-sounding voices whispering terrible things to us when we played in the woods over the hills." She reached for Liz's hand and squeezed tight. "What's it doing here?"

Moira moved forward and inspected the dead giant, awestruck. "It's resting here. The resting places of the great ancient race need protection. Which I am sure your parents and family before them amply provided." She carefully touched some of the cold, black steel on the side of the monitors. "What I'd like to know is what the purpose of all this other stuff is."

Quincy shone the flashlight across the rows of flickering machines. From the outside, they looked like the exact same dark material and build they had seen with the God-machine in the Arctic. But where that machine had a near-impenetrable shroud of importance and soul wrapped around its very core, this one felt more like what a computer generally does: compute things, keep track of stuff, have a database.

Quincy's hand hovered toward an elongated green button—he pushed it. He didn't need to think about it, it was as if some invisible force pulled him toward it and guided him to it.

A big green flare lit up against the smooth cavern

wall. It was a map of the Earth, with about fifteen flickering red dots blinking, indicating places all over the planet. A purple rectangle framed a part of Europe.

"Wow, it's stunning." Liz gasped. "What do you think the red dots mean?"

Sean clicked his tongue. "I'm sure the answer to that can be found somewhere in here. On any of these screens, or perhaps some of the paper rolls in the corner there. There's even a couple of books over there on the—"

Lilly was already over near the simple wooden desk and had thrown one of the big brown books open when she jumped up and sucked in her breath. "This is Dad's handwriting!" she called out excitedly. "There's all kinds of research notes here. He studied in here. He studied all of this!"

Quincy was next to his sister in a heartbeat. "This is unbelievable. So many years, and still, we probably only know a mere fraction of what kinds of secrets our parents really kept from the rest of the world."

"Which is probably for the best," Moira added. "Glad you lot are as good at keeping them as you are at uncovering them."

Quincy chuckled at that then turned back to Lilly, asking, "What's it say?"

"Listen to this." Lilly stopped and gasped before continuing:

"I have recently returned from England with new information about the whereabouts of the Supreme Being of the Gibbous Horde. These horrific god-like entities lie dormant for now, but when awakened… I fear not even the Celestians, their most ancient of adver-

saries, could stand a chance, even if they would've still had a significant presence on Earth.

"I must dig deeper.

"Yet, every time I leave, I fear more and more for the lives of my beloved Emily and the twins. I feel like I'm being followed. Or at least spied upon. What kind of knowledge would be too much for me to bear, and thus, in the wake of it I were to be deemed too great a hazard?

"Quincy, Lilly…Emily. They are my life. But what kind of life can I offer them if everything we know and love teeters on the brink of oblivion?

"The horde, they…they get under your skin. Figuratively so. They have the power to alter consciousness. They can inspire madness or chaos in anyone they please for hundreds of miles in their vicinity. If only one of them would awaken it would… They can't be stopped, not individually. Not by us mere humans.

"Why didn't the Celestians try to stop them? The notes they left on these ancient apparatuses is all I have. The Gibbous Horde are a hive mind. They act upon the wishes of the Supreme Being. But nobody knows where it slumbers…save for that it's somewhere beneath an age-old cathedral in Eastern Europe. That's…something, at least.

"I'm pretty sure I can crack the code. There is more to be found in England to start. I must return. Perhaps this time I will take Emily with me, we could cover twice as much ground. I must be foolish to leave the twins alone, at merely sixteen years old, but the quicker Emily and I can work, the sooner we can return, and we can keep this secret until I can find significant forces to help me destroy this monster.

"It's the only chance we have.

"I shall inform Emily tomorrow."

"Fuck, man!" Lilly threw the book across the room

and screamed. It wasn't physical pain or anxiety. It was the realization that whatever thing their father was rolled up in, whoever was following him, they were probably responsible for their parents' demise. The plane crash that Emily and Tobias Swansong were caught up in was a private charter to London. It was the first time their parents had left the twins to their own devices. It was also the last time, for they never saw their parents again.

Both Liz and Sean bolted forward to make sure Lilly was okay when she started pacing, but Quincy shook his head at them. "Just leave her for a moment, okay? I feel what she's going through… There's like a whole mix of emotions bubbling up for me too. I think…I'll need a moment. If only to get a grasp on what all of this means, and what it has to do with us."

Moira had been staring at the world map the entire time, though she had listened carefully to what Lilly was reading aloud. Her eyes were focused on the red flickering dots—on one of them in particular.

"Quincy," she called, "I know you need your moment, but I could really use some help in topography. Liz, can you come too?" Moira looked grave. "I'm pretty sure I just tied a couple of strings together, and it ain't pretty." She pointed at the southern US part of the map. "That glowing bit right there. That's Darkness Falls, Isn't it? That thing that likes to be called *Mother*…" She winced. "Oh man, there's no arguing that that's apparently one of the beings your dad described. And it's awake."

"That's no coincidence," Liz murmured, a wave of defeat washing over her.

"Fuck," Sean hissed. "We need to head over there and stop it right now."

"And do what? End up how Lilly and Quincy did in the first place?" Liz retaliated. "No, we need to think about this, and we need to think about it well. We just need some time. Time to get everything sorted."

Quincy slammed his hand on the table, which startled his sister, who had just taken a seat. "We don't have time! Sean is right, we need to act fast. Think about what that one thing has done to most of the people we have encountered. We can't let another of them awaken. We…"

"Ha," a gurgling voice said, emerging from the darkness. It was Agent Dutch, who was crawling across the floor, leaving a streak of blood in his wake all the way from the hewn stairwell and beyond. "You…you have already lost." He coughed. Blood and mucus spattered the floor in front of him. "Four more…Four more have already awakened. You are too late. We shall find the… We shall thrive in Europe… We…"

Agent Dutch reached for his radio and started summing up a series of numbers that sounded suspiciously like coordinates to certain trained ears. Sean ran over to him and buried his boot in his face before he could finish. He lifted it up again, but hesitated. "Dammit, he's not worth it," he said, flustered, while holding his hand over Agent Dutch's mouth. Sean's boot found a new target in the little radio, which quickly broke apart under its heavy weight.

"We need to get out of here, ASAP." Sean nodded at the group, who were still kind of in shock from the sudden re-appearance of the Haven agent. Sean was aware there was no other course of action than to leave him down here to rot. His eyes met those of Agent Dutch, whose mumblings had gone silent under the force of Sean's foot. "I-I can't help you. I— Look, we don't have time for this now." He turned to the group. "Please, let's just go. We're probably going to need to bury this place, or burn it, or…I don't know."

Liz and Moira nodded.

"Yeah, but I'm taking Dad's research with me, no discussion. Let's go." Quincy told him.

"That's fine," Sean answered. He turned to Lilly. "Are you ready to go as well? C'mon, Lil'. We need to scram."

Lilly sat in the chair, quiet as a mouse. There wasn't a drop of emotion on her face. It was as if all empathy, all feeling had erased itself from her soul. It was the never-ending curse of the Swansongs. That horrid black stain in history that had followed her family from one place to the next, always lurking in shadows. That incessant need to uncover the secrets of the universe and all dangers that lie within.

Somehow it was no surprise, as it couldn't really have been any other way. But now it was all too clear. It was that same drive to uncover lost knowledge, *useless* lost knowledge that killed their parents. As only the so-called excitement of a new discovery could sway them away from their children and off across the ocean to a place which they would never arrive to see. A piece of Lilly Swansong had broken off that day, and another piece broke off just now. It would take a very long time for those pieces to heal.

If they would at all.

"Yeah," Lilly answered coldly. "Coming."

Chapter 20

THE THING about finality is that you finally feel as if a humongous weight has been lifted off your shoulders. Your demons will not haunt you anymore. You can breathe easy again, your sleep is mercifully dreamless, and you get a tremendous appreciation for time; one you never knew you could conjure up at all.

The thing about finality is the realization that you probably can't do anything about it. It's a reassuring, comforting thought. There are no surprises. No revelations. There is just time to spend. Until there is no more time. And you'll know when that is.

The thing about finality is peace. And peace is love. And love is remembering.

I hope you will remember me.

A couple of hours later, underneath one of the small piers lining the coast of Massachusetts, a dinghy rowboat tapped its bow against one of the wooden beams sticking out from the water.

Sean was the first to climb out onto the wooden pier. He took a sniff of salty ocean air and stared up at the sky.

It was almost morning, probably only another hour or so to go. He reached down and helped Liz up.

One by one, the group plopped onto the creaking boards of the small anchorage.

"We've got to keep moving," Sean told them. "It's not safe here. If they're acting up the same way they usually do, soon the entire coastline will be swarming with agents."

"I just hope destroying that support beam down in that tomb was enough to bury most of the machinery. We can't let Haven get their hands on it." Quincy lifted his father's diaries out of the boat and pushed it back into the sea. "What the hell are we supposed to do now?"

Sean's cell phone buzzed. Worried faces rose among the group, but Sean waved his hand in way that tried to convey that they shouldn't worry. "It's just my buddy, Harold. Damn, I totally forgot to text him back. It's been like days. He said something about being tracked… I need to take this."

"Hey! Woah, now, what exactly will you be discussing?"

"Quince, man, chill," Sean told him. "I trust the guy, but I really don't trust him *that* much." He tapped the blinking green button. "Harry Mason speaking," he joked, winking at the rest. "Yeah, slow down, chief. What do you m—Hey, *H.* take a deep breath, okay?"

Sean started nervously tapping his foot against the stiff wooden post of the pier.

"Are you serious? Washington, Colorado, California, and Oregon… Disappeared without a trace. You can't get in contact with any of them? Yeah, I know Haven is probably listening right now. Look, I'm going to be off the grid for a while, anyway—some stuff has come up. I'll be in touch when I can. *We'll meet at the place where the unclear birds gather.* Okay, bye."

Sean hung up and stared at his phone. It buzzed a couple of times more after the call, and Sean scrolled through the messages before cracking the phone in half, taking the sim card out, and throwing the broken electronic remains into the water.

"Care to tell us what that was about?" Liz asked. Her voice was drenched in skepticism. "And what the hell is an *unclear bird?*

Before he could answer, an otherworldly howl rang through the pink sky of the breaking dawn. They heard the flapping of heavy wings overhead, but couldn't see where they were. Several loud explosions went off just a few miles north of them, and people could be heard screaming in terror. Gunshots started going off in the distance.

Through instinct, Lilly started to push the group off the pier and onto the solid ground up in front of them; Sean followed suit. Lilly remained quiet except for the few words of urgent 'encouragement.'

They started moving up the road at a brisk pace.

"There should be a safe house a few miles from here. If it still stands," Sean told them between hurried breaths. He flinched when a hollow cry shot through the woods on their right, and one of the big red maple trees crashed onto the road in front of them.

Liz grasped her bag of magical doodads tightly; she couldn't afford to lose them. "If it still stands?" she mimicked Sean. "What does *that* mean?" The screeching of something enormous nearby made her gasp. "Well, I can imagine *something*, but..."

"In here." Sean gestured toward a narrow tunnel that ran straight through the woodland hills to the side of the main road. "It should be in here; I think it'll be okay," he said.

"You *think* it'll be okay?" Moira protested. "Sean, I'm serious, if we came all this way and accomplished all of this just to die sad and smelly in a sewage drainage pipe, I...I'll haunt you to the ends of the Earth itself." She looked more determined than ever.

Quincy chuckled.

"I promise, I promise." Sean replied. "If we'd all die here, you'd have no one to haunt anyway."

"Oh, I *will* find a way," Moira countered.

One by one, they all went inside and braced themselves against the inner wall.

"I'm not sure how many of my contacts are still alive," Sean told them somberly. "That guy I just spoke to on the phone, he and I were one of the first to get in touch right after the twins started to lay low in New York. Same ideals. Protecting people who can't protect themselves. It all started as this group of people who hunted down malicious creatures or helped people get to terms with things they couldn't understand." He paused for a moment as the earth shook around them. Something big was pacing around above them.

"I think it's gone," Moira whispered when the shaking stopped. There was fear in her voice. If this was what revenge by Haven was like, she had no idea how Sean and the twins had lasted so long.

Sean scurried further into the tunnel. He held his

flashlight in front of him and sighed with relief. There was a metal door on the left-hand side. "Yes!" he spouted. "It's still here."

Liz raised an eyebrow. "You thought a *door* would be gone? As in missing? How? Magic?"

"If by magically missing, you mean the very real possibility of it being blown off its hinges and the place on the other side of it unceremoniously being on fire, then *yes*. It could have been missing and I, for one, am very glad it's not."

Quincy groaned. "Good grief, how did you two get anything done before with all this bickering?"

"We didn't work any cases *together*," Liz told him. "Not if you don't count whatever this is."

"I kind of saved her whole coven from a particularly nasty pickle." Sean grinned.

"It was just me and three other witches. Besides, there were *twelve* of you. You could have levelled a freaking dinosaur with the amount of firepower you all were carrying."

"I made the killing shot. You'd all be Wendigo brunch if it wasn't for me."

"Bullshit."

"Quincy and I tracked a Wendigo once," Lilly suddenly interjected. "Pretty horrifying, all in all. Tell them, Quincy."

Quincy scratched the itch that had been building over his eyebrow during this whole exchange. "Perhaps we should get on with getting inside, first?" The ground rumbled, and bits of dirt and small gravel drizzled down from the tunnel. "Quickly?"

Sean fumbled for a bit with a small metal grate a few

feet from the door. "Shit," he concluded. "Key's gone. We're gonna have to—"

"Let me," Liz interrupted. She pulled out her favorite pair of makeshift lockpicks from her bag and started working on the lock immediately.

"Picking locks? That's a different side of you," Quincy commented. "Well, I had no idea. Doesn't really seem to suit you."

Moira laughed. "I had that reaction at first as well. But it is what it is. And I'm glad to tell you it got you your car back."

"You got the Fiesta back?"

"Say '*thank you.*'" Liz grinned and winked at Lilly, who smiled weakly as

Quincy chuckled.

Liz bent one of the little metal rods in her hands into a peculiar shape. "Hey, Sean, why don't you finish your story about you and your old hunting buddies, huh?" It wasn't necessarily spiteful, the way she said it, but from the tone of her voice, it was clear she wasn't entirely enthusiastic about it.

"Okay," Sean said, either oblivious to, or ignoring the snarky tone. "Let me see, where was I... Oh, yeah. So this group started out just like the twins did, just helping folks out. They took cases that were deemed too small for the GDF. Started spreading across the States."

"But how many innocent creatures did your friends rip from their nests, unsuspecting of any danger, just because they thought they might be a threat someday?" Liz asked bluntly, still fiddling with the lock. She had one of the lockpicks clenched between her teeth while rubbing some sort of greasy substance on the metal.

"I-I don't know, Liz. You know *I* never did, and probably most of my friends didn't either."

Liz scoffed.

"Hey, we can't dwell on that now, okay? In fact, I'll make this really short and sweet. This group of hunters eventually turned into some sort of rebellion against Haven when the GDF disbanded, and all these people started to forget the dangers around them. Haven started screwing with us, throwing dirt in our plans. And we found out so much of their experiments... Bad news, man."

Sean looked down at the ground. "This past night? Haven marched full-force against every group they caught wind of. Lot of people disappearing, snatched up in their unmarked vehicles. Harold was in full-fledged panic mode when he called me, and he's the chillest dude I know. *Nothing* fazes him, usually. I got all these texts... I even got one from a guy I trust—says his wife was shot dead on the spot in front of him, like a warning..."

"They're retaliating," Lilly whispered. "It's because of us. All these people are dying because of us." She was mortified; her face had gone pale like a ghost's.

Quincy shook his head. "No, Lil'. Haven is just bending everyone to their will. They're cleaning up so there's nobody to thwart their plans anymore."

Moira cleared her throat. "I'd like to take this moment to change the subject from one mortal peril to another. Do any of you think it's true what Agent Dutch said? Four children of the Gibbous Horde already awakened?"

"Did he tell you anything? Anything at all?" Sean

asked her. "While you were working for them in Darkness Falls, I mean."

"No," she answered. "I was kept in the dark for most of it. I just knew about the thing they call *Mother*. Damn. That wall of blubbering insanity was powerful enough to make the most rational man or woman go stark raving mad in a matter of seconds. If there's really four of them now…"

"That's an apocalypse scenario, right there," Quincy breathed out slowly.

The lock clicked and the metal door creaked open.

"Got it!" Liz told them with bated breath.

A terrifying cry came from the entrance of the tunnel. It sounded as if the concepts of death and decay were transposed to an audible noise of terror.

The group hurried inside the hunter safe house. Not looking back, Sean slammed the door closed and bolted it with a big metal beam from the inside.

"Heh. Little hut here is still doing exactly what it's supposed to." He chuckled.

From one underground shelter to another in a pretty short time span, they hid in the tunnel bunker for more than twenty-four hours until the noise and violence above them finally subsided.

With nothing more to eat than stale canned beans with less spoons than they could divide between the five of them—a fact of which Moira, recently de-cursed, was the butt of many jokes of for the first couple of hours—and nothing else to read except some encyclopedias on monsters and an unfortunate hunter's terrifying account of her encounter with Black-Eyed Children, there really wasn't a lot to do. Quincy had perused his father's notes a couple of times, but he kept quiet on them for the most part. Most of them were unintelligible scientific theory crafting anyway—interesting, but probably *only* to Quincy.

The rest of the bunker was drab and empty. It was stuffy and full of dust, laden with only the bare essentials for survival.

After the initial few hours had passed and stories had been swapped around, they all fell into a deep sleep, one by one.

Upon waking up, the noise that emanated from outside betrayed the ominous fact that things were still havoc and mayhem. And so, they stayed put.

Throughout the ordeal, the mood was tense to say the least.

Sean tried to keep their spirits up, but deep down, he was worried sick of the implications of the last night. Moira kept casual conversation with Liz and Quincy, sharing stories of growing up in the bayou and learning about all kinds of strange and scary things before those things became the norm.

Lilly was quiet for almost the entire stay. She had been writing mostly non-stop in the journal which she had kept closely by her side this whole ordeal. She directed most of her attention on it during their hiding, writing down her thoughts as they came to her. Quincy thought it was for the best for the rest of them to leave her alone for a while. He, for a fact, knew exactly how she felt: They each had to deal with their troubled minds in their own way.

For him, it was keeping up light conversation and keeping that small spark of hope alive while he tried to keep his mind from being devoured by dark thoughts, while Lilly tried to come to terms with everything by separating herself and giving those dark memories a place on paper, or so he thought. Quite strange, Quincy then realized, that this was playing out in the exact opposite way for both of them. They appeared to have adapted each other's methods of dealing with grief and sorrows.

When the group finally emerged from the hillside tunnel many hours later, half of the woodland around them was either burned to cinders or in the process of reaching that state. A few cars had swerved off the road and collided with the trees on the slope of the hill. Their occupants were nowhere to be seen.

It was dawn again. Only, it was an entire day later.

The pretty orange slit of horizon that promised a beautiful late fall day yesterday had made way for another batch of grey storm clouds and freezing eastern winds. Their only hope was that the blanket of rain that was to be expected any moment now would douse most of the flames licking at the high branches of the age-old trees that lined the New England coast.

Liz gasped with terror as she saw the tree line burn in front of them. In a panic, she ran toward the smoldering flames, then back again. "Bastards!" she yelled, and plopped onto the ground.

Lilly ran after her and quietly embraced Liz, letting her bury her head in her arms.

Quincy tried reaching out, but Moira grabbed him by the arm and held him back. "Don't," she whispered, shaking her head. "This is something neither one of us can solve."

Quincy solemnly nodded. "Any luck?" he asked, turning his attention to Sean.

Sean popped the sim card he had been carrying around in the flip phone he found in the bunker and turned the phone on. He held it up in the air, waved it around for a bit, then checked the screen. "Nothing," he said cautiously.

"Any bars, at least?" Moira asked.

"Yeah, yeah," he answered back. "I just meant I haven't received any messages or anything anymore. That can be good or bad, depending on your view of things, ha." He wiped a bit of sweat off his brow. "C'mon, man. Not even one?" he whispered quietly to himself.

"Hey, they probably just did the same rational thing you did. They got rid of their phones and hid until it's safe for them to come back out," Quincy reassured him.

Sean ran a hand through his hair. He looked worried. "I don't know, Quince. I can't be the first one out, can I?"

"We have no idea what's going on everywhere else at the moment. We've got to keep going."

"What are you proposing?" Moira asked carefully.

Quincy knelt down and took a pebble off the road. He threw it up a few times, each time catching it back in his hands. He wandered around, pondering. After about half a minute or so, he stopped: "I might know a guy. I hope he still lives near here. He's a pilot—does private flying tours and stuff. He *could* get us to England. It's the only lead we have at the moment. We need to find this Supreme Being or whatever it is before Haven does. Or else…"

"Game over." Sean grunted.

Quincy nodded. "Listen, I don't think Haven knows Lilly and I are alive again, so we could scout ahead and—"

"*Lilly* and I?" Lilly overheard the conversation and stomped over to her brother. "What makes you think I agree to any of this?" she asked. She was visibly furious. Tears were streaming down her face.

Quincy was clearly taken aback. "Lil'… Hey, it was just a suggestion. We just need a little faith. You know, to—"

Lilly screamed in frustration, her hands balled up in fists. "Faith?" she yelled. "You don't get it, do you? I'm not going anywhere anymore. I'm done!"

"W-what do you mean?" Quincy asked. "Lilly, I can't do this without you. What are you saying?" His eyes welled up.

"You're trying to save the world from the apocalypse," she told him. "It's useless. One way or another, it will still happen. It's bound to happen. Always. But I can't live with the delusion anymore that it's somehow our responsibility to solve everything. I just *died*. *We've* just died. We only *just* came back. A one in a million shot, *a second chance,* and you're getting ready to storm off and die all over again in a blaze of glory trying to delay the inevitable. I want to die on my own terms. I want to live the life I've dreamt of since we were little. Just for this little while longer. To be happy. Just for the few months we still have left."

Tears started dripping down Quincy's cheeks. "Stop. Please. I really can't do this without you, Lilly. Come on, I really think we can do this. I truly do. And with the help of everyone here, I'm one-hundred-percent sure. You just got to have a little faith, you know."

"Stop!" Lilly yelled so loud, it startled everyone around. "You're not getting it—you're not getting *me*. If there's anyone who can stop the world from going to hell, I know it's *you*. I truly believe that. But Quincy..." She grabbed his shaking hands. "I am tired. I am tired of feeling responsible for cleaning up the mess other people make. There is no obligation to any of this. But it so often felt like there was, simply because of the last name we share and the legacy of our forbears' dive into the occult."

Quincy scoffed. "What about all of the times where you told me you never knew what to do with your life? That helping people gave you a sense of pride and purpose. Are you telling me that was all bullshit? All a ruse to keep me, your brother, happy?"

"Of course not!" She squeezed his hands hard. "Everything I have *ever* told you has been nothing else than the absolute truth all the time. I wanted to help people, the little man, those who couldn't stick up for themselves or were deathly afraid of the things happening around them. But now? For me, there's no glory to be found in undermining some secret agency's diabolical plans to destroy the world. They'll just move over to the next plan if this one doesn't work."

Lilly glanced over to a worried-looking Liz. "I've found a new purpose. I want to lead a simple, semi-sane life with someone I care deeply about. And I want nothing more for you to be a part of that life. But you're...you're going somewhere I can't follow. Not now."

Quincy simply stared at his sister in disbelief. "No,

this can't be happening. I need you. What if something happens to one of us and we're not together?"

"I'm sorry, Quince." She sniffled. "If you're really doing this, it will be without me." She stepped back. "I'm really sorry."

"I'll miss you." He wiped the tears from his cheeks.

Lilly broke a smile and laughed for the first time in a while. But it was a sad smile, and the laugh was to mask her pain. "I'll miss you too."

Quincy took a few steps backwards. "I understand. I really do." He nodded at her. He turned around and paced off to the other side of the road, where the cliffs overlooked the ocean. Here he stood still for a while, until he was joined by Liz.

"You'll take good care of her, right?" he asked, giving her the smile of a man with a broken heart.

"I will." Liz told him. "I just wanted to come over and say thanks."

"Thanks? For what?"

"Quincy, the impact you two have on people is… extraordinary. I haven't felt loved like this, like I belong somewhere important, since I joined the Night Lights. And with most of the coven in hiding or avoiding big gatherings, I've found so much purpose now, with you two. And it's not just me; it's Moira and Sean too. You've given them a reason to fight and the feeling that they belong."

Quincy sighed; he felt restless.

"She just needs time, you know?" Liz continued. "You two have learned so much from each other. This isn't an impulse. She's thought about this for a very long time. I could see it in her eyes and hear it in her voice. Jumping headfirst into an adventure in Europe—she's just not ready for that." She paused for a second and looked at him, then tugged his hand. "But one day soon, she might be. And if she is, so will I." She looked back for a second. "Hey, at least you got Moira and Sean. They both seem eager to stop the apocalypse from happening or die trying to."

"I'm terrified." Quincy admitted and laughed nervously. "Not of what's to come, really. But rather deathly afraid I'll never see her again."

"I know." She gave his hand a squeeze. "Remember what I said way back? When the shadows grow longer and deeper and the sunlight is chased away, the demons of the fall will rear their ugly heads and manifest in the deepest, most broken parts of our minds?"

"Yes, I do. But why are you telling me this?"

"Because, Quincy Swansong, I now know what demons torment you. *You* know what demons torment you." She paused. "Now, fight them."

———————————————

Chapter 21
REFLECTION

———————————————

TWO MONTHS LATER

R-O-O-K... T-O... B-5... The magnifying glass shot across the Ouija board.

Lilly looked over the board quizzically. "What's that? Is that...?"

C-H-E-C-K... the spirit of the board announced triumphantly.

Lilly dove for her *how to play chess* guide and retraced the steps of the last few plays. "Wait, no, it's not! You're cheating!" She pointed the book at the board.

Liz walked in with a mug full of tea and a grin on her face. "Well, would you look at that? I didn't know Ouija boards had eyes nowadays. That move's perfectly legal, by the way."

S-E-E-? whoever was controlling the board agreed.

"Ugh!" Lilly threw the book away and took the mug out of Liz's hands. "Thanks. You know, for someone who can actually *see* the board and therefore can think ahead about their moves, I'm really getting my ass handed to me right now."

Liz laughed. "Who are you playing, anyway?"

"Mr. Mortimer. He decided to teach me how to play well so I can surprise Quincy one day by kicking his ass in chess. If it comes to that…you know."

Y-O-U… S-T-I-L-L… S-U…

"Would you shut up, please?" Lilly slapped the little glass away. It flew off the board against the wall of the cabin. "The nerve."

"You realize you're playing, and messing with, the Grim Reaper, right? Just want to get things straight, here."

"Oh yeah, I figured that out ages ago. Mr. Mortimer and I have an understanding, you see."

Liz sloughed onto the couch next to Lilly and cuddled up against her. "And that is?"

"He told me it could get quite boring there, beyond the veil in the realms of the dead."

"Really?"

"Totally. So, in trade for me keeping him some company now and again, he'll keep me in the loop of anything weird or fishy going on across the entire spectrum of the afterlife."

"Huh, that's not the worst of deals, actually." Liz shrugged and grabbed the remote from the table in front of them. "Speaking of weird and fishy, I just got a message from my friend, Anatole. You know, from the north-west?"

"Uh-huh," Lilly responded vaguely. She was reaching over the side of the couch, trying to get a hold of the

Ouija board magnifying glass. "You talked about him. Great at healing spells, etcetera."

Liz pulled Lilly back so they were eye-level. "Well, you might want to sit down, pay attention, and take this in, because it's apparently not good. Not good at all." She turned on the TV and pressed the volume button all the way up.

A figure in an orange and red cloak appeared on the TV. He was in a church of some kind; its architecture appeared to be Catholic Christian in nature, but there was a distinct lack of recognizable symbolism present. Liz and Lilly tried their best, but they could only see the bottom half of the figure's face; his eyes and nose were obscured in shadow.

Several similarly dressed men and women stood to the side of the altar on which the man stood. There was an ominous figure dressed entirely in black, with a full-pointed hood on and a noose in his hands. It stood motionless in the background.

The speaker tapped the microphone and began to preach with a heavyset southern accent:

"Brothers and sisters, the time is near.

"We have waited too long for this moment in good faith, but alas the day has come for us, humankind, to say farewell to our home of Earthly delights. We must pass on, on to the great beyond in the darkest sky, for we are not worthy any more to dwell here on this fine Earth we have created, and destroyed, for ourselves.

"We have forgotten. Forgotten the true hardships of what it was to be alive, and to live a life worth living and worth fighting for. Earth is no longer ours, my friends… There is a new power here, new life. Unfit for our sinning eyes to behold."

"Liz!" Lilly pointed at the TV.

Liz saw it too; Haven agents were gathering in the back of the church. They stood in silence, just watching, waiting for something to happen. It was truly unnerving. The hooded figure still did not move an inch.

"*Do not fear, however!*" the strange priest continued.

For it is our *duty. The duty of the Esoteric Order of the Final Dawn to see you through these final moments on our planet. It is our duty to safely escort your heavenly bodies back into the fluttering dance of the rolling cosmos. Can. You. Feel. It, brothers and sisters?*"

The camera zoomed in on the wicked grin of the priest. Right before the congregation was swept out of view, Liz and Lilly could swear they saw the glistening of knives and the barrels of guns appear among them: Lilly squeezed Liz's hand tight.

"*The apocalypse is coming. And you are nearly saved, my blessed children*"—he spread his hands—"*and must let the Order guide your way. Walk toward that blazing hellfire looming right at our doorstep and look it straight in the eye. The end of days is coming. Save yourself, my brothers and sisters. Save yourselves.*"

The camera loomed on the sickly grinning priest for a few seconds more before the nauseating sound of metal ripping through flesh and the blasting of gunshots exploded through the church just off-camera.

And just like that, the broadcast was suddenly ended.

Lilly felt sick to her stomach. "Wha-why are they doing that?" She was in total shock.

Liz took a moment for herself as well. She took a few long breaths, in and out, and sipped her tea. She made a face when she realized it had gone cold. "Anatole told me" —she took one last deep breath through her nose, urging herself to calm down—"that gatherings like this have been happening all over the country, all over the world, even. It's the same everywhere. Creepy priest or priestess of this… apocalypse cult preaching to people to save themselves, and all of a sudden, there's a mass suicide going on."

"It must be the *Mother* creatures," Lilly concluded. She anxiously bit her nails. "The Gibbous Horde…"

Liz nodded. "Yeah, that's what I was thinking as well. No human has this amount of charisma to pull it off. But the thing that's bugging me is that it's been happening all over the world—"

"Oh no!" Lilly bolted up. "It means that a lot more of those…*things* have started to awaken… Did Anatole tell you where the first cult gathering was? The first known one?" Lilly had a nagging suspicion and prayed to whatever benevolent god was left in the universe that she was incorrect.

Liz began viciously tapping her phone. "Asking right now…" Her eyes grew wide. "It says the first gathering was in…England."

"Quincy!" Liz shouted. "Oh, shit, *shit*! I need to know if he—" Her eyes flashed toward the Ouija board. "He's not in there with you, is he?" She grabbed the board and shook it. "*Is he?*"

NO, it said. The glass then slid over to the letters G-T-G and then GOODBYE.

"Ergh! Useless!" Lilly threw the board and began pacing.

Liz carried away the tea mugs so they wouldn't be unfortunate passerby casualties of Lilly's anger. "Quincy's alive," she said. "That's really good news, isn't it?"

Lilly plopped down on the couch. "Yeah, I guess so. I

just hope he's alright…that he didn't get himself in a boatload of trouble."

"You're dodging the fact of why he went there in the first place," Liz said in her most sincere tone. "He's learned everything he needs to know about wit and cunning from you. If he isn't with Death himself in the afterlife, he's probably doing fine."

"I guess so."

"And Moira and Sean are with him. He's probably in some old library, peering through books, trying to find the location of this Supreme Being so Sean can dowse it in gasoline and light the match to end the end times in style."

Lilly laughed. "Yeah, he's a Swansong. And he's the rational, brainiac kind. What could possibly go wrong?"

A Teaser for Book Three

The Apocalypse Rebellion, book three of The Eldritch Twins!

Sussex, England — 5 days, 14 hours, and 23 minutes until the end of the world

Quincy dashed down the flight of stairs with such incredible speed, he had to restrain himself and think rationally before he'd jump out of a window to get an even faster, and more painful getaway.

"Stop right there, *scum!*" A frail, but very agile and quick on his feet man dressed in red robes ran after him. He was fast and unrelenting, often trailing Quincy by mere inches, grabbing and snatching at his collar and the book he was clutching under his arm.

"Drop that tome this instant!" the cultist yelled. "You have no idea what powers you are meddling with!"

Quincy, panting and sweating, looked behind him and threw a sly smile at the aged face beneath the bright-colored robe. "Trust, me old timer. There's little to nothing that can faze me anymore. I have died and have experienced rebirth, both of my frail body, but also of my soul. I have seen the black abyss yawning and churning beneath the wobbling, thin thread that separates rational human thinking and utter and complete madness."

Quincy ran out into the broader, open monastery hallway that overlooked the inner garden. The weather was typically English, gray and drab. He looked behind him to see the man in the red robe losing distance on him. He smirked. Perhaps the old geezer wasn't so fit as he might have thought. Or rather, perhaps his words really did resonate with the guy?

He always wondered how it would be just to make the most terrible and cursed statements regarding to humanity's survival and the crisis of existentialism. Quincy *did* think his words had some sort of profound impact on the somewhat frailer members of the *Esoteric Order of the Final Dawn*, but only for a second or two, right before several more cultists appeared in front of him with shining silver daggers which they were waving menacingly toward his face.

"Ah, shit!" Quincy exclaimed before jumping and diving through one of the open arches that lined the right side of the half-open hallway. He landed on his shoulder, painfully, but managed to roll through most of the impact —a maneuver Lilly once taught him to, in her words: '*You know, not die so quickly.*'

Before long, Quincy was back on his feet, adrenaline pumping through his veins like crazy. He crossed over the courtyard diagonally and was on the other side in a matter of seconds. The bright mass of orange and red-cloaked individuals scampered over the little knee high-way, but with a lot more trouble than Quincy had antici-pated. *Good*, he thought, right before instinctively ducking upon seeing the glimmer of the mace heading toward the general direction of his face.

Quincy pushed the somewhat clumsy, mace-wielding cultist back. Putting all of his weight into it, he managed to knock him on his butt. The heavy mace landed right onto the heavy guy's chest, and a gust of strained breath released from his mouth as he blacked out. Now, Quincy waited a couple of seconds. His eyes darted from left to right. Nothing.

Good, he thought again, and brought the walkie-talkie speaker to his lips.

"Okay, so I met with way more resistance than we thought," he panted, still dashing toward any possible exit. "How are things on your end?"

"Sean ran into some 'red-hoods' when getting the crucifix relic, but nothing too bad. We're ready to pick you up at the parallel road next to the woodland inn, right on-cue." The familiar voice of Moira came up through the walkie-talkie. "That all right with you, Quince?"

"Sure, I..." Quincy had sped through an apparent servant's corridor of the monastery and emerged outside on the north-facing side of the old structure, where a quiet graveyard full of weathered and overgrown graves and headstones was found, surrounded by rusty iron fence and thick oak trees.

This was not the most peculiar thing, however.

Because there was something that instantly shut Quincy up. In the middle of the old graveyard stood a strange man. He was of average height, sported an impressive, but finely kempt beard, wore peculiar 17th century nobleman's clothing, and (this is the big one) was literally ripping Final Dawn cultists in half and spreading their viscera all across the yard.

"Come out and fight. Do not stand on ceremony in front of *me*, evildoers. You slick orange lapdogs of Satan, you swine of Beelzebub—come forth and face the wrath of your Maker!" The man's face contorted. "BLOOD FOR THE GOD OF DEATH, FACE ME, MORTALS, AND TREMBLE IN FEAR. YOU KNOW NOTHING!" he yelled, shook his head in confusion, and closed his eyes for a bit. "You cannot control me, demon! For the righteous will always prevail."

Quincy looked behind him. There was a distinct lack of any pursuers. In fact, he saw one of the windows above him slam to a close and heard what sounded like boards being nailed over it from the other side.

"Quince? Are you still there?" the walkie-talkie crackled.

The crazy man's eyes flashed toward Quincy, who started sweating profusely. "Who stands before me now? Another pawn of the Antichrist? Perhaps another shadowy denizen of Carcosa in disguise, flaunting itself like a scholarly individual, hmm?" His eyes grew wide. "GO ON, GASH OUT HIS EYES AND HIS TEETH AND HIS... MASTER SWANSONG?"

Quincy's jaw dropped to the floor. If this was who he thought it was, the world had officially started to end, for pigs flying was definitely a sign of Final Dawn's Apocalypse. "Tim?" Quincy asked carefully. "Tim, is that you? W-what are you doing here?"

"RIDING THE COATTAILS OF THIS ONE; A MOST PECULIAR ONE, I'D S—" The man stuck out his tongue, started blowing raspberries while looking crooked-eyed. He then spoke again, though it was the other voice now:

"Do not listen to that devil that has attached itself to me and is trying to trick me into using my glory for nothing else but its own nefarious ways. I have returned from very far away, for evil once again walks the land of old Europa, and it is up to me to cleanse it. In the name of our Lord, I am a warrior of God almighty, and nothing will stand in my way. Jolly good times, old chap, I'd say!"

Quincy stared, not quite knowing what to say or think anymore. He looked hard at the pale, somewhat flaky skin. He also looked deep into the cold, lifeless pupils that bore down into his soul. This man was dead. Or at least, he had been. Quincy cleared his throat. "And who…*are* you, exactly?" He popped the question as lightly as possible.

"FEEBLE M—frail youth, how can anyone not recognize the master in front of them, *pip pip*. My name is Matthew Hopkins, Witchfynder General and—HE IS WEAK FLESH AND BONE, MOTTLED—I am pleased to make your acquaintance. Will you ride with me, youth—AND ONCE AGAIN BASK IN THE GLORY OF TIMAXOATILACILUZIPTA, BANE OF THE ANCIENT COSMOS—and become my apprentice in banishing evil from this land? AND KILL EVERYONE THAT STANDS IN OUR WAY?"

Quincy had no words. He dropped the walkie-talkie on the ground and scratched himself on the back of his head.

"Quincy? Are you okay?" Sean yelled through the speaker. "Do you need a pickup? Quince?"

A Request...

Did you enjoy Nearly Departed*? Reviews keep books alive . . .*

Leave your review on either GoodReads or the digital storefront of your choosing.

We thank you greatly!

Acknowledgments

I don't think I have to explain much when I say that the year 2020 has been a terrifying and horrible year for just about everyone. During the writing of this book we were smack dab in the middle of it all. Even though I had started *The Nearly Departed* back in 2019, had the general plot down and knew it was going to be darker than its predecessor, I did not yet know how much real world circumstances would seep into the pages as the writing process carried on through the next year. I think some passages speak for themselves really channel that insecurity, fear and uncertainty. Then again, the book also covers hope and perseverance. Quincy and Lilly know like no others what it is like to stand up for yourself and for what you believe in, but also to have hope. To believe in themselves and to believe in humanity. To persevere.

From the bottom of my heart I would like to thank everyone who stuck by me last year, whether it was close by, at safe distance, or miles apart. Your kind words have helped me a lot, as I'm sure they helped others. I would also like to once again thank The Parliament House for their support and belief in my as an author. Publishing my first novel was a dream coming true. All hail the Literary Luminati! And to you reading this: Believe in yourself, help others and help make the world a safer place. Together we have the power to change the world for the better, let's act on this now.

Eldritch Twins fans, see you next year at the end. *The Apocalypse Rebellion* is coming.

About the Author

Nick Vossen was raised on blockbuster films from the 80s and 90s as well as fantasy and sci-fi novels, comics and games. No matter the medium, his love for storytelling grew ever larger. Having always had a fascination with the fantastical and weird, he quickly grew fond of authors such as Terry Pratchett, H.P. Lovecraft, Neil Gaiman and many more. During the winter of 2017 Nick released an anthology of short, weird fiction entitled The Fissures Between Worlds, which delves into the strange places on Earth where time does not flow as it should. It was received quite favourably, and so Nick's desire to tell more stories grew. He has since been privileged to appear in several other anthologies, magazines and short story compilations and has quite a few projects still in the works. His biggest fascinations and inspirations are old forgotten woodlands, the deepest depths of the oceans and the unsettling, uncanniness of retro futurism.

Nick graduated in Media- and Culture studies at Utrecht University in The Netherlands. He is currently working as a freelance creative writer and author. He also frequently works on projects in the Dutch indie-film industry, putting his talents to use in art-direction, set-dressing and of course screenwriting.

Nick has been working on and off on The Swansong Conspiracy since the tail-end of 2017. The idea first came when Nick wanted to give Lovecraftian Horror a much lighter and charming edge. But what started as a 'Monty Python-esque' parody eventually turned into a tale of equal suspense and horror but also humor and personality. Nick likes to write fluently and to the point, resulting in fast-paced action and quick & witty dialogue. It is also no secret that The Swansong Conspiracy is dripping in pop culture references and easter eggs, all done in loving tribute. Nick is extremely proud of the little strange world he created, and is ecstatic to be able to work on its two sequels for The Parliament House, as well.

www.nickcronomicon.wordpress.com

Also by Nick Vossen

If you loved *The Nearly Departed*, check out these fantastic titles
from within the Eldritch Twins series:

www.ingramcontent.com/pod-product-compliance
Lightning Source LLC
Chambersburg PA
CBHW031314210726
48287CB00005B/1552